CLAY

LIGHTHOUSE SECURITY INVESTIGATIONS

MARYANN JORDAN

Cover Design by: Designs by Stacy

ISBN ebook: 978-1-947214-68-2

ISBN print: 978-1-947214-69-9

❀ Created with Vellum

Author's Note

Please remember that this is a work of fiction. I have lived in numerous states as well as overseas, but for the last twenty years have called Virginia my home. I often choose to use fictional city names with some geographical accuracies.

These fictionally named cities allow me to use my creativity and not feel constricted by attempting to accurately portray the areas.

It is my hope that my readers will allow me this creative license and understand my fictional world.

I also do quite a bit of research on my books and try to write on subjects with accuracy. There will always be points where creative license will be used in order to create scenes or plots.

It was a black night, but not the darkest he'd ever experienced. Time spent in the Afghan mountains on cloudy nights without a hint of a campfire in sight anywhere in the distance had caused the kind of darkness where it was easy to become disoriented and fear sucked at your soul. No, this night was not like that. Not by a long shot.

Tonight, an occasional glimpse of moonlight peeking through the drifting clouds, plus the fact that he had two teammates nearby and wasn't in peril of an enemy ready to kill, made this mission seem like a leisurely stroll in the park compared to earlier years.

Surrounded by thousands of acres of woods, disorientation would affect most men. But then, as a former Ranger and CIA operative and now employed as a Keeper for Lighthouse Security Investigation, he was not *most* men.

Massive, thick trees covered the area. In the daylight, the lush green forests nestled at the Maine-Canadian border would have been the stuff of dreams for campers, hikers, and nature lovers. Although to get there would have made the trek unpleasant for vacationers. The deep-rutted road he had just driven would have given the heaviest lumber truck difficulty, not to mention the heavily-fortified military SUV he'd traveled in. Now, with his vehicle tucked away, he was settled in the crook of a thick limb of a large tree, his night vision goggles providing eerie visibility.

The calendar might indicate spring, but the cold breeze blowing was an easy reminder that he was in one of the most northern sections of the mainland United States. Leaves rustled all around, and the fresh scent of uninhabited, unsullied, unpolluted air filled his nostrils.

For Hank Claiborne, known as Clay since his first day in Army boot camp, it was just another day at the office. He'd earned the nickname when he'd stumbled on a long walk and the drill sergeant claimed he had feet of clay. Later, proving he was anything but clumsy while in the Army Rangers, he was recruited to be a CIA special operator where he met Mace Hanson, his boss once they both got out of the service.

Mace had started his own business known as Lighthouse Security Investigations, hiring men and women who had served with special operations in the military or CIA. Known as the Keepers, Clay had developed his closest friendships with his coworkers.

He grinned, thinking of earlier that evening. He and two of his fellow Keepers, Tate and Walker, had stopped at a local bar en route to the mission for a bite to eat. Clay munched on his burger, keeping an eye on the small crowd, chatting with the others. Just as they were walking out, the sound of drums and bagpipes filled the back of the bar. Twisting his head around, he watched as a small band belted out Celtic rock. A singer added his voice to the ensemble, and then a woman jumped onto the stage playing an electric violin. Her dark hair swirled around her shoulders as she played. Entranced by her performance, he wanted to walk back toward the front just to get closer, but Tate's voice cut through his musing.

"Clay!"

He startled, cursing both the disruption of his appreciation of the fiddler and his inattention to their mission. "Fuck," he mumbled. Hustling after the others, they climbed into their vehicle and got back onto the road.

Now, perched in the tree, he heard the whistling of the wind through the branches and thought of the music. *I wonder if I could find out who they were—*

"Incoming."

Josh's voice in Clay's ear kept him grounded in the vast forests of northern Maine even though his teammate was back in the compound, eyes on the satellite and real-time images coming from their contacts. "Copy that."

Even though he could not see them, Tate and Walker would also have the rutted logging road in their sights. It only took a moment before he began to hear the rumbling sounds of a Hummer and see the lighted pinpricks of headlights in the distance. Grinning, he shifted ever so slightly, ready for the waiting and watching to be over.

He had chosen his position at the sharp curve in the winding road, knowing the vehicle would either need to slow greatly to make the turn or skid into the woods. Either was fine with him.

Shifting slightly, he waited patiently. Patience was truly a virtue to a man in his field. As a Ranger, he'd learned to not rush a mission, enjoying the careful planning while knowing it would assist in keeping his squad safe. As CIA Special Ops, those skills had served him well. And now, he was in no rush to allow his prey to discover his presence.

"I've got a visual," he said, the Hummer rumbling toward him, now completely in his sights. The vehicle was equipped with upgrades, but he was surprised they had not opted for a full military Humvee bought on the black market. His prey must have been overly sure of their success. From the sound of the tires on the gravel, he knew they weren't reinforced. A slow grin spread over his face. *This'll be fuckin' easy.*

The Hummer continued forward, moving steadily. But, just as he anticipated, it slowed at the curve. Taking aim with his long-range sniper rifle, Clay shot into both back tires, knowing that Tate would be taking out the front tires at the same time. The sound ricocheted throughout the night, music to his ears, knowing the hit was successful.

Again showing that the smugglers had no military training, the passenger threw open his door to see what had happened. Walker fired tear gas inside, and the two men stumbled out, making more noise than Clay could have imagined. Walker approached with his gun raised, and Clay dropped to the ground from his tree perch. Approaching from the back, he held his weapon on one while Tate and Walker secured the other.

The men were huge, and the tats on their knuckles and neck indicated their gang affiliation. *Minotaurs... fuckin' drug smugglers.* The Minotaurs MC gang was affiliated with Hell's Angels and plied the drug trade in Montréal.

As Tate and Walker had secured the second man, Clay opened the back door and peered inside. Camping equipment, tool chests, dirty boots, and extra clothing filled the space. "Looks like we've got a couple of campers," he said, catching Walker's grin.

The toolboxes were locked but he gained access with ease. Flipping open the lids, he spied plastic-wrapped bricks. Pulling out his knife, he slit the top of one, exposing compressed powder inside. Using the color strips for a quick initial test, he radioed, "Suspects secured. Got the package. Heroin."

Tate called out, "FBI and International Drug Task Force are on their way. Their contacts were apprehended on the Canadian side."

During the two-hour wait for the members of the task force to arrive, Clay, Tate, and Walker secured the vehicle and the heroin along with the prisoners. Finally, once law enforcement made their way to the obscure location, the government agents took over. Clay, Tate, and Walker finally walked away from the scene to their vehicle parked a mile away. By now, daylight streaked the dark sky with pale blue.

"Once again, we do the nasty and they take the glory."

Clay looked over at Walker and shook his head. "That's what we're hired for." His grin widened, and he added, "And what we get paid very well to do."

Tate and Walker laughed as the three pulled off their equipment and stowed it in the back of their vehicle. With Tate behind the wheel, they made their way out of the thick Maine forests, glad when they finally felt their tires land on paved roads.

"It took the shipment so long to get there, I thought we were going to spend all night up in the trees," Tate said. "At least Nora isn't on duty today, so she'll still be home when I get there."

"Nothing better than coming home from a mission to a beautiful smile and a warm body," Walker added before sighing heavily. "Of course, Julie will already be at work by the time I get home. She'll be itching to find out how everything went. I'll probably have ten texts by the time I get back."

"You can't talk to your wife about a mission," Clay said, twisting around in his seat to glare at Walker.

"Seriously, man? You gotta give them something. I don't care how adept they are at being in a relationship with a Keeper."

Glancing toward Tate, he asked, "What about Nora?"

"Hell, these women know what it's like. I may have known Nora for a long time, but it wasn't until I was involved in a rescue mission with her that she really understood what I do."

Walker barked out a laugh. "Considering I met Julie

on a mission, she gets it, also. She knows I don't go into details about missions, but she just wants to know that I'm safe... and that I caught the bad guy, as she says."

Clay remained quiet, but his thoughts were swirling. With no one waiting for him at home, he was used to ending a mission on his own with a cold beer or glass of whiskey, sitting alone on his deck. He had to admit he welcomed the idea of being with someone special, but his fellow Keepers had a penchant for falling for women during missions, right in the middle of a fuckin' nightmare. And that held no appeal to him.

Closing his eyes, he allowed the movement of the vehicle to lull him to sleep as they headed toward the coastline... and the lighthouse.

2

A WEEK LATER

Clay closed his eyes for a moment, allowing the music to swell within him. The first note resounded throughout the concert hall, giving evidence that every instrument in the orchestra was playing. Each section appeared to vie for dominance. Woodwinds against the brass. Reeds against the percussion. And the strings chiming in, each section adding their own layer.

For a moment, he was taken back to his childhood. Mr. Olaf had attempted to lead the middle school orchestra through their paces. His mother had insisted he learn music but vetoed his request to play the trumpet or percussion. That was how he ended up with a violin tucked under his chin and his clumsy fingers attempting the notes when he was in seventh grade. He loved music but knew that creating it himself was not his aptitude. While he no longer played an instrument, his mother's love for a beautiful symphony had been passed along to him.

He glanced around the interior of the Portland

Concert Hall, noting the architecture was perfectly created for the resonating tones. His attention was jerked back to the stage as the music halted except for a single violin holding a long note. The orchestra had moved into Bach's Air On The G String. His breathing slowed to the song's measure, the violin solo creating a longing inside with its haunting melody.

Inwardly cursing his choice of seats in the house, he was unable to identify the violinist capturing his attention. Equally cursing that the symphonic director was not having the soloist stand so that they could receive their due, he closed his eyes again for just a moment, the melody pulling him along.

Sitting next to him was an older woman, and while he didn't want to make her uncomfortable, he shifted ever so slightly to peer up toward the stage. With all of the instruments now down, he caught a glance of the solo violinist as she continued to weave magic through her strings and bow.

Dark hair pulled back tightly into a bun. Pale complexion. Glasses perched on her nose. The hint of long fingers as they moved over the instrument. With his imperfect view, he was unable to discern more.

Catching a movement from his side, the older woman pursed her lips, and he shifted back, mumbling an apology. His movement sent the soloist out of his sight once again, and he felt a strange loss.

The other musicians joined in, and once again the music swelled deep inside. This time when he closed his eyes, he was no longer transported back to his childhood's feeble attempt at playing in an orchestra, but instead had a vision of the woman… serene and calm as she created music that filled his soul, offering the peace that he craved.

He had come to the symphony in Portland alone, but that was fine with him. Not many of his friends cared for driving two hours to listen to an orchestra concert. In fact, none of them had that desire. But Clay used the driving time to think about missions and upcoming cases, then usually on the way home he listened to music from the orchestra that he downloaded. Having heard the violinist, he was anxious to replay the music from Bach.

Too soon, the concert was over. When the applause began, he hoped to catch a glimpse of the violin soloist. Just as the conductor waved his hand toward her and she rose to her feet, the person in front of him stood, crying out, "Brava!" By the time he scrambled up, the others on the stage had stood as well, once again blocking her from view.

Knowing that members of the orchestra would often mingle with patrons after a concert, he hoped to get to the lobby in time to meet her. Unfortunately, his seat was in the middle of an aisle, and it took all his patience not to push past the people blocking his path. Fifteen minutes later, he made it to the lobby and was surprised at the crowd. Glad for his height, he scanned the tops of heads, looking past the hues of gray, red, brown, or blonde, searching for dark hair pulled tightly back. *Not exactly unique in this crowd.*

With all the women musicians wearing long, black dresses, it only made it that much more difficult for him to ascertain individual differences. Stalking around the perimeter, he gradually worked his way toward the center, his gaze continually sweeping the area, finally landing on the object of his interest.

Once more attempting to push people out of his way in the politest manner possible, he made it to a cluster of musicians surrounded by patrons and well-wishers. Now that he was closer, he understood why it was so difficult to find her. She was so petite her head would easily tuck under his chin. She was chatting with others, but now so near, he allowed his gaze to be filled with her.

With her hair pulled so severely away from her face, it was easy to discern her delicate features, and he blinked at the sight of her eyes. Grey? No, blue-green... more like aqua. He wasn't sure he'd ever met anyone with such striking eyes. Silver glasses framed the beautiful orbs. Her black dress was fitted through the bodice, showing soft curves before flaring out over her hips and ending at her flat black slippers. He stared at her quietly for a moment as she was accepting the congratulations from others, but eventually, her eyes shifted toward him.

They widened slightly as her gaze moved upward, landing on his face, an action he was not unfamiliar with considering his height. Her head tilted slightly to the side, and he jolted, realizing that he was staring. "My apologies for interrupting," he said.

A soft blush appeared across her cheeks, highlighting her face as she inclined her head. "Of course."

Her voice, with only those two words, was as melodious as the tones from her violin had been, and he wanted to push everyone else away so that he could focus her attention solely on him. But just as quickly, someone else moved forward to congratulate her, and she was maneuvered toward another group of patrons.

"Clay."

At the sound of the name, he turned, recognizing the politician standing next to his wife. The previous year, he'd met the congressman and his wife while working on a security detail for their house. Nodding politely, he greeted, "Congressman and Mrs. Bennett. Nice to see you again."

"Wasn't the concert lovely?" Mrs. Bennett asked. An attractive woman, her pleasant smile was welcoming.

"Absolutely. I was late getting a ticket and wasn't sure I was going to be able to make it since I was traveling. I'm thrilled that I was able to be here."

A teenager who looked like a younger version of Mrs. Bennett popped into their circle. Mrs. Bennett smiled wider and wrapped her arm around the girl. "Our Amelia is going to learn how to play the violin, so we wanted her to come tonight so that she could hear the entire symphony."

He smiled politely at the bright-eyed young woman before turning his attention back to the congressman. After another moment of small talk, he was finally able to say his goodbyes. Turning, his heart fell when he realized the hall was emptying, and the beautiful violinist had disappeared before he had a chance to talk to her further.

Clay loved the early morning deep in the caverns before everyone else arrived at work. Mace had created the headquarters for Lighthouse Security Investigations in the caves underneath the decommissioned lighthouse he now owned, having explored them as a child.

As he passed through the kitchen when entering the house, he greeted Marge and Horace, the couple Mace had hired to keep LSI running smoothly. Horace, a retired Navy Seal, kept his gray hair cut high and tight. To the casual eye, he would easily seem to be the laid-back caretaker of the grounds. But Clay knew Horace's eagle-eyed gaze was on every aspect of maintaining and securing LSI. Marge, with the looks and demeanor of a grandmother drill sergeant, eagerly accepted her duties of taking care of the Keepers with as much dedication as when she'd first met Mace on a CIA Special Operation.

Now, down in the main compound room, he munched on one of Marge's famous breakfast biscuits while fixing his coffee. Josh walked up beside him, refilling his mug. Glancing down, he asked, "You on your second cup?"

Josh laughed and shook his head. "Third."

"Damn, you did get here early." He and Josh often worked security from inside the compound. He enjoyed fieldwork but also enjoyed the mental stimulation from puzzling together investigation clues of the information they divined electronically.

Rank and Blake walked in together, and he offered a

chin lift in greeting. They were soon followed by their newest Keeper, Levi.

"Are you and Claire getting settled?" Rank asked Levi.

"Yeah. We're doing great. I'm afraid her introduction to Maine was wild considering that somebody was trying to kill us on the way here, but she's enjoying it now."

Shaking his head, Clay said, "You're crazy! Every one of you is a magnet for relationships that start out with drama."

"That's what keeps everything lively," Babs said, laughing as her fellow Keeper and husband, Drew, leaned over and kissed her with a large smacking sound.

Sylvie placed several files on her desk and turned to smile at him. "Don't you think a little bit of excitement is good?" Mace had stepped in when Sylvie's son witnessed a murder and was threatened. Now, happily married, she was not only Mace's wife but also chief administrative assistant at LSI.

Shaking his head slowly, Clay emphasized, "No, not for me. I think calm, quiet, and easy is the best relationship to have." He kept his reasons private, but his parents had been the poster family for loud, dramatic... and angry. Very angry. It might be Psychology 101, but he knew there was no escaping the chaos that had been his childhood without making sure his adult life was orderly.

Mace walked in, winked at Sylvie, then settled into a chair as the other Keepers filled their seats at the large, round table in the middle of the room. "The International Joint Drug Task Force has offered their official congratulations and thanks for our assistance. The two men that Tate, Clay, and Walker apprehended and turned over were part of a Montréal drug gang, the Minotaurs. The head of the Task Force has asked if we're available for future endeavors."

He looked around the table, every Keeper nodding their acquiescence. Mace's gaze landed on Clay. "You had point on this one, any problem with working with them again?"

Shaking his head, Clay responded, "Nope, not at all. With Levi acting as our FBI liaison, it was smooth sailing."

"Good to hear, because we've got a new assignment."

Chuckling, Tate said, "Hell, that didn't take long."

The others laughed as well, then turned their attention back to Mace. "Continuing to use Levi as our FBI liaison, the Task Force is looking into an American with political connections."

"Who's the target?" Tate asked.

"State Congressman Bennett's closest friend and campaign manager, Jerry Kincaid. The congressman already had basic security set up by our company on his estate, but our target is his campaign headquarters and the residence of Jerry."

"Their suspicions?" Josh asked, tapping on his computer to bring up pictures of the congressman's headquarters. With a few more clicks, he also brought up Jerry's condo.

"His name came up in an investigation of drug trafficking to Canada. So far, the Bureau has nothing concrete, and because of his political and judicial connections, they're trying to keep this under wraps as they dig further. But since they're limited in the scope of what they can do at this juncture, they've asked for our assistance."

Clay rubbed his chin, the vision of the congressman, his wife, and teenage daughter coming to mind. "The Bureau doesn't suspect Congressman Bennett?"

As he looked across the table, he noted Mace's raised eyebrow. He recognized the unasked question in their iconic leader. "I actually saw the congressman and his wife at a concert last evening. Since I was one of the ones who'd initially set up the security for their estate he remembered me."

Nodding, Mace continued, "At this time, the Bureau has no indication that the congressman is involved in anything untoward or illegal. It seems their entire focus is on Jerry Kincaid. Granted, they have nothing concrete, but with his name being linked to the congressman, they want to follow this through. Since you've met with the congressman and have actually been in his campaign headquarters, I'm putting you on this."

"Is the congressman aware of the investigation?"

Mace leaned back in his chair, the metal squeaking with his weight. "No. There's nothing on the congressman, but Jerry is his closest friend and business associate. The Bureau doesn't want to tip their hand to the congressman with their suspicions." He looked toward Clay. "Do you want in on this one?"

"Absolutely. Got no problem working this mission."

"Cobb, I want you on this assignment as well. Your particular expertise will be helpful. Levi will continue being our liaison, and others can help as needed."

With the next assignments divvied out, Clay walked over to Josh and Cobb, settling into their station to plan the first steps of the mission. Thinking of the beautiful violinist he'd just met when the congressman interrupted, he smiled. Having tickets to another philharmonic concert on Friday evening, he'd have the opportunity to meet her again. With that in his mind, he turned back to business.

3

During the entire two-hour drive from his house to the Portland Philharmonic Concert Hall, Clay listened to their music, having downloaded anything he could find that included violin solos. Of course, over the years there had been many soloists, and he had no idea how long the beautiful violinist had been with them. By the time he'd parked and made his way in, he breathed a sigh of relief at having snagged a seat that afforded him a much better view than the previous weekend. This time, having chosen one in the balcony, he'd be able to find her with ease.

While the sound system in his SUV was excellent, it was nothing compared to the actual music created by the instruments as they weaved their magic amongst those present in the hall. From his vantage point, he could now see the violinist that had captured his attention the week before.

Not usually purchasing a program, something he'd regretted last week when he was unable to discern her name, he made sure not to make the same error. Quietly flipping the pages, he scanned the program but discovered the orchestra members' names were listed alphabetically by instrument, still not giving him a clue to her name.

Tonight's concert did not include a violin solo, but he couldn't take his eyes off her nonetheless. Her body swayed gently as her nimble fingers danced over the strings and the bow in her right hand moved with a fluid motion, eliciting pure sounds. While playing, she didn't smile, instead focusing on the music in front of her as her eyes darted between the stand and the director.

When the concert was finally over and the members stood, her lips curved into a smile. He wondered if she was pleased with her performance, simply glad the concert was over, or if there was something else in her life that made her happy. Desiring that smile to turn toward him, he made his way quickly to the entrance lobby, determined to meet her tonight.

His observational skills were keen, and soon his gaze found her. Tonight's long black dress was different from the one she wore last week, and he wondered how many different performance dresses she owned. The square neckline and fitted bodice only hinted at her curves, while the skirt flowed to her low-heeled black pumps. Her hair was once again pulled severely into a bun, and her minimal makeup showcased a pale complexion with just a hint of color on her cheeks and lips.

Approaching with haste, he slowed his steps at the

last minute, not wanting to intimidate with his size. She was once again engaged in a conversation, but he stood to the side and waited. As soon as she turned, he stepped closer. Her gaze landed on his chest before her head dropped back and her eyes lifted to his. His breath caught in his throat at the sight of her pale, aqua eyes pinned on him. "Excuse me, miss, but I wanted to tell you how much I enjoyed the concert. Your Bach solo, in particular."

Her lips curved slowly into a smile, and he was as ensnared by the expression on her face as he had been enraptured by her music.

Inclining her head ever so slightly, she replied, "Thank you, but I didn't have a solo tonight."

Now, it was his turn to smile. "That's true, but I was here last week. I wanted to speak to you after that concert but unfortunately was detained before I was able to fully express my gratitude."

Her brow lifted and her smile widened. "So, you came tonight just to make sure that you could pass on your appreciation?"

"At the risk of sounding a bit stalker-ish, yes. I try to catch several concerts during the season but definitely was hoping to hear you play again."

"I'm flattered, and the orchestra certainly appreciates your dedication to the arts."

Her voice was exactly as he remembered—soft and lyrical.

He stuck his hand out and said, "I'm Clay."

"And does Clay have a last name?" she asked, her head tilted slightly to the side as she peered up at him.

The motion pushed her chin out, exposing the pale expanse of her neck, making him wonder if it tasted as delectable as it looked. Clearing his throat, he added, "Actually, my name is Hank Claiborne. But everyone calls me Clay."

"Everyone?"

"Well, my friends. I suppose everyone except my mother." He shrugged and added, "It's a nickname from my days in the military."

She reached out and placed her hand into his much larger one. "Christina. Christina Monroe."

He wrapped his fingers around hers, just enough to feel the tingle spread throughout his arm while not crushing her hand.

Her gaze dropped to where their hands met before lifting back up to his face. "You have a delicate touch, Mr. Claiborne."

"I would never crush a woman's hand in a hand-shake, but I'm especially careful when greeting someone whose fingers elicit such beautiful music. And please, call me Clay."

Her smile widened and her eyes sparkled. "Ah, but you said that your friends call you Clay. We don't know each other well enough for me to take that liberty."

"I'd love to ask you for coffee, and we can rectify how well you know me."

"Now?" She blinked as the word held a sense of incredulity.

"There's no time like the present."

She rolled her eyes and shook her head. "I'm very

sorry, Mr. Claiborne, but it's ten o'clock at night. If I had coffee now, I'd never get to sleep."

"Tomorrow is Saturday. Can you not sleep in during the weekend?"

"My sleeping habits are not up for discussion," she said, her eyes twinkling and her lips twitching upward. "Actually, I'm very busy, even on the weekends." Her top teeth landed on her bottom lip, now snagging his attention as he stared at the reddened flesh. Her delicate shoulders lifted. "Anyway, I'm afraid I don't know you well enough to accept an invitation to coffee."

Just then, a server passed by with a silver tray filled with champagne goblets. Snagging two, Clay handed one to her. "Well then, if we have drinks now, we can consider this our first date. Then perhaps meeting for coffee would not seem quite so forward."

She threw her head back and laughed, and his eyes were once again drawn to her neck. In fact, everything about her drew his attention. Her dark hair, pale complexion, blue-green eyes, petite stature—

She clinked the edge of her glass against his and said, "Then here's to our first date."

"While it's not a perfectly planned first date, the fact that I'm in a beautiful place with a beautiful woman sipping champagne makes it perfect."

"My, my, you do know how to make a girl feel special even in the middle of a crowd of people!" She sipped more. "Do you always come to the concerts?"

"Not always. Sometimes work interferes. But when you're in season, I try to get to as many concerts as possible."

She appeared to carefully consider his words. "What work are you in? Or is that too many questions for a first date?"

Chuckling, he shook his head. "I think it's important to get as much information as possible out on the table for a first date. After all, I know what you do." He shrugged and said, "I work for a security company."

"Oh, I remember when a security company was installing the locks on our instrument rooms in the back."

He smiled and nodded politely.

"So, what else should we get out of the way on our first date?" she asked. "Favorite sports team? Favorite color? Favorite drink? Oh, how about most embarrassing childhood story?"

"I'm game for whatever you want to tell me."

"Okay," she said, drawing out the word. "Let's start easy… my favorite color is blue."

"The color of your eyes blue or a different shade? Cause I've got to tell you that I didn't have a favorite color until I saw your eyes. And now, aqua is absolutely my favorite."

She laughed again and gently pushed her glasses up on her nose. "Oh, my, you are really good at this first date stuff!"

Now it was his turn to smile as they finished their champagne. He slid her empty glass from her fingers and handed both back to one of the servers without ever taking his eyes off her. "I'd like to see you again. I definitely think we're ready for a second date."

"Well, next Friday night, I'll be right here at the

concert hall. That will be the first chance I have to see you. No pressure, though. If you're here… then you're here. So, goodbye, Mr. Claiborne." Inclining her head, she smiled, turned, and quickly walked through the doors leading to the area behind the stage.

Clay watched her disappear and sucked in a quick breath before blowing it out slowly. It had been a long time since he'd felt such a pull toward a woman. Still smiling, he walked out the front and down the street to his vehicle. He knew she didn't expect it, but he planned on being in the same place next week. And that would count as date number two.

Clay easily disabled the security at Congressman Bennett's campaign headquarters, and he, Blake, Tate, and Levi slipped inside. The headquarters' security was not elaborate, but Clay was methodical, checking each step as they went. With night vision goggles, they deftly maneuvered through the mass of desks, tables, chairs, and boxes.

Tate and Blake installed cameras and audio surveillance, taking a few extra minutes to explain their system to Levi, who was used to the constraints that the Bureau placed on him and appeared glad to be able to focus on the mission at hand instead of legalities imposed by desk jockeys.

Opening one of the boxes, Clay peered inside, seeing reams of printed flyers, each pronouncing the congressman's achievements in his bid for reelection. Looking at the others, there was nothing suspicious in the office at all.

The headquarters was simplistic in layout. The main area was a large workroom where most of the volunteers would spend their time on the first floor, along with several smaller, utilitarian conference rooms. A few tiny offices, bathrooms, and a break room completed that space. Once the surveillance cameras were in place, they slipped up the stairs to the second floor.

This floorspace was broken up into carpeted rooms and larger offices with furniture that was a cut above the metal tables and chairs found below. While the others placed cameras and microphones around, Clay made his way into Jerry's office, finding it more elaborate than the rest of the floor. A heavy wooden desk sat on the plush carpeting. He was sure Jerry kept his personal laptop with him, but there was another one on the desk.

Using a drive that Josh had created, he popped it in and within a few minutes set up the parameters so that Josh would be able to see what was on Jerry's computer at all times, including the history.

A quick glance at files in a drawer gave him nothing, and he checked inside a few more cardboard boxes in the corner, each revealing more of the congressman's flyers. Installing the surveillance equipment in this office as well, he left it as he found it and made his way back to the others. "Ready for a check."

"Affirmative," Josh replied.

Clay waited for a few more minutes until Josh gave

them the all-clear to leave. Making sure the building held no clues that they had ever been there, they slipped out the back. Once they left the area, he radioed Josh to have him reinstate the outside security on the building.

"Hey, Nora is getting Babs to teach her and a few of the other wives how to scuba dive," Tate said as they pulled up to their vehicles they'd left at the LSI compound. "Levi, you should ask Claire if she wants to join."

Shaking his head, Clay chuckled. "How the hell do you do that? I thought it was just us that were adrenaline junkies, but now it seems like your women are, too."

"What plans do you have this weekend?" Blake asked.

"Me? I'm driving down to Portland where I have tickets to the Philharmonic Orchestra."

Tate blinked slowly. "Seriously? You're going to put on a suit, drive two hours, and listen to highbrow music? Music that you can't even tap your foot to or dance to?"

"Gotta tell you, Tate, there's more to music than honky-tonk." Clapping him on the back, Clay jogged to his SUV with the sound of laughter coming from the others. That was okay by him. He couldn't wait for Friday night and the chance to hear Christina play once again. Especially since this would be their second date.

4

The decorated lobby with its red carpet and gilded portraits hanging on the walls offered a festive vibe as white-coated servers carried silver trays of champagne goblets. Snagging two flutes of the amber bubbly, Clay waited anxiously by the door where the musicians would appear after the concert was over.

As soon as Christina walked out, he stepped forward. Her eyes widened as her feet stuttered to a halt, and a smile curved her lips. He grinned as he held out the glass. "You look surprised."

"I didn't really think you'd come tonight," she admitted, accepting the champagne from him. "Three Friday nights in a row... I don't know whether to be flattered at the dedication to our symphony or concerned about being stalked."

"I assure you, Ms. Monroe, I'm not stalking. Admiration for your music? Absolutely. Want to get to know you better? Definitely. But I would never want to make you uncomfortable, so if you'd like me to leave you alone, I'll respect your wishes. Regretfully but respectfully."

Behind her eyeglasses, her blue-green eyes appeared larger as she held his gaze with an intense one of her own. "I appreciate your honesty," she said, lifting her champagne flute.

He clicked his with hers, then asked, "And may I ask what we're drinking to?"

As though unable to hold back her mirth, she smiled widely. "To our second date, of course."

Relief coursed through him, and he laughed. Finishing his champagne, he replaced their empty flutes onto the passing server's tray. She was jostled from behind by a large man walking past, and Clay stepped closer, his hand sliding around her, his fingers lightly touching her back. He could not help but notice her dress, the sweetheart neckline hinting at cleavage and a long skirt that was not as full as the one she'd worn the week before. With her standing this close, it was easy to see he was right in his first assessment. Her head would fit underneath his chin.

"You're staring," she stated, peering up at him. "I can also tell that you're pondering something, but what, I have no idea."

"I was simply admiring your dress and couldn't help but wonder how many black dresses you own."

"Don't you know? Women are supposed to have lots of little black dresses." Waving her hand down the front, she admitted, "Of course, this isn't exactly little."

"Well, if you consider how petite you are, then it could be considered little even if it goes to the floor."

She cocked her hip and tapped her toe as her eyes narrowed. "Are you cracking a short joke?"

Shaking his head slowly, he continued to hold her gaze. "I assure you, Ms. Monroe, I think every inch of you is beautiful." His gaze dropped from her eyes to her mouth where once again her top teeth pressed against her bottom lip.

"You certainly know how to turn a phrase, Mr. Claiborne."

"Hmm... when will you call me Clay?"

She rolled her eyes toward the ceiling and tapped her forefinger against her chin. "Considering this is our second date, I think we're *almost* to the first name basis."

"Is there any chance I can entice you out to eat? I know it's late, but I thought you might be hungry." He saw interest flare in her eyes. "Oh, I seemed to have hit upon the right subject. Food."

She hesitated before admitting, "I skipped lunch today—"

Not waiting for her to say anything else, he guided her back to the door leading to the area behind the stage. "Please, allow me to take you to dinner. I know a little diner where you can get breakfast food all day and all night."

Her eyes brightened, and her hand landed on her chest. "Oh, my God, that sounds amazing."

He smiled at the enthusiastic comment. "Then gather what you need backstage, and I'll be right here waiting for you."

She smiled and nodded, then disappeared through the door. While waiting, the thought struck him that if she was like the women his friends were with, then right about now she'd get kidnapped... or shot at... or disappear suspiciously, leaving him to search for her. Another moment slipped by, and his heartbeat increased as he waited. Lifting his hand, he placed it on the door, determined to go look for her. Then suddenly, the door flung open and she reappeared.

No longer in her black dress, she wore black slacks, a demure white blouse, and carried a royal blue coat along with her violin case. Silently chastising himself for his ridiculous thoughts, he helped her slide her arms into her coat. With his hand once again on her back, he gently guided her toward the door.

Before walking out, she placed her hand on his arm. "I texted a friend of mine, and she asked who I was going out with. I realized that I should see some ID."

"Smart woman," he rushed, shaking his head. "I can't believe I didn't think of that. To be honest, I'm embarrassed that I didn't."

She laughed as she squeezed his arm. "Well, we can just say that you were dumbfounded by my beauty and couldn't think of anything practical."

He didn't laugh along with her, instead holding her gaze. "You're not far from the truth." He pulled out his wallet and handed his driver's license to her.

She looked at it carefully and then said, "It's nice to see that your name really is Hank Claiborne." Pulling out her phone, she quickly typed a message and hit send. "I'm sending your name and license number to my friend. I know that doesn't sound very trusting—"

"Don't worry about it, Christina. You're being smart and doing exactly what I want you to do." Waving his hand toward his SUV, he said, "Now, let's eat."

The diner was a quick drive, and after they ordered, he glanced around the restaurant he'd eaten at several times. Red vinyl seats, plastic menus, paper napkins rolled around the silverware. Swinging his gaze back to her, he cringed. *I should have taken her somewhere nice.* "I'm sorry that this place isn't... um... well, quite so..."

Her large eyes blinked at him from behind her glasses. "Isn't what?"

Pulling at the collar of his shirt, he held her gaze. "I should have taken you somewhere much nicer."

"Somewhere fancier?"

When he nodded, she grinned. "But then I couldn't have ordered French toast, which, by the way, is my all-time favorite breakfast food." Her smile dropped slightly as her brow crinkled. "Well, that and scrambled eggs. Oh, and bacon."

His nerves easing, he chuckled. "So, you're saying this simple diner is not turning you off of our second date?"

"Quite the contrary. If you'd tried to pawn off fancy-schmancy food this late at night, I would have gagged!" She looked around before settling her gaze back on him and a gentle smile crossed her face. "This place is perfect. And now you know more random facts about me."

When their food arrived, he watched as she dug into

her favorites with obvious joy. She drank juice instead of coffee but appeared to appreciate every bite.

"So, what's your favorite food?" she asked, licking syrup off her lips.

His focus zeroed in on her lips and his brain threatened to short circuit. "Uh... what?"

"Your favorite food," she laughed.

"Right... well, to be honest, I like a lot of things." When she lifted her brows in a prodding manner, he continued, "I love a medium-rare steak but can chow down on a hamburger."

"Oh, a meat and potatoes man."

"I can give equal devotion to seafood, pork chops, barbeque chicken, and right now, eggs and bacon."

"I knew we had that in common!" she exclaimed, biting into another piece of bacon.

He loved her enthusiastic responses. "Do you usually skip lunch before a concert?"

Shaking her head, she swallowed. "No, not really. Today I was busy with practice and just didn't have time." She held his gaze for a moment before asking, "Did you enjoy the concert tonight?"

His lips curved slightly at the memory, and he nodded slowly. "It was beautiful. I confess that I've never heard the Mahler Symphony No. 5 in person before. It was exquisite." She smiled at his response, and he chuckled. "Are you testing me?"

"No," she replied, shaking her head. "I was just curious. Have you always loved orchestras?"

"My mom used to listen all the time. She had some old LPs and tons of cassette tapes. She was not particularly musical herself but loved all types of music. We listened to jazz, symphonies, bluegrass… she loved the music from the '60s and '70s as well."

"So, you're a fan of The Mamas and the Papas as well as Bach?"

"Absolutely. In my house, there was equal respect for Beethoven as well as The Righteous Brothers."

She laughed as she pushed her glasses up on her nose, and he stared into her twinkling eyes. *Sucked in.* That was the only way he could describe what he was feeling at the moment. Absolutely sucked into her beauty, her words, and her music. Suddenly, wanting to know everything about her, he asked, "What do you do besides make music so beautiful that it could make a grown man weep?"

Her mouth dropped open. "Wow, what a job description you've just given me!"

"I never lie," he said, his voice now solemn.

She inhaled deeply then let her breath out slowly. "Okay… well, let's see. I practice my violin. I work with the symphony as well as practice with a string quartet and a small group of like-minded musicians. I also teach privately but only have a few select students. I'd like to teach more but there's only so many hours in a day."

"So, you really are a full-time musician."

Nodding, she sipped the last of her juice. "Many in the orchestra work other jobs but it's a competitive business. Keeping my musical skills up is the way to stay where I am, make enough money to live on, and I get to do what I love all the time."

"I admire your skills but confess I also envy your natural talent, something I didn't have."

Her head tilted slightly to the side again, her chin jutting out in a way that he now recognized as a sign that she was considering his words carefully. He wasn't surprised when she asked, "That sounds like you played at one time."

"You can imagine with my mom loving music the way she did that she insisted I learn an instrument. I wanted to play the drums." His forearms were resting on the table, and he turned his palms up as he shrugged his shoulders. "But she insisted on the violin."

"The violin?" she asked, incredulity dripping from the two words.

"I was in the middle school orchestra, but I'm afraid I just didn't have the aptitude. My fingers simply did not want to move the way they should. Then, by eighth grade, a growth spurt caused the delicate instrument to feel too tiny for my large hands. My mom wanted to push the cello on me, but I'd discovered two other things that pulled my attention—sports and girls. By the time I hit high school, I was over six feet tall, a heavy hitter baseball player, and... um..."

"Don't stop your story now! I have a feeling this is going to be where the girls come in."

His face heated as he admitted, "I discovered a cute cheerleader was way more impressed with me in my baseball uniform than she'd ever been when I was wearing my dark suit for the orchestra."

Her smile widened as her eyes drifted over his torso. "While I've never seen you in a baseball uniform, I can only say that you cut quite an impressive figure in your dark suit."

As he paid the server, she stifled a yawn. "I hate for our date to end but can tell you're exhausted."

"I am," she admitted. "I'm afraid it's been a long day, but I love how it ended."

He escorted her back to his SUV, holding her hand as he assisted her into the passenger seat. The drive back to the concert hall was much too short, and before he was ready for the evening to end, he parked next to the vehicle she indicated was hers. Shutting down the engine, he made no move to exit, instead turning to face her. "I had a really nice time, Christina."

She unbuckled and twisted to face him, a smile on her face. "I did too, Clay."

"Clay? I've made it to first name status." He rested his arm on the back of her seat and leaned forward slightly. "Do I dare hope that we might have a third date?"

"I'd like that. In fact, it doesn't even have to be on a Friday night after a concert." As soon as the words left her mouth, her brow scrunched slightly, and she sighed. "Although, this week is going to be a bit crazy. A group that I play with is laying down tracks for a demo. I'm not sure how much free time I'll have."

"That's impressive," he said, leaning even closer. He lifted his hand and slid his fingers over the soft skin of her neck, his thumb sweeping the apple of her cheek. Hesitating, he wanted to give control over to her. As she leaned her face into his palm, he closed the distance, stopping a whisper away.

Her eyes remained open, pinned on his until dropping to his mouth. She shifted in her seat, drawing nearer, her lips molding to his. Just as he thought, she tasted as sweet as she looked. Her mouth was soft and warm, and with the slightest bit of pressure, she angled her head so that their noses wouldn't bump as their mouths devoured each other. His tongue swept inside, tangling with hers, and he swallowed her groan. For a moment, he reveled in making out with her before pulling back, not wanting her to think his romance skills ended with the cheerleader in high school.

He glanced down at her kiss-swollen lips now curved into a smile, knowing a smile was plastered on his face as well. Glancing at her purse resting beside her, he said, "Give me your phone."

Without hesitation, she reached inside her bag, pulled out her phone, unlocked it and handed it to him. He tapped the keys, then handed it back. "I just put my name and number in your contacts. I won't ask for yours, but if you want, send me a message or give me a call and then I'll have your number on my phone." He kissed her lightly once again, then added, "I really hope you do. I'd love a third date."

He stepped out of his SUV and jogged around the front, offering his hand to assist her down. Making sure she had her purse, keys, phone, and of course, her violin, he waited until she was safely inside her vehicle. Waving as she drove away, he climbed back inside his SUV and started the engine. The screen indicated a message had been sent to his phone. Glancing at it, he grinned.

Can't wait for a 3rd date. Now you have my number.

Chuckling, he began the two-hour drive home, listening to violin concertos as he smiled at the thought of seeing her again.

5

"My liaison at the Bureau says that our surveillance on Congressman Bennett's headquarters has given them no evidence. They're still convinced that Jerry Kincaid is quite possibly involved in illegal drugs as part of the pipeline that goes from Mexico up the East Coast through Maine and then jumps to Canada," Levi reported at the LSI meeting.

"Jumps?" Clay asked.

"The cartels use their connections with motorcycle gangs to transport over land and air. They may also be taking small boats from the coast of Maine and transporting them short distances to Canada."

"What about the Coast Guard?" Rank asked.

"So far, if the drug runners are using very small boats, they've managed to slip past the Coast Guard monitoring."

"I've been keeping track, but for the past month, Jerry has only spent two nights at his condo," Josh reported. "Travel takes up some of that, but has the FBI looked to see where the man is laying his head at night?"

"Jerry still owns his condo but now lives on the congressman's estate, but not at the main house," Levi said.

Josh tapped on his computer, bringing up pictures of the congressman's home and the security system LSI had installed.

"I remember doing this work last year," Clay said. "It was specialized security cameras on the main house outside doors and windows. That was all."

Mace said, "Then we need to get more eyes on where Jerry spends his time. That's what makes you perfect for this. You've been on the estate."

Clay and the others glanced up to the screen and the image Josh had produced. He nodded. "There were a number of buildings on the congressman's estate. He inherited it from his father, and besides the main house where the family lives, there are several smaller buildings where live-in servants stay, and near the coast is a house that was often used for family and friends when the congressman's father entertained friends from D.C. Congressman Bennett had newer guesthouses built closer to the pool. Jerry lives in the guesthouse right by the water."

"What's that? A boathouse connected to the guesthouse?" Tate asked, leaning forward to stare at the image.

Clay nodded. "Yeah, we didn't have security placed there. At the time, Congressman Bennett simply wanted the main family home to be wired for security. None of the servants' houses or guesthouses were involved." Turning his attention from the screen back to Mace, he asked, "What's the assignment?"

"Our security is already set up so that we can see what's going on. I want to get eyes and ears on the guesthouse. The FBI has the boathouse monitored, but we don't have the same limitations they do for getting into the guesthouse."

Rank grinned and shot a raised-brow expression toward Clay. "Hell, Mace, you should send in a SEAL, not a Ranger."

"Right, like you know what kind of security to lay down," Clay fired back, his lips quirking upward.

"Before we get into a pissing contest about which former military career had the biggest dicks, let's get back to what we need." Mace glanced toward Sylvie, mumbling, "Sorry, babe."

She laughed, shook her head, and continued typing on her keyboard. Babs rolled her eyes, grinning as well.

"When do you want me to go in?" Clay asked.

"Congressman Bennett, his family, and Jerry are all going down to the Hamptons on Friday. Once we confirm their itinerary, we'll get you in."

Clay nodded his acquiescence, then moved to Josh's station with Blake, Levi, and Tate to plan.

Tate clapped him on the back. "Sorry, man. That'll cut into your Friday night with your girl."

Shrugging, he replied, "I'll see if she can get together a different day next weekend."

"A month of Friday night orchestra concerts... that's dedication," Josh laughed. "She must be something else."

"She is, believe me. Pretty. Sweet. A fuckin' talented musician."

"So, is it getting serious?" Tate asked, bringing up the congressman's security on his tablet.

"Not yet, but I'm hopeful. With her schedule and mine, it gets hard to squeeze in more dates than just the orchestra and dinner afterwards." He smiled at the thought of their more-frequent late-night calls and texts over the past several weeks.

"That grin says she's something special," Blake said, walking over.

Turning back to the screen in front of him, he murmured, "Yeah, she is."

Christina rushed through the door, crying out, "I hope you're finished in the bathroom! Sorry I'm late!"

Her roommate and best friend, Amy, laughed. "No worries. I'm ready, so you jump in and do what you need to do."

Throwing off her clothes, she grabbed the long, black dress that Amy had laid out for her. "I couldn't believe the studio was backed up, and of course, my student was the one whose parents insist that they get their full hour. Even when I cut it short five minutes to tell her that I had to get home for the concert, she rolled her eyes as though that was the biggest inconvenience she'd had all week."

"Is that gorgeous boyfriend of yours coming again tonight?"

Christina looked over at Amy and smiled. She was already in her dress, hair pulled back into a bun, and was slicking on the barest hint of lip gloss. Turning back to stare at her reflection in the mirror, Christina tucked one more bobby pin into her own hair, making sure no strand was out of place.

Amy was right about Clay being gorgeous. The first time she stood near him in the lobby of the concert hall, she had been struck with his square jaw, piercing eyes, and tall, muscular body in the perfectly fitting suit. Standing near him made her feel even more petite, but he was so careful with her, she felt protected. And every time since that first moment, her knowledge of him had confirmed her first impression—gorgeous, inside and out.

"First of all, he's not my boyfriend—"

"Well, he's been waiting for you after every concert and taking you to dinner afterwards. In my book, I'd say that makes him your boyfriend."

She sighed. "He won't be there tonight. He said he had business to attend to."

"Business? On a Friday night? Are you sure that's legit?" Amy walked into the living room, grabbing her instrument case.

Checking her appearance one last time, Christina adjusted her black orchestra dress. Her hair was slicked back away from her face and her makeup was minimal, two things the conductor preferred for all the women in the orchestra. He wanted everyone in the audience to focus on the music and not the individuals playing instruments. Following Amy into the living room, she picked up her violin case and checked her slim leather bag to make sure she had the music she needed.

"Again, he's not my boyfriend so it doesn't matter if it's legit or not. But he doesn't seem like the type to lie. I don't know a lot about what he does, but I know he works for a security company." Shrugging, she added, "Let's face it, I have to work Friday nights most of the time."

"You're right, I hadn't thought about it like that." Amy wiggled her eyebrows as they left the small apartment, locking the door behind them. "I have to admit, he's dreamy, Christina. And he loves to listen to the orchestra."

Sucking in her lips, she nodded as she followed Amy down the stairs to her car. "Yeah... he does," she whispered under her breath. "He loves the orchestra."

With the congressman, his family, and campaign manager out of town on their trip, LSI was free to set up surveillance at the congressman's estate. Josh, back at the LSI compound, monitored the cameras while Blake, Levi, and Tate assisted Clay on-site. Levi had continued being the liaison with the local Bureau. Slipping into the guesthouse that Jerry occupied, they maneuvered amongst the furniture with night vision goggles.

Blake whistled softly. "Damn, no wonder Jerry lives here. This may be the congressman's guesthouse, but it's a fuck of lot nicer than where most people live."

"The congressman's father was a U.S. Senator and his grandfather was friends with the Kennedys. From what I understand, they've entertained a lot of rich and famous people at their estate."

The Keepers stood in a three-story great room, with stairs leading to the third floor visible from the balcony above. Several doors opened from the second-floor balcony, possibly bedrooms. While Blake and Tate quickly fitted the rooms with cameras, Clay and Levi headed upstairs. Just as he surmised, three bedrooms led from the second-floor balcony, each with their own en suite. The largest was obviously Jerry's bedroom. After installing cameras there, Clay jogged up the stairs to the third floor. Much smaller, it was still larger than many people's apartments. Furniture was arranged for social gatherings, and the windows offered an expansive view from all sides. A wet bar, including a full-sized refrigerator, was on one side.

Turning around slowly, Clay commented, "Jerry has a visual on the whole estate from here, including the ocean."

Blake nodded as he peered out a few of the windows. "From up here, he could keep an eye on anyone coming and going from the main house as well as any boats nearby."

The four Keepers checked the area, but it didn't appear that Jerry had installed any security or cameras of his own.

"He must be very trusting," Levi murmured.

"I think he probably feels very safe here," Clay added, his gaze scanning the area as he tried to see it through

Jerry's eyes. "He has the absolute trust of the congressman, therefore the trust of anyone who's around the congressman. They've been friends since childhood, so no one has a reason to think he has an ulterior motive." It was easy to see from the furniture cushion indentations as well as the placement of two telescopes that the room was well used.

"It doesn't appear that the cleaning staff has been through this week," Blake said, pointing to the trashcan containing a couple of imported beer bottles.

"If I had to guess, this is a place he spends a lot of time. Private. Quiet. There's an extra laptop charger and phone charger on the counter. He can conduct business while keeping an eye on the comings and goings at the main house, the boathouse, and the water."

"It's fuckin' crazy, man," Tate said. "It's like he's got his own hideout in plain view."

"Yeah, a hideout where he can keep track of everything going on with everybody around him, and yet no one knows what he's really up to."

"Well, until now." Installing the last camera, Blake turned around and grinned.

Slipping outside under the cover of darkness, they made their way back to their boat with stealth, then quietly up the coast back to LSI. Entering through the caverns, they secured their craft and headed up to the workroom.

"I swear, I don't know how you get used to this," Levi said, walking behind Clay. "First time Mace took me down here, I couldn't believe it."

The others laughed while nodding. "As he hired us,

he was still working on this," Clay said. "If I hadn't run special ops with him, I would've thought he was crazy to create this space in the caverns. As it is, he's fuckin' brilliant."

Checking with Josh to make sure all the cameras were functional, the group headed to the elevator and left the building.

6

A week later, Clay reached for Christina's violin case, sliding it from her fingers as she tossed a shawl over her shoulders to ward off the spring night's chill. Wrapping his arm around her shoulders, he escorted her to his vehicle, assisting her inside. Flipping on the radio, the sound of the '70s filled the air.

"Oh, the Doobie Brothers!" She grinned, looking at him. "Favorite Doobie song?"

"Their Michael McDonald years and probably Taking It to the Streets," he answered easily, turning to look at her face glowing in the streetlights. "You?"

"Tell Me What You Want and I'll Give You What You Need," she answered just as quickly.

Chuckling, he said, "I like that song... I like that title."

"I'll bet you do. So, if I tell you what I want, you'll give it to me?"

The interior of the SUV filled with sexual energy and the only reason he looked away was because he was still driving. "You can tell me what you want anytime." Her smile speared straight through him.

Her head swung around as they drove past the diner and she turned her attention back to him. "By the way, why did you want me to stay in my concert dress tonight?"

"Because I'm finally taking you somewhere nice."

Lifting an eyebrow, she remained quiet as he drove several blocks before parking outside a small Italian restaurant. Her eyes bugged, but he rushed to say, "I know you're not in the mood for a big Italian dinner this late at night, but to celebrate, I thought at least dessert and wine would be appropriate."

"What are we celebrating?"

"Being together and... well... just getting to know each other more and more."

Still sitting in his parked SUV, she leaned forward and placed her hands on his thigh. Her soft breath puffed over his face as he leaned toward her as well. "I think that sounds wonderful," she whispered. "And what would you say if I told you that what I wanted was a kiss?"

"Your wish is my command," he assured just before closing the distance.

Her lips were soft and sweet, and he suddenly wished that she didn't have a roommate or he didn't live two hours away. Sliding his arms around her, he pulled her close, angling her head so that when his tongue slid inside her mouth, they both could take advantage of their positions. Her breasts were crushed against the hard planes of his chest. The wet kiss continued as their tongues tangled, filling his senses. His cock was at attention, pressing against his zipper, desperate to sink inside her sweet body. She finally pressed lightly on his shoulders and they separated, her chest heaving with deep breaths.

"Wow," she whispered.

"Yeah, wow." Grinning, he asked, "I swore we were going to take things slow, but are you sure your roommate is back in the apartment?"

Her expression fell as she nodded slowly. "Yes. Amy has an early morning practice tomorrow and was heading home as soon as the concert was over."

"Okay, then let's get some tiramisu and wine. I'll feed you and fantasize."

A giggle slipped out, and he kissed her lightly again before escorting her inside the restaurant. Even with the late hour, the inside was crowded with patrons, but he'd had the foresight to call ahead. Following the hostess to a small table covered in a red-checkered cloth near the back, they settled into the wooden chairs. Ordering wine, tiramisu, crème brûlée, and a coffee for him, he turned his attention back to Christina.

"This is nice," she said. "I've never had anyone so infatuated with my music that they came to see me for all my concerts."

"I'm not like most guys."

Her gaze held his and she reached over to take his hand resting on top of the table. "You're right, you're not."

"Your music is enrapturing, Christina, but that's not

why I'm infatuated. It's you. Everything about you. Your music, your beauty, your gentle spirit, everything."

"You're not like anyone I've ever met." Shrugging, she kept rubbing his hand. "Now that I think about it, it seems like I've only been around musicians for a long time."

"Speaking of musicians, have you talked to your parents lately?"

Her smile widened. "Is that your way of asking if I've told them about you?"

Laughing, he nodded. "Busted."

"Actually, yes. I talked to them earlier today. They were asking about the piece I was playing tonight."

"That's right, you said it was difficult."

"Sometimes it's scoffed at since Mozart No. 3 in G is one of the first pieces that violinists learn, but it's still a Mozart concerto. In some ways, it's one of the easiest of the three major Mozart openings, but it still ranks high in difficulty because it's also easy to sound really bad!"

As she spoke, he watched her hands as they fluttered about. The way she expressed herself, both with words and music and even the way her hands moved when she talked, was one of the things he loved about her. *Loved.* Blinking as that word reverberated through his mind, he forced his thoughts back to what she was saying.

"Mom and Dad also told me that the L.A. Philharmonic Orchestra is going to be traveling to three countries in the next several months."

Brows raised, he asked, "Is that something that you want to do, also?"

Her nose wrinkled slightly as she shook her head.

"No… not with the orchestra. Mom and Dad's musical goals are… different… from mine." She huffed. "It's hard to explain to someone not in the industry."

Squeezing her hand, he said, "Then just tell me. Honestly, Christina, I want to know everything about you." Something flashed through her eyes but quickly left, leaving him uncertain if his mind was playing tricks in the dark restaurant lit mostly with candlelight.

"My father is a concertmaster—the lead violinist. It's a coveted position that comes with not only status but a higher salary. My mother is the cellist which, like my father's position, means she is the top cello player. You know, they used to be with the New York Philharmonic Orchestra and then both received offers to move to California to participate in the L.A. Philharmonic. They were ready for a change and the timing was right. I was out of college and already employed by the Portland Orchestra. They wanted me to come with them, but it was never my goal."

"You wanted to strike out on your own."

Eyes bright, she nodded and smiled. "Exactly. I know, I know, it's very common for any young person to want to separate from their parents. I was no different. Only, since we were all in the same business, it was even more important for me to have a separate professional identity from them. Plus, my musical goals are different."

"Different?"

She nibbled on her bottom lip as her brow scrunched again. Lifting her gaze, she said, "I enjoy teaching. I enjoy a variety of music, not just playing in the orchestra. I'm completely dedicated to the orchestra, but it's a much smaller, less prestigious one. I have time to pursue other musical interests. Believe me, with an orchestra like New York or L.A., you are one-hundred percent dedicated and invested in that job."

The server interrupted with their desserts, and for the next several minutes their talk halted as groans of delight left their lips. Looking across the table toward her, a tiny dab of chocolate on the corner of her mouth snagged his attention, and he wanted to lean over to kiss it off. Instead, he lifted his finger and gently swiped it away. Startled, her tongue darted out over her lips.

"I wish I'd done that."

Tilting her head to the side, she asked, "Done what?"

"Licked the chocolate off your lips."

Her breath hitched. "I wish you had, also."

"Don't tempt me. I'm barely hanging on not grabbing you, tossing you over my shoulder, and dragging you out of here."

Her fingers covered her mouth as she stifled her mirth. "That might sound caveman-ish, but I'm barely hanging on not saying to hell with the tiramisu and leaping across the table and landing in your lap."

He jammed his hand into his back pocket and grabbed his wallet. Tossing enough money to pay for their food, including a huge tip, he grabbed her hand and gently pulled her from the chair. With a head nod toward the server, he guided her outside. His intention had been to get to his SUV as quickly as possible, but his movements were thwarted when she rounded on him, plastered herself to his front, lifted on her toes, and wrapped her arms around his neck.

"I'm a little short, so I could use some help," she said, her words filled with desperation.

His answer was to wrap his arms around her waist and lift, bringing her lips straight to his. With his back resting against the brick building, their kiss flamed hot. She tasted of wine and sweet dessert. Her legs separated as though she wanted to wrap them around his waist, but her long skirt didn't allow the movement.

"Get a room," someone called out from the parking lot, laughing loudly.

With her still in his arms, they separated, breaths coming in pants.

"I wish we could," she said.

He growled, "Change of plans."

Thirty minutes later, after checking into the Portland Harbor Hotel, clothes flew off as they stumbled around, each trying to undress the other while maintaining their kiss.

"Christ," he mumbled after he grabbed a condom, barely catching her as they fell onto the bed. "I had more finesse as a teenager."

Laughing, she tossed her eyeglasses to the nightstand, then cupped his jaws, holding his gaze while wrapping her now-free legs around his waist. "I think your technique is perfect."

His cock settled against her core, but afraid of crushing her on the soft mattress, he flipped them so she was on top. She lifted and impaled herself on his erection, eliciting a gasp from his lips and a moan from her.

"Christina, I didn't get you ready—"

"I'm ready," she rushed, her eyes finding his. "I've been ready ever since I first laid eyes on you."

If her words were meant to excite, they had the desired effect. Grabbing her hips with his hands, he lifted her slightly, steadying her movements as she allowed him to thrust upward. Her fingers clutched his shoulders before dragging her short nails over his chest. Her breasts bounced to their rhythm, their two bodies working together.

His hands glided up to cup her full breasts. "You're just as beautiful as I imagined... and I've imagined you like this more than I want to admit."

Leaning down, she kissed him, mumbling, "This is better than what I've been fantasizing."

Her hair was still in its bun, but a few strands were now loosened and waving around her face. Her pale eyes were hooded with lust.

He lifted his torso enough to capture a taut nipple in his mouth, pulling it deeply. Sliding one hand down to press his thumb against her clit, she shuddered, crying out as her orgasm hit. Her nails dug in, and he knew he'd been marked with little crescents.

She fell on top of him, and with another flip, he continued to piston his hips, driving his cock inside her pulsating core. A smile curved her lips as she met him thrust for thrust, and soon, he threw his head back, his neck straining with his own release. Falling to the side, he could barely catch his breath and wondered if death by orgasm was possible.

Sex for Clay had usually been with a semi-committed partner. Not a man who participated in one-night stands since getting out of the military, he preferred sex with a woman with whom he at least had shared a few dinners and conversations. It was still just sex. A physical release with someone interesting, but he'd never found anyone he cared about. Even though he and Christina were new, she was different. *God, I hope this isn't one-sided!*

Opening his eyes, he found her staring intently at him, her lips curving slightly.

"I was going to ask you what you were thinking about, but then I thought you might just be trying to recover," she said.

Chuckling, he rolled toward her, keeping her tucked into his embrace. "Yeah, I am trying to recover from an orgasm that nearly killed me." He brushed the loose lock of hair back from her face. "But I was also thinking that I want to see more of you."

Brows lifted, she quipped, "Clay, I'm naked. How much more of me can you see?"

Squeezing her hips, he growled, "Smart-ass."

She laughed, then cupped his jaw with her hand. "So, this goes beyond just concerts, dinner, and sex?"

"Oh, yeah. I'm interested in a lot more." She nibbled on her bottom lip. Leaning forward, he mumbled against her mouth, "Stop thinking so hard."

"It just seems... I don't know... like there's so much more to know about each other."

"You're right, babe. And that's what we're doing."

"Not just sex—"

"I'm not talking about just sex," he said, holding her gaze. "Yeah, sex is part of it, but I want to know everything. I think we've already got a good start."

"We only get to see each other on weekends, and that's if I don't have a music event to attend."

"Then stay here tonight."

She sucked in a deep breath before letting it out slowly. "All night?"

"Yeah. Stay here with me. Sleep with me. Let me hold you all night."

The corners of her lips twitched upward. "Okay... you and me... all night." Shifting slightly so she settled into his arms, she asked, "And in the morning?"

"Then we've got our start." Kissing her smile once again, he tucked her underneath his chin, a smile on his own lips.

7

The clink of the weight bar on the metal hanger resounded throughout the LSI gym.

"I'm telling you it's going to be a great festival," Babs said, walking into the room.

"You just want to go so that you see big guys in skirts," Drew retorted.

Lifting a brow, she replied, "First of all, if I want to stare at a big man's legs, all I have to do is look at you. Second of all, it's not a skirt, it's a kilt. And third of all, shut the fuck up, sweetie. You know you'll be in the beer tent enjoying the music!"

Drew grabbed Babs and swirled her around, planting a smacking kiss on her lips. "Yep, you're so right, babe."

"Eew! Put me down! We might be married but that doesn't mean I want to be around you when you smell like a man who's just worked out!"

The others laughed, used to Drew and Babs' banter. Clay once wondered if Drew and Babs would ever get together after making eyes at each other for so long, but their relationship kicked into high gear even more with wedding bands encircling their fingers.

"I confess," Clay said, "I'm a Celtic festival virgin."

"Well, the food is great, the music is great, and heavy athletics are impressive," Babs responded, her smile wide.

"Babs has convinced the rest of the women that it's the place to go this weekend, so it looks like most of us will be there. You coming?" Walker asked.

Shrugging, he replaced the weight bar and nodded. "Sure, I'm game."

"You mentioned music," Tate said. "What kind of music?"

"Considering you only listen to country, I'm not sure that's what you'll find there," Clay laughed.

"Celtic bands will be playing," Babs said. Turning to Clay, she narrowed her gaze at him. "I thought you were the resident music lover of all types."

"My mom passed along her love of music, but gotta admit Celtic music was not something she listened to."

"Is that why you've been hitting the symphonic concerts lately? A love of music?" Blake asked, a grin on his face.

Clay smiled but remained quiet.

"Whoa, what brought that smile on?" Babs asked, her brows wiggling. "That is the look of a man who met someone." She looked around at the men and grinned. "Come on, guys. Have you been holding out on me?"

"Not me," Drew said, throwing his hands up in

supplication. "You'd have my balls, babe, if I kept gossip from you."

"So, did you? Meet someone?" Mace asked, sitting up on the weight bench.

"Y'all are worse than the women gossiping—"

"Hey," Sylvie fussed, holding her nose as she walked into the room and handed Mace a file. "We women don't gossip, we're just involved." Turning back to Mace, she said, "Sign here quickly before I have to have the room fumigated." Mace handed the file back to her, and she held Clay's eyes while still pinching her nose. "So... did you meet someone?"

"Might as well tell them," Tate advised, unwrapping his hands after pounding on the weight bag.

"How do you know something?" Drew asked, tossing a towel at Tate.

"Right time, right place, man." Tate grabbed the towel and tossed it right back, hitting Drew in the head.

"Shut up and let him confess," Babs shouted, popping Drew on the shoulder.

The room grew quiet and Clay realized all eyes were on him. Sighing, he shook his head in defeat. "Christina Monroe... concert violinist."

The others shouted congratulations as they grinned and went back to their workouts.

"Is it serious?" Sylvie asked.

"You've been bitten by the love bug," Babs said, tapping his arm. "Hang on, guys, this means someone else to rescue!"

"No way! She's a classical musician, not a magnet for

trouble. It won't be like the rest of you all. Me? I want simple, easy, no drama in a relationship—"

"That sounds like a turtle," she quipped.

"No, just a beautiful violinist." Thinking of Christina as he continued to press weights, he wondered if she would enjoy a Celtic festival. *She likes music... she'd probably love it.*

Clay had to admit the Celtic festival was a blast. As the Keepers and their women sat in the stands around the athletic field, the World Competitors in Highland Games hurled sheaths and hammers, threw stones, and tossed cabers. Since one of them was a native of Maine, the hometown boy had the crowd cheering.

"Hey, Mace, are we going to add this to our regimen?" Rank called out. "I could get into throwing heavy stones!"

"Honey, you can wear a kilt anytime you want," Helena said, receiving a wink from Rank.

Mace grinned, nodding. "Don't think I haven't thought about it. We've got enough room behind the lighthouse."

"These guys are fuckin' titans." Clay watched one athlete after the other lift the telephone-pole-sized cabers in their hands, carry it several feet, and then toss it end over end.

"They'll take a break in just a little while," Babs said, looking down at the schedule in her hands. "A couple of us thought about grabbing a big table in the food and entertainment tent. We can even take orders from everyone and get lunch from the food trucks."

"Are you going to try haggis?" Walker asked, throwing his arm around Julie.

She shook her head. "I don't think so. But I'm gonna go with Babs. I'll get you some."

After the others called out orders for meat pies, pastries, Scotch eggs, haggis, and fish and chips, several of the women left to place orders from the food trucks before the crowds descended after the athletic games paused.

"I thought you might bring your new girlfriend here," Bray said. He had been on the other side of the country on a mission for LSI and had just gotten back into town. "Babs says it's getting serious."

"I thought about it. I asked if she had plans today but she said one of her music groups was working."

"So, does Babs have it right? Is it getting serious?" Cobb asked.

A grin spread across his face. "I guess you could say that. We finally had several dates that didn't involve the orchestra, although I've got no complaints listening to her play."

Mace turned around and held his gaze. "Well, bring her by some time. The other women will want to check her out."

That thought sent shivers throughout him. "I don't know if that's such a good idea. Even the quietest of your women tend to get a little wild. I just don't see Christina doing that. I wouldn't want to overwhelm her."

"Why? She's not breakable!" Josh laughed.

Shooting a stink eye toward Josh, he said, "Yeah, well, when you get ready to introduce a woman to this group, you can throw out a comment from the peanut gallery."

"It's just... damn, it's hard to find someone special," Cobb grumbled.

"Don't I know it!" Bray agreed.

Mace pulled out his phone and glanced at the screen. "Sylvie said they just snagged two tables in the food tent and pushed them together. She said the others have the food ordered and by the time we get there, it'll be ready."

"I hate to miss any of the games, but I'm getting hungry," Rank said, standing.

The others followed along, making their way toward the huge tent where music was playing, laughter was ringing out, and the scent of food pulled everyone along.

Reaching the table, Clay kissed Nora on the cheek and said, "Thanks for getting my food."

She leaned forward and winked. "Tate says the others are ragging on you about the girl you're dating. I really wish you'd introduce us to her." Before he had a chance to respond, she threw her hands up in front of her. "I get that she's quiet. I am, too, but if she's special to you, then we'd like to meet her."

"Maybe I'll see if her string quartet or another group she's in besides just the orchestra is playing sometime, and we can get a group of us to go," he suggested.

As Tate wrapped his arm around his wife, Nora

glanced between them and smiled. "I think that sounds lovely."

Sitting down to eat, he had to admit the women had bought everything they possibly could. The food trucks had made quite a bit of money on the hungry Keepers. The music group on stage consisted of one man with a guitar and the other one singing Irish lullabies.

As they finished, everyone clapped and the MC stepped up to the microphone. "Okay, you've had a little soft music while some of you were eating, but now it's time to raise the roof! Let's give a big welcome to Amhrán M'anama!"

Clay watched in amazement as a drummer took to the stage and began pounding out a beat to the shouts and cheers in the crowd. He was soon joined by two long-haired young men in kilts, both playing bagpipes, their boots stomping the time on the wooden platform. The music was lively, filling the tent, and everyone tapped their feet in time to the beat. Another man with long hair pulled back into a ponytail, a kilt, and heavy boots ran onto the stage, heading straight to the microphone. He began singing a Celtic rock song.

"Damn, they're good!" Walker said, his head bobbing to the beat.

"I love this music!" Babs agreed, jumping to her feet and clapping.

Clay grinned and nodded. He had no idea if this band was the same as what he'd heard in the remote bar but couldn't deny that the music was just as good. The men on stage continued belting out the fast tune, the vocalist encouraging the crowd to clap. Suddenly, another musician bounded onto the stage, causing the crowd to cheer even more. This member was a woman, wearing a miniskirt in a Scottish plaid, spike-heeled boots that went above her knees, and a tight black tank top showing off her curves. Her long, dark, wavy hair tossed wildly about her head as she danced and twirled while playing the fiddle.

Her violin was electric with a wireless amplifier, giving her the freedom to move around as her sound meshed perfectly with the bagpipes. In awe, Clay watched as her hair swirled about her head in wild disarray. Her fingers and bow flew across the strings and as the music mingled with the bagpipes and the drums, her feet alternated between skipping across the stage to the beat and twirling in circles. She was a whirling dervish, never stopping, never hesitating as the music continued to pour forth.

"Holy hell, she's fuckin' fantastic!" Blay enthused.

Clay agreed, but a strange wave of possessiveness grabbed hold, and he fought to keep from telling Blay to keep his eyes in his head and his tongue in his mouth. As soon as that thought slammed into him, guilt followed quickly. *Christina... I'm involved with Christina.* He had never stepped out on a girlfriend, thinking men who cheated were weak. But watching the stage as the fiddler continued to twirl and toss her long hair, seeming to emit the lively music from deep within her soul, he cursed his weakness.

On the last note of the song, she turned toward the drummer, laughing as he grabbed his whiskey and downed it in one gulp, much to the delight of the crowd who roared with approval.

"Meet the members of Amhrán M'anama," the lead singer called out. "I'm Steven. Dunk is on the drums. Mike and Jamie are on the bagpipes. And, I know you want to know our fiddler... Tiny Monroe!"

The crowd stomped, clapped, and shouted as Clay took to his feet to get a better look at the dark-haired sprite who made magic spark from her fingers. She tossed her hair from her face, offering a wide smile to the admiring gathering. It was when a pair of large, blue-green eyes landed on him, growing wide as her mouth dropped open in surprise that it hit him—he was staring at Christina.

8

Christina?

"That's your Christina?" Tate asked, standing next to him.

Not realizing he'd spoken aloud, he was barely aware of the other Keepers and women as Christina stepped down from the stage and walked through the crowd toward him. The band was taking a break while the Massed Bagpipe Bands marched onto the athletic field to welcome the athletes back from lunch. Not replying, he watched as she continued forward, only hesitating long enough to accept the compliments from the crowd. She stopped directly in front of him, her boots giving her enough added height so that her eyes now came to his chin.

Her chest still heaved with exertion and she pressed her ruby-red lips together as she held his gaze. "I had no idea you were going to be here, Clay. Was this what you were going to invite me to?"

He opened his mouth to speak, then snapped it shut.

Sucking in a breath, he finally nodded. "Yeah." A strange battle of emotions hit him—glad to see her but pissed he knew nothing about this part of her life. "Where are your glasses?" As soon as the words popped out, he winced at the ridiculous question.

She grabbed a handful of hair and pulled the heavy tresses away from her face. "I have contacts. I don't like them, but it makes dancing around easier. Otherwise, I'd have to keep pushing my glasses up when I sweat."

"You never mentioned anything about... uh... this," he waved his hand toward the stage, but his eyes were on her outfit.

Shrugging, she said, "This is one of the bands that I play with."

"Just one?"

"You know about the orchestra and the string quartet. But yeah, this is another part of my musical life." With her violin tucked under one arm, she pushed a long strand of wavy hair behind her ear, and her eyes darted around to the others standing nearby.

"I've got to tell you, your performance was fuckin' magic," Babs said, stepping closer with her hand lifted toward Christina. "I'm Babs. I'm one of Clay's coworkers."

"Oh, hello. I'm Christina."

"She's right," Drew added, wrapping his arm around Babs. "Your music's the shit."

Her lips curved. "Thank you. I'll tell the band... or you can tell them yourself. They love hearing how great they are, although to be honest, I don't think their egos need stroking."

Clay sent a glare toward the other Keepers and turned back to Christina. "Tiny?"

"You're not the only one with short jokes. I have to put up with it from the guys in the band all the time."

A bolt of jealousy shot through Clay at the realization she had more guys in her life than just the men in the orchestra, and he felt certain none of the men in the orchestra had groupies. His jaw tightened as he battled those feelings as well.

She glanced back up at him and licked her lips. "I get the feeling that you're not too happy with me right now."

"And that's our cue to give them some privacy," Nora said, pulling Tate backward. Clay was barely aware that the others followed suit, leaving him and Christina standing to the side by themselves.

His hands landed on his hips as he dropped his head and stared at his boots for a moment. Lifting his eyes, he held her gaze. "No, I'm not upset with you. I mean, your music up there was crazy good. I've never seen anything like that. It's just... I guess I never really thought about you professionally in any other way than in the orchestra."

They were silent for a moment. Finally, she sighed. "Do you remember how you told me your mother liked all kinds of different music?"

He snorted. "You're gonna tell me this is the same thing."

Nodding, she said, "Yeah. Kind of. I love the violin. I love the music it makes and the way it makes me feel when I play. I once played in a bluegrass band in college. I even filled in for a friend of mine with country music one time on a record demo. But it wasn't until I took a trip to Ireland that I really fell in love with Celtic music. So, I divide my time. Yes, I can play Mozart with the Philharmonic and Gaelic music with this band."

His gaze dropped from the top of her wild-haired head, black-lined eyes, and ruby-red lips down to her curves shown to perfection in her tank top and miniskirt, ending at her heeled boots. "Okay, I have to admit, you also look fuckin' hot. How can you look so amazing in a black orchestra dress *and* in this outfit? Hell, both are a real turn-on."

She threw her head back and laughed. "So, tell me, Clay, were you getting hard just watching me play up there and then felt guilty about cheating on me?"

Narrowing his eyes, he pretended to glare. "Busted."

"Then I'm glad to know I can make you hot no matter what I'm wearing."

"Tiny! Come on!"

Looking over her shoulder, she lifted her bow and waved toward Steven. Turning back to Clay, she said, "Are you going to stay for the rest of the set?"

"I wouldn't be anywhere but right here." Before she could walk away, he placed his hand on her waist and pulled her forward, bending to take her lips in a kiss. Part of him wondered if it would feel different. It wasn't. Tiny was just his Christina.

"You okay, Tiny?" Steven asked as Christina made it back up onto the stage.

"Yeah, of course, I'm fine." She hid the fact that when she first laid eyes on Clay in the audience, her heart had threatened to pound louder than Dunk's drums. She had agonized over how to tell him about the group and suddenly, the choice was taken away from her.

"Hell, girl, you were standing over there with a bunch of hot guys. I know you can attract them, but what was up with that?" Dunk asked, his words slurring slightly.

"None of your business." As soon as the words left her mouth, Dunk adopted a kicked puppy expression. "Sorry, guys. It's actually the man I've been dating. I haven't told him about any of my side gigs. He's only seen me with the orchestra—"

Barking out a laugh, Dunk said, "He's just now seeing you out of that old lady black dress and in this outfit? He had to think he'd hit pay dirt, Tiny!"

"Oh, shut up, Dunk," she groused as he winked and twirled his drumsticks between his fingers.

Before she had a chance to say more, Steven walked up to the microphone. "Are you ready for more?"

The crowd roared.

"Then lift your drinks... it's time for Whiskey in Me Tae!"

The shouts brought on the next song, and she glanced out toward Clay, seeing him smile. Heaving a sigh of relief, she was thrilled he wasn't angry about what she was doing. She closed her eyes and felt the beat of the drums and the bagpipes move through her.

Lifting her fiddle, tucking it under her chin, she began to play and dance, the music flowing from her soul.

Thirty minutes later the set was over, and Clay approached as she placed her violin back into its case. "Are you free now?"

Looking up at him, she nodded. "Completely. What do you have in mind?"

"Do you ever get to just enjoy the Celtic festivals?"

Glancing past him to the athletic field, food trucks, and shop vendors, she realized she never had. She lifted her gaze back to his and smiled. "No, not really. I just come with the band."

"It's my first time here. How about we spend the rest of the day together?"

Her breath rushed from her lungs. "I'd love it!"

He glanced back down at her heeled boots. "Can you walk around in those?"

She lifted one leg and wiggled her foot. "I admit the only time I wear these are when I'm performing, but I've gotten used to dancing around in them. I'll be fine, I'm sure." Turning, she handed her violin case to Steven and said, "Secure this with the other instruments, and I'll get it tomorrow."

"Who's the dude?" Dunk asked, his eyes slightly glazed.

"Dude?" Clay rumbled.

Placing her hand on his, she squeezed. "This is Clay, he's a—"

"Her boyfriend," Clay interjected, the two words firm.

"That's cool, man," Dunk grinned, swaying slightly.

"He's not driving, is he?" Clay asked.

"No, I got him," Jamie replied, stepping up to Clay. "Nice to meet you. I'm Jamie."

She watched as Clay shook hands with Jamie, Mike, and Steven, and offered a chin lift to Dunk.

"Loved your music," he said, and she breathed another sigh of relief, noticing the guys in the band smiling as well. Waving goodbye to the others, she linked fingers with Clay and followed him out of the tent.

"How long has the band been together?"

"Steven and Dunk—Duncan—go way back, even to high school. At one time, they had a garage band. Then Steven heard Mike on the bagpipes at a festival and figured rock bands were a dime a dozen, but a niche like Celtic could really go places. Mike knew Jamie and that's how they were formed. I joined a couple of years later."

Walking past the food trucks, she was assaulted by the scents, and her stomach growled. Clay grinned and asked, "What would you like?"

Glancing at the menus, she gushed, "I'd love a Scotch Egg and a beer. Nothing dark, just a pale ale."

They moved through the line together and he placed the order. A few minutes later, she bit into the fried sausage-covered hard-boiled egg and moaned in delight. "I was so hungry." She swallowed the bite, wiping her mouth with her napkin. "God, that's so good."

Laughing, he said, "Glad I could make you happy."

As they walked past the vendor tents, her hand was

linked with his. The woolen goods, silver jewelry, Scottish plaids, sweaters and hats, and a myriad of other items were all displayed. She stopped at a silversmith's booth, fingering a few of the Celtic cross earrings and necklaces. Glancing at the price, she moved on past, her gaze drifting over the butter-soft wool scarves.

Her perusal was interrupted from loud cheering coming from the athletic field, and she twisted her head to look up at Clay. "What's going on?"

His brow furrowed as he asked, "Have you ever seen the heavy athletics?" She shook her head, and he continued, "I thought you'd be used to Celtic festivals."

Shrugging, she sipped her beer as they continued walking toward the field. "We usually just get to the stage area, set up and tune, and then play our set. We often leave without even eating. For me, this is a real treat."

His gaze shot past her back to the vendor booths before he grinned and said, "Come on, let's find my friends. There will be room at the athletic field for us."

"All of those people that were around you in the tent were your friends?"

"Yeah, and I know the rest of them would love to meet you."

They made their way to the stands, and he held onto her arm carefully as she teetered up the steps. Maneuvering down the row to where she recognized some of his friends, she started to sit, but Clay kept his arm around her.

"Everyone, I'd like you to meet Christina. You just

saw her as the band's fiddle player, but she's also the concert violinist that I've been seeing."

Eyes wide, she tried to follow as he introduced the men and women in the large group filling the area.

"Don't try to remember all our names," one of the women said, smiling warmly.

She recognized her as being with the boss, Mace. "It's nice to meet all of you." Accepting the congratulations on the band's music, she was relieved when everyone shifted, and she and Clay could sit. It didn't take long for her to learn that one of Clay's best friends was Tate, and his wife, Nora, was sitting next to them. Directly behind were Walker and Julie, Blake and Sara, and Levi and Claire. Babs and her husband, Drew, were sitting in front of them. On the other side were Rank and Helena. There were others, but the mass of testosterone and beautiful women around all seemed like a blur.

Now, with her eyes on the field, she watched the athletic competitions. The crowd cheered for each competitor, and she soon learned about the different Highland games. Twisting her head toward Clay, she said, "I can't believe I've never watched any of this. I've only been with the band for two years, but we've been to a bunch of Celtic festivals. I've never stayed to enjoy anything other than just our own music."

"Stay here," Clay said. "I'm going to run and get a funnel cake."

"Do you want me to go with you?"

"Nope. You and your feet need to rest. After the

performance you gave, I can only imagine your toes are screaming."

Crinkling her nose, she said, "You're not far from the truth."

Squeezing her shoulder, he kissed her lightly. "I'll be right back." Getting some orders from the others, he and a couple of the men headed toward the food trucks.

The seat gaps around her quickly filled in by the women who slid closer.

"It's so nice to finally meet the woman Clay has been dating," Babs said. "I told him he needed to bring you around."

"He's mentioned me?"

"Well, we don't have a lot of secrets amongst us," Helena said.

"And everyone works with a security company?"

She watched as the women's eyes shifted back and forth amongst themselves, and Sylvie simply replied, "Yes."

That one-word answer seemed to be the cue that she shouldn't ask any more questions about Clay's work. Now feeling self-conscious, she turned her attention back to the field where the athletes were ready for the caber toss. It reminded her of when she first joined the orchestra and felt as though 'New kid on the block' should be tattooed on her forehead. At least then, her musical ability gave her a way to gain the acceptance of the others in the violin section. But now, she felt out of place with the group of women who all seemed close.

A touch on her arm drew her attention toward Julie.

Cocking her head slightly, she waited to see what the other woman had to say.

"I know this is a lot to take in," Julie said. "Most of what they do, they don't talk about. So, please, don't feel self-conscious or left out."

Her smile stayed but felt more genuine as she said, "Thanks for that. Clay and I are still new."

"Just remember to duck when the bullets start flying," Babs said from behind.

"Bullets?"

"Oh, ignore Babs," Sylvie said. "She's exaggerating."

"Exaggerating?" Babs said, rolling her eyes. "These men have a type of woman that catches their eye. And that type usually means exciting things happen!"

Brow lowering, Christina shook her head slowly. The idea that she didn't fit slithered in deeper. "Then I'm afraid I don't fit that type. Believe me, all I do is play the violin."

Before the women had a chance to say anything else, the men came back, their arms loaded with sodas and funnel cakes. Thrilled when Clay settled close to her, their legs touching, she accepted the paper plate from his outstretched hands. Munching on the fried, sweet goodness, trying not to breathe in all the powdered sugar, she mumbled, "This is delicious."

Clay scooted closer, his gaze holding hers as he leaned forward and gave her a sugar-coated kiss. Smiling widely, she mumbled against his lips, "That's the sweetest kiss I've ever had." He chuckled, and she decided kissing him while he smiled was even better.

9

"Do you have to go back tonight?" Clay asked as he escorted her to his SUV, his arm slung about her shoulders.

"Back? To Portland?"

Nodding, he said, "Yeah."

She cocked her head to the side, unsure what he was really asking. "What did you have in mind?"

"What about my place? We can go to my house."

It had been a while since she'd dated anyone seriously and hadn't been invited to a man's house in a long time.

"The look of concern on your face is making me wonder what you're thinking," Clay said, his gaze penetrating.

As he helped her up into his SUV, she said, "I'm sorry. I'm probably overthinking everything. Actually, I'd love to go to your place."

With him still standing in the open door of his SUV and her buckled into the seat, they were on the same eye level. He leaned forward and kissed her lightly. "Christina, I don't just take random women back to my place."

Grinning, she slid her lips over his face and kissed the underside of his jaw. "Nice to know I'm not just some random fiddler you picked up at the festival."

He barked out a laugh, shaking his head. "Well, I've fantasized about asking my concert violinist girlfriend to come to my home, never imagining that I'd also ask a Celtic fiddler to do the same. Lucky for me, that it gets to be the same person."

"I am, you know."

"You are what?"

"The same person. Tiny's outfit is just part of the act. But the music... it comes from deep inside. It's why I gave the band their name."

He settled into the driver's seat and turned toward her. "What does the band's name mean?"

"Song of my soul. Amhrán M'anama is Gaelic for song of my soul."

She watched, mesmerized as his lips curved upward. His already gorgeous face morphed into something even more spectacular.

They drove for several miles, listening to classic '60s. "Okay, I've got to ask... what's your favorite?"

She blushed and said, "You're going to think it's cheesy, but Elvis Presley's Can't Help Falling in Love With You."

His head jerked to the side, eyes wide. "Didn't expect that, but it's a great song and a great rendition."

"Why didn't you expect that?"

"Because it was my mom's favorite," he said, his words hesitant. Glancing to the side, he asked, "Why that song?"

"I'm a sucker for a deep, male voice that resonates and words that touch my romantic heart. Elvis. The Righteous Brothers' Unchained Melody. You've Lost That Loving Feeling."

"Gary Puckett and the Union Gap—"

"Oh, my God, yes!" she exuded. "All those songs... they weren't just songs of easy love, but of love that is born of real life."

"You and my mom would have gotten along so well," he said. Now his voice held sadness. With her hand on his arm, her fingers flexed.

He spoke in past tense and she wondered if his mother was still alive. Not wanting to ask, they continued in silence for several minutes until he pulled into a drive. "Welcome to my home."

The sun was already setting, but she could see water in the back. "Nice view!"

As he assisted her down, he said, "It's home for now."

"For now? Are you planning on leaving the area?"

"No, no, not that. But it's a small house, as you'll see. It only has two bedrooms, and one of those is in a small loft upstairs. When I decided to buy, I wanted to be near water, didn't want to spend a lot of money, and this place is perfect for just me. But, I figure that one day I'll want a bigger place."

She wondered if that was because he would want a wife and children in the future but didn't ask. Somehow, a new girlfriend asking about the long-term housing aspirations of her boyfriend seemed to be rushing things.

As they stepped inside, she saw that it might be small for such a large man, but the space was much bigger than her apartment. The living room opened into the eat-in kitchen with a hall running down the middle of the house. Assuming the two doors along the hall were for the bedroom and bathroom, she looked up and spotted the small loft over the living room. "As big as you are, it was hard to imagine you living in a little house, but this is really spacious on the inside."

"And I thought it would just fit you, Tiny," he said, earning a narrow-eyed glare from her. "Actually, when I bought it there was a wall between the kitchen and living room, but it made the place feel closed in. I worked with a contractor, and we opened it up so it appears larger."

Looking down at her feet, she twisted her head back around him. "Do you mind if I take these things off? I mean, I know most men have a sex fantasy about a woman in heels or boots, but my feet could use the rest."

Laughing, he said, "I have a lot of sex fantasies about you, Christina, but in every one of them I want you happy and comfortable. So let's get those boots off."

She followed him to the sofa, and once she sat down, he knelt at her feet. Unzipping the boots in the back, he slid them over her feet and carefully set them to the side. The immediate ease of pressure off her toes felt delicious, and she leaned back against the sofa cushions. Wiggling her toes, she groaned.

He grabbed one foot and began massaging her arch

and toes, eliciting more groans from her. "Oh, my God, your hands are magic."

"That's what I think about your hands when I watch you play."

He continued his ministrations on her feet for several minutes before moving up to her calves and eventually working his way to her thighs. Dropping her chin to her chest, she noticed the twinkling in his eyes and the smirk on his lips. A tingle had started deep inside and now shot straight from her core to her clit as his thumbs slid to the apex of her thighs. Biting her lip, she sucked in a quick breath as he slid a long, thick finger underneath her panties, gliding it through her slick folds. With her skirt now pushed up around her hips, he leaned forward and breathed in deeply. Grinning, she asked, "Are you sniffing me?"

"Abso-fucking-lutely, yes!" With his hand pulling her panties to the side, he dove in, licking her folds and sucking her clit as his finger moved in and out deep inside.

Her hips undulated in concert with his rhythm, and her fingers dug into his scalp as her body began to quiver. As her orgasm rushed through her, he continued to lick. Boneless, she wondered if she'd ever be able to move from this position on his sofa and decided she didn't care if she stayed there the rest of her life.

He stood, slid one arm underneath her knees and the other behind her back, and picked her up. She threw her arms around his neck and tucked her head underneath his chin as he carried her to his bedroom. Setting her feet onto the floor, she once again remembered how tall he was as she had to lean her head further back to hold his gaze. "This was easier when I was in my heels," she jokingly complained.

"Babe, I'm discovering all sorts of facets to you and love each one, but there is not one thing wrong with your height." His hands slid under the bottom of her black tank top and pulled it upward until it skimmed over her head and was tossed to the floor. He dove his fingers through her hair, and it dawned on her it was the first time he'd been able to run his fingers through her tresses.

While she unzipped her plaid miniskirt and shucked it and her panties down her legs, he divested himself of his shirt and pants and boxers. She watched as he grabbed a condom and tossed it onto the bed before snatching her up again. Holding her tight against him, they kissed, and she could still taste her essence on his tongue.

She reached down and wrapped her hand around his erection, sliding her fingers up and down, feeling him shudder. She was ready to drop to her knees when she was suddenly lifted and tossed backward on the bed. Bouncing on his mattress, her laughter caught in her throat as he crawled over her, kissing his way from her stomach up over her breasts to her mouth.

He shifted to the side and rolled on the condom before settling between her thighs. With his weight resting on his forearms and his fingers threaded through her hair, he plunged into her waiting sex. She wrapped her legs around his waist, digging her heels into his ass. As he groaned, she kissed him.

They thrust and parried, tasted and tangled, kissed and licked, and rolled back and forth, each vying for dominance as the crescendo threatened to drown out everything. She finally cried out again, her core clinging to him. She watched as he gritted his teeth and threw his head back, and the long growl he emitted sent shivers throughout her.

He crashed on top of her then quickly rolled to the side, pulling her with him so that she was now resting on top with his cock still buried deep inside. Her body rose and fell as he dragged air into his lungs, his chest heaving. Slowly, his spent cock slipped from her body, but she remained wrapped in his arms.

He finally opened his eyes, and his gaze roved over her. She knew her dark hair was wild, and she had no doubt her makeup was smeared over her face.

"You are so beautiful," he said, his voice soft, almost reverent.

"I'm a mess. I think I was a lot more put together last time."

A chuckle rumbled from his chest, and her whole body moved again.

"Whether you're Christina or Tiny, you're beautiful."

She held his gaze and saw nothing but honesty in his eyes. "Thank you. I've never had… well, thank you."

He rolled her to the side gently and mumbled, "I'll be right back."

She watched his taut ass as he walked to the bathroom to deal with the condom and propped her head on her hand as she lay on her side, smiling as he walked back to the bed. He crawled in and leaned against the pillows piled next to the headboard. She scooted upward, his arm wrapping around her shoulders and pulling her in tight. Her arm lay across his tight abs and she rested her head on his chest.

"Today was wonderful, Clay, and I have to confess that I love being here."

His hand gently moved up and down her arm, his fingers trailing along her skin, tingles spreading from his touch. "You're not the only one with a confession. You being here means everything to me as well. You mean a lot to me, babe. I feel things for you that I've never felt before."

Smiling, she lifted her hand and cupped his stubbled jaw. "It's the same for me."

They continued to kiss as he slid down into bed. Rolling to one side, he turned off the lamp on the nightstand. Tucked into his embrace, they worshipped each other's bodies again, only this time it felt more like making love.

Clay's phone vibrated on the nightstand, and his eyes jerked open. Glancing down, he could see that Christina was still asleep. Shifting slightly, he grabbed his phone. "Yeah?"

"We're needed."

Recognizing Tate's voice, he whisper-growled, "You've gotta be fuckin' kidding me."

"Shit, man. I can tell just from your tone you've got her with you. Sorry, but this shouldn't take too long."

"Headquarters?"

"Yeah. Thirty minutes."

Disconnecting, he sighed heavily, scrubbing his hand over his face. Sliding from the bed, he headed to the bathroom, then quickly dressed in dark pants, a tight, long-sleeve dark shirt, and pulled on his socks. By now, Christina was sitting up in bed, looking adorable. Her hair was a tangled mess around her face, and she blinked in the faint light coming from the bathroom.

Holding the sheet around her, she asked, "Are you okay?"

Bending, he kissed her. "I've just been called out, but I want you to stay here. I'll be back as soon as I can."

"Is it your work? You get called out in the middle of the night?"

"Sometimes, babe, but we'll talk about it later. Stay here, sleep, have breakfast, and I'll be home as soon as I can."

Swiping her hair back from her face, she said, "Clay, I've got orchestra practice tomorrow afternoon..." Looking at the clock, she amended, "Actually, later on this afternoon since it's already tomorrow."

"I'll be back and can drive you into Portland."

She nodded and yawned widely. "Okay, be safe doing... whatever it is you're doing." Cocking her head to the side, she asked, "It is safe, right? I mean, we've never really talked about your job in detail, but—"

"Sweetheart, I've got to go. I promise I'll be safe and see you later. I'll get you back to Portland in time for your practice."

He kissed her soundly, watched her slide back

underneath the covers, and then left quickly. Driving straight to the LSI headquarters, he pulled up next to Tate's truck, seeing Cobb and Levi already there. Climbing down from his SUV, he asked, "What's up?"

"Josh has been working on the historical data from Jerry's computer. Both his work and personal laptops were clean, but he just intercepted a message from an unidentified source that said the shipment was in trouble. The only other things were coordinates that are north of here, just over the border. Mace said our FBI liaison wants to meet us at the border but then needs us to take it from there."

Nodding, he hated that he wouldn't be crawling back into bed with Christina, but the chance to have the morning with her at his house before driving her back to Portland would make it all worthwhile.

Over an hour later, they met with the FBI liaison, Mack. He immediately filled them in.

"Got a snafu with us and the International Drug Task Force in this area. The coordinates from the message are at a small outpost where we assume a drop-off was to occur. A small boat was found just over there, wrecked on rocks." Mack pointed a short distance away and they could see the wreckage. "Our guess is the drugs came in and the Minotaurs were supposed to pick up the shipment. Wrecking the boat, they didn't get the handoff completed. The Task Force stopped some gang members near the area, but they had nothing on them."

"How did the drug shipment get this far?" Clay asked.

Mack grimaced and shook his head. "No idea. There

are a fuck ton of boats in the area but no sighting of a drop-off. Although air surveillance indicates something out in the water, it's in the area between the two countries and jurisdiction problems are cropping up. We called you in to see what you can find."

It did not take them long to scramble over the rocks between Maine and Canada, and in the early light of dawn, they made it to the boat that had run aground, discovering it was empty.

"It looks like the whole boat was wiped down," Levi grumbled, radioing back to Mack.

Having used color strips to test for drug residue, they could tell that the boat had held heroin. But with it cleaned out, there were few clues to go on.

"Is there anything to tie this definitively to Jerry?" Clay asked and Levi relayed his question to the agent.

Mack's voice came over the radio, "I listened to the message that your people discovered. And even that was just vague enough that if you hadn't pieced it together, we wouldn't even have this."

"Our boss is sending someone with scuba equipment." They did not have a long wait for Rank to arrive, and Clay knew what was in the back of his SUV. Nodding toward Levi, he said, "We'll get suited up and go for a dive."

Rank, Tate, and Clay pulled on their wetsuits and fins. This time of year and this time of day, the water would be cold, so they used hoods and gloves as well. Completing the checks of their regulator, power inflator, buoyancy compensator, and octopus, they stepped into the water.

Using lights, they swam in a pattern, moving toward the coordinates Josh had secured from the Task Force underwater sighting. He looked for a reflection that the drug runners would have used so they'd be able to come back and retrieve whatever they had sunk into the watery depths. Moving in an ever-expanding circle, Tate signaled he'd found something.

Clay and Rank swam over, seeing the bright orange tape wrapped around the plastic container. Working together, they cut off the weights attached to the container, and while Tate lifted it to the surface, Clay and Rank carried the weights up so that they could be investigated for evidence as well.

Once at the surface, they could see the shore and swam toward the rocky coastline where Levi and Mack were waiting. By the time they arrived, several more FBI agents and investigators had made it to the scene. On land, Clay pulled off his mask and hood, moving with the other Keepers to where the agents could take possession of the container and weights. Sitting down on a large rock, he pulled off his fins then walked over to see what their bounty contained.

Carefully opening the container, they revealed it was filled with plastic-wrapped bricks of what Clay assumed was drugs. As the agent tested the powder inside, he nodded. "Heroin, for sure."

"If the Minotaurs were transporting this north and ran into trouble, they were prepared to dump it overboard. They might have come back for it later until the Task Force picked them up, tipping them off that they were suspected."

Looking toward Levi, he said, "We need more to tie this in with Jerry. Right now, there's not enough evidence."

"We'll increase the surveillance on the guesthouse that Jerry stays in on the congressman's estate."

Clay nodded, then added, "And that fuckin' boathouse." Stalking over to Rank's SUV, he peeled off his wetsuit, placing all his equipment into the back. So involved in his mission, he just then realized how high the sun was in the sky. Grabbing his phone from the pack with his clothes, he looked at the time. Almost noon. *God dammit! Christina needed to get back to Portland!*

He tried to call her, but it went straight to voicemail. *Shit!* Sending a text, he hoped she would open it. Slamming the passenger door closed, frustration raged through him.

"She'll understand—"

"She shouldn't fuckin' have to," he growled.

Continuing as though Clay hadn't interrupted, Rank said, "Maybe not, but they all do. That's part of a relationship, Clay."

He remained quiet, thinking of how much understanding his parents had toward each other... *not a fuckin' lot.* He sucked in a deep breath and let it out slowly. Christina was not his mom. He couldn't imagine that she would specifically look for something to be pissed about, but this was different. Either she'd had to find a way to get back to Portland, or she was going to miss her orchestra practice, something that would hurt her career.

Tate flipped on the music in the SUV, and Clay

closed his eyes as he ground his teeth together. For the next hour, he listened to country musicians sing about lost loves and love lost. *Jesus, shoot me now.*

By the time he was dropped off at LSI to get his own vehicle and drive home, he was not surprised to see that she was gone. Racing inside, it was obvious she had left. He moved to his laptop and checked his outside security camera feed. There she was, walking out of his house in her miniskirt and tank top, carrying her boots in her hand and getting into a waiting cab. Her head turned to the side as the cab pulled from his driveway and her face was visible in the window. Unable to discern if she was angry or sad, he sighed heavily, embarrassment filling him that she was forced to endure the walk of shame. *Fuck!* She looks like she spent a night with a guy who didn't give enough of a shit to get her home.

Growling, he stalked through the house, pacing. He thought of driving to Portland but had no idea where she lived. Picking up the phone, he called Josh. "I'm at home and need a favor... an address."

10

Christina had attempted every way she knew to calm her anger. Counting. Humming. Reading a book on her phone. Listening to music. None of them worked.

The cab driver had attempted to make conversation during the first thirty minutes of their two-hour drive, but after her numerous one-word responses, he gave up. Guilt had slithered through her but was quickly gobbled up by her anger toward Clay.

Now, as she swiped her credit card in the card processor hanging on the back of the front seat of the cab, she swallowed deeply. She added in a tip and tried not to think how the fee would cut into her account. Between her job with the symphony, the band gigs, the weddings and events she played with her quartet, and the private lessons, she made enough to live on and save a little. But she was far from rolling in riches. It was fine most of the time because she was living the life she loved. But occasionally, splurges dug a little deep. And a two-hour taxi bill definitely stung.

The conductor of the orchestra had zero patience for tardiness, so she ran past Amy, who was standing at the door ready to leave.

"I had no idea if you were going to get back in time!" Amy said.

Christina ran to the bathroom to tame her unruly hair, then changed into clean and more appropriate clothes. "Grab my music and my concert violin!" she yelled, sliding her feet into her flats, remembering she would need to get her electric violin from Steven as soon as possible.

"Are you gonna tell me what happened?"

"Yes, but you're going to drive. I'll tell you on the way."

The two raced out of their apartment, and once on the road heading to the concert hall, she leaned her head against the headrest and sighed heavily. "The short version of my story is that I ran into Clay at the festival yesterday, and—"

"Oh, my God! So, he saw you playing with the band?"

"Yes. At first, I think it really shocked him, and I don't think he was terribly happy. But we chatted, and he admitted that he really liked the music, thought I was hot, and—"

"You are hot! With that outfit, those boots, dancing around while you play... damn, he'd have to be blind or dead to not think you were hot!"

"Well, hot or not, he admitted he liked it. He asked me to stay for the rest of the festival, so I did. I met his friends, we had a good time, and then he asked me to go back to his place. I agreed and—"

Amy jerked in and out of traffic as she continued to interrupt. "You spent the night at his house? I knew he liked you!"

"I was going to give you the short version, but if you keep interrupting, I'll never get my story out!"

"Sorry! I'll zip my lip. Promise."

Chuckling, Christina shook her head. "You're fine. Honestly, I'm just in a pissy mood. He got called out in the middle of the night for work and left. He knew I had to be back in Portland for practice, and he promised that he'd get me here. By ten o'clock, he still wasn't back, and I couldn't take a chance on missing practice. So, I had no choice but to call a cab."

"He just left? He didn't tell you where he was going or what he was doing?"

"I told you that he works in security. I honestly don't know what his job is. Maybe he chases bad guys and dodges bullets." She looked out the window as Amy continued to hurry down the road, that last thought not settling well even if she was angry. "You should've seen his coworkers that I met yesterday. These guys are huge. All ex-military-looking, secret-ops kind of guys. I know I probably watch too many movies, but these guys looked like the real deal."

"Honey, when you told me he worked in security, I just thought maybe he installed systems in homes, you know, like ADT or something," Amy said, pulling into a parking spot close to the concert hall.

They grabbed their instruments and music and

hurried up the steps. "I know, that's what I thought, too."

Just as they arrived at the door, Amy reached out, placing her hand on Christina's arm. "I know you're upset, honey, but please, promise me that you'll give Clay a chance to explain. I can tell you really like him. And maybe his job isn't what you thought it was, but... well, just give him a chance."

She looked down at her feet, worrying her bottom lip. Finally lifting her gaze, she admitted, "You should've seen the other women that were with these men, Amy. Beautiful, smart... but they all had something... oh, I don't know. They all look like they could handle whatever these men might need from them. I'm just a musician." Closing her eyes tightly, she shook her head, trying to clear her mind. Breathing deeply, she opened her eyes and said, "Ignore me. I'm tired, grumpy, and we have four hours of practice in front of us that I'm not looking forward to!"

"Afterwards, why don't we get some wine?"

"Seriously? After I paid for that two-hour taxi ride, I don't have enough spare money for wine."

"Fine, then I'll go buy a cheap bottle, and we can drink it at home."

Throwing her arms around her best friend, they hugged. Grinning, she said, "It's a date." Pulling open the door, they hurried inside, racing down the hall to the stage.

Hours later, as Amy drove back to their apartment, Christina felt the pull of exhaustion and wondered how she could even keep her head upright. A lot of sex and very little sleep the night before combined with the anxiety and anger earlier that morning plus a long practice with the conductor who picked apart everyone's performance had her close to tears.

"Oh, I think you're going to need some privacy," Amy said, her voice soft.

Opening her eyes, she turned toward Amy only to see her roommate staring out the windshield. Following Amy's gaze, she looked in the same direction. There, leaning against his SUV, was Clay. "No. I'm not kicking you out just because Clay is here."

Pulling into the parking space, Amy shut down the engine before turning toward Christina. "First of all, you're not kicking me out. Second of all, I can easily crash at Carol's place. Third, remember what I said? If you two are going to be a couple, you need to talk. He now knows about your band gigs, and you need to find out more about his job."

Her chest depressed as air rushed from her lungs. "What if... what if I find out that I don't like what he does? Or I don't think I can handle it?"

Amy reached over and held her hand, giving a little squeeze. "Then you'll know. It's the *not* knowing, like this morning, that made you doubt."

Nodding, she sighed. "You're right. Thanks." Climbing from the car, she grabbed her music and violin case and waved as Amy pulled out of the parking lot. Turning, she watched as Clay pushed away from his SUV and stood, waiting for her.

"I tried to call," he said.

Lifting her chin, she held his gaze, uncertain how to

read him. "We're not allowed to have cell phones during practice." She hesitated for a second, then added, "I missed your first call this morning, then saw your texts. I knew that you were safe, but I wasn't really in the mood to talk."

"I was worried. I have outside security cameras, so I knew you'd taken a cab, but I didn't like not knowing where you were or what was happening."

"Well, then, you had a taste of what I was feeling this morning."

His brow lowered and he sighed. "I was at work, Christina. You knew that."

"Yes, and you knew I was stuck at your house with no transportation and had to get back to the city. You leave in the middle of the night and then you don't come back. Nor do you call to check on me or tell me how you are. I'm not trying to be whiny, or controlling, or a bitch, but I don't really know what you do, Clay. This morning was an example of how it impacts me."

They held each other's gazes for a long moment, then finally he sighed and nodded slowly before jerking his head toward her apartment building. "You're right. Can we talk?"

She threw her hands to the side. "We are talking." He didn't reply, and she pinched her lips together, regretting her snippy comment. "Yeah, I think that'd be a good idea. My roommate saw you and said she was going to visit some friends." Leading the way, she climbed the steps and unlocked the door to her apartment. Moving inside, she set her belongings down and walked straight into the kitchen. Throwing open the refrigerator door, she said, "I can make sandwiches."

"How about we just focus on us, and I'll call out for pizza?"

It was on the tip of her tongue to snap that she couldn't afford take-out pizza, but she knew Clay was going to pay, so that comment would be just as snippy as her previous quip. "Okay." As he made the call, she grabbed two bottles of water and walked over to the sofa. Piling up on one end, she nodded toward the other and watched as he sat down, twisting his body to face her.

"I've got to start out and just say, Christina, that I don't want to fuck this up. I really like you."

Her shoulders drooped, fatigue still pulling. "I don't want this to get fucked up either. I know my being in a Celtic band surprised you yesterday. I had my reasons, although now, they seem a little silly."

"And I realize I've been too vague about my job. Honestly, I've never dated anyone long enough for me to really explain what I do. So I guess this is all new for me, too."

Somehow, hearing that this was uncharted territory for Clay lightened her anxiety. Her lips quirked slightly, and she said, "So, who goes first?"

"We can do this however you want. I'm just glad you're giving me a chance."

She chewed on her lip for a moment and then blurted, "As soon as I saw you yesterday, I thought we were over." Seeing his furrowed brow, she continued. "In the past, I either managed to date someone who'd met me through the orchestra or through the band. Not both. Depending on which, they formed an opinion about me based on their interpretation of the music. It's stupid really, but there it is. Those who knew me through the orchestra hated the band."

"Hated the band?" he asked, his head tilted to the side. "I mean, it was a shock to see you on stage, but why would someone hate it?"

"They liked dating someone from the symphony. They liked the social aspect and class of that type of musical endeavor. But they hated the band that played in bars. Hated that I wore a short skirt, or hated that the other band members were all guys, or that so much of my time was taken with them."

"And the others?"

Snorting, she said, "When I met someone at a band gig, they loved the get-up—the outfit, the music, the idea they had of me being in a band. They liked that they were dating someone who played music in bars. When they found out that I also play in an orchestra, especially when they saw my formal dress or found out that my Friday nights were with the symphony, well, that blew their image of me." She hefted her shoulders in a shrug. "Now that I say it out loud, it sounds rather stupid."

"I agree. Someone who cares about you should care about all of you."

She jerked her head up, her breath catching in her throat, but a knock on the door stalled her response. Clay jumped up and threw open the door, took the pizza from the delivery guy, and paid. Moving into the kitchen, she grabbed two plates. The scent of pizza wafted past, and her stomach growled. "I'm starved."

"Good. I've felt guilty all day about leaving you, so the least I can do right now is make sure you're eating."

They filled their plates and moved back to the sofa. Neither talked for a few minutes as they relaxed, eating their fill. Finally, she leaned back and said, "I really needed that. Thanks."

He leaned forward, took the empty plate from her hands, and placed it along with his on the coffee table. Settling back against the cushions, it did not escape her notice that he shifted forward, sitting closer. He stretched his long arm along the back of the sofa, and his fingers drifted through her hair. Her scalp tingling, she leaned her head into his palm, and a sigh slipped from her lips. "Your turn," she whispered.

11

"I was a Ranger." As soon as those words left his mouth, Clay watched as Christina blinked and then a crinkle slowly formed across her brow. He gave his head a little shake and said, "I suppose that was a rather dumb opening remark."

Her brow eased as her lips curved slightly. "Clay, I just want to know more about you. You can start any way you want to."

"I really should start further back than that." He sucked in a deep breath, hating how he needed to draw strength to talk about his parents. *And this is why I never do this.* "Just as your parents worked well together, mine didn't. As your parents were dedicated to their music and had no problem putting in the time it took to work toward a common goal, mine didn't share those traits."

She leaned forward and placed her hand on his, rubbing her thumb over his rough knuckles. "I'm sorry, honey."

"My parents argued. A lot. As in I can't imagine why

they ever got together because they didn't seem to like anything about each other. But weirdly enough, they both liked me. When my dad wasn't around, my mom was funny, she baked cookies, and she put on her records, and we'd listen to music. But as soon as my dad got home from work, she groused and complained, ignoring me just to argue with him.

"And my dad was the same. If Mom was out working or shopping or visiting a friend, Dad and I tinkered in the garage. We worked on the car, built model airplanes, watched old movies. But as soon as Mom got back home, they'd devolve into their petty, screaming arguments that often ended in doors slamming, leaving me in the middle, not knowing who to turn to."

"Were they... um... physical?" She bit her lip and continued to rub her thumb over his hand.

He sighed at the soothing gesture. "They never hit each other, although my mother was known to throw things when they fought, and my dad punched a hole in the wall a few times in anger. Sometimes I think they did those things just to piss each other off. And they never did that if I was in the room. But believe me, when the screaming started, I got out of there."

Shaking his head, he winced, the memories still able to sting. "As an adult, I can compartmentalize. My parents should never have gotten married because they truly didn't like each other. I even wondered if they got married because they were pregnant with me, but I checked their marriage license against my birth certificate when I got older." He shrugged. "I was born a full year after they got married. I once asked my dad why he married my mom, and his only response was that it seemed to make sense at the time." Christina's eyes bugged, and he couldn't help but chuckle. "Yeah... not exactly the answer I was looking for."

He turned his hand over so that their fingers were now linked. Hers were so small, so delicate against his much larger, much rougher hand. And yet there was strength in her fingers. The pads were calloused from untold hours of practicing her instrument. His were calloused from untold hours of practicing with firearms. He wondered why that thought didn't bother him, and yet seeing their hands together, all he could think was how perfectly they fit together.

"Did they stay together?"

Lifting his gaze to hers, he continued. "My upbringing was so chaotic that I craved order. Discipline. I joined the Army as soon as I graduated from high school. My dad came to my boot camp graduation and informed me that as soon as I'd left home he and my mom filed for divorce. I asked him why they'd stayed together all those years only to divorce as soon as I left." He snorted as he continued to shake his head. "He claimed they wanted to give me stability even though they knew they weren't right for each other. Stability... Jesus, seriously?"

"Wow, I don't even know what to say to that, Clay."

He lifted his free hand and gently brushed his fingertips over her forehead, smoothing the line. "There's nothing to say to that, sweetheart. My parents were fucked up as a couple but thought that staying together while I was growing up was the right thing to do. Mom died from breast cancer about seven years ago. Before that, the few times I'd go home, I'd spend a day or so with her and we'd have a good time. She'd bake and we'd listen to music. Then I'd go to my dad's place, enjoyed time with him as well. I've often thought how much better my upbringing would've been if they hadn't tried to live in the same house. Anyway, I stayed in the Army, got into the Rangers, had missions all over the world. The discipline I craved I got from the military. The family I'd never had I got from my fellow Rangers."

"If you loved the Rangers so much, why did you get out?"

He shifted and now wrapped his hands around both of hers, holding them in his lap. "I was chosen for some special operations with... well, let's just say with a special group. It was an honor, and I was proud to be part of it. That's where I met Mace."

"Your boss?"

Nodding, he said, "Yeah. He was in charge of our missions. Through him, I met some of the others. After a couple of years, Mace was getting out and had a dream of starting a security business. He hand-picked some of the people that he'd worked with and extended invitations to come work for him when they got out of the service. I was one of those people and considered it even more of an honor."

"So, when you said you worked in security, you weren't just talking about setting up run-of-the-mill security systems on people's houses, were you?"

He hesitated, uncertainty filling him. He wanted to

tell her as much as he could, and she was so easy to talk to. But the unknown of her reaction was creating tension in his shoulders and neck.

Clearing his throat, he admitted, "No, I don't. Mace's business is called Lighthouse Security Investigations. It's no secret that he runs the business, but our clients know that they can count on our complete discretion. It involves security of all types as well as assisting clients or our government with criminal investigations."

"Wow," she said as her breath left her lungs in a rush. "That's why you have a lighthouse tattoo on your shoulder? I thought it was just a really cool tattoo."

"We all have them. They were designed just for those of us who work for LSI."

They remained quiet for a moment and he could tell thoughts churned behind her eyes. Lifting her gaze to his, she stated, "I take it you get called out a lot. Nights, weekends, maybe even weeks at a time. Going places you can't tell me about. Doing things you can't talk about."

His chest squeezed, uncertain if she was leading up to a declaration of not being able to handle what he did for a living. While he'd never been in a relationship that had lasted this far, he'd always known that one day he might have to face the possibility that the woman he was interested in would not be interested in what he did. "Yeah... sometimes, yeah." The answer was pulled from him, dragged from the depths of insecurity.

Her head moved up and down slowly, but she continued to hold his gaze. Finally, lifting her shoulders in a slight shrug, she replied, "Okay."

He blinked slowly. "Um… okay?"

Her nod this time was more rapid. "Yeah, okay. Clay, it's your job. It's your career. It's what you love to do. If I'd known that this morning, I wouldn't have waited to see if you were going to make it back in time to take me home. We could've made alternate arrangements before you left. I know that now, so it'll be easier to plan in case you get called out suddenly."

The tension that had crept over his shoulders, increasing with each hour since he first realized she'd left his place in a cab, eased. "That's it?"

"We're still getting to know each other, but it's not like I have a nine-to-five job, either. During concert season, every Friday night is with the orchestra. My Sunday afternoons are usually in orchestra practice during the season, also. My Saturdays are often with Amhrán M'anama, either in practice or at a gig. There will be times when you're not working and would like to be with me, but I'll be working. It just means that we have to figure out our schedules to make the most of our time."

Slumping back against the cushions, he squeezed her fingers. "You really are easy, aren't you?" Seeing her eyes widen, he rushed, "That didn't come out the way I meant for it to! I just mean that you're easy to get along with."

"That's important to you, isn't it?"

She was right, her words hitting exactly what he felt. "Yeah. Everything with my parents was not easy. And my friends? They all met their women on missions. Dangerous situations, investigations, rescues."

Her head jerked back. "You're kidding! I know one of them mentioned something about bullets flying, but I didn't understand that. I liked them, but they all seemed... well, rather intimidating."

"Bullets flying?" His eyes widened as his voice rose. "One of them mentioned bullets flying?"

"Uh-huh. I thought maybe they were kidding, but the look on your face right now makes me think that they might not have been."

Dropping his chin, he grimaced. Looking up, he held her gaze. "Look, most of the guys happened to meet someone on a case. So, yeah, in those cases, they might have been in dangerous situations and things got pretty intense real quick."

Her mouth opened but no words came out. After a few seconds, she snapped her mouth closed.

He lifted his eyebrows in silent question, hoping she'd say more, but she remained quiet. "What are you thinking?"

"Clay, I'm... I'm not very adventurous. I'm just a violinist... my life is practice, performances, and throw in a little travel to venues. That's all." She looked down, her hands pressed together before she shook her head. "The other women... they appeared very close. The kind of sisterhood that occurs when people share their lives. It's... well, it's intimidating."

"Listen, Christina, they're great women. You'll love getting to know them, and you'll fit right in."

"I liked meeting them. I don't want to give the impression that they weren't friendly when we met yesterday." Giving her head a shake, she added, "Wow, was that just yesterday? I swear, it seems like it was forever ago."

They sat quietly for a moment, him giving her a chance to digest all that he'd shared. Finally, she looked up and asked, "If you go on a trip for work, will you be able to tell me?"

"Yes and no. The actual case that I'll be on, no. But you can know where I am and when I'll be back. We do some work overseas or in other states, but we're never gone for very long. A lot of the work we can do from LSI's headquarters."

Her brow scrunched again. "So... do you often meet women on cases? I mean, if all the others did, I must seem rather boring—"

"Don't even go there. First of all, you're not boring. And second of all, I happen to like a relationship that's not mired in chaos. And third? I'm glad you're giving me another chance."

She let go of his hands and crawled onto his lap. With her core nestled against his cock, he cupped her face, bringing her closer. Leaning closer, their lips were a whisper apart. "Is Amy coming back tonight?"

Grinning against his mouth, she replied, "Nope. She went to a friend's place to give us some privacy—"

He cut off her words as he stood, lips locked, and his arms banded around her middle. Carrying her toward the hall, he followed her grunting directions to get to her bedroom. Once inside, he showed her just how much he liked the chance she was offering. He planned on making the most of it.

Used to being at work early, Clay looked up at the screen, stifling a yawn. He'd left Christina's bed early in the morning with a kiss and a promise to call her as soon as he could—a promise he intended to keep. During the two-hour drive to get back to his house in time to shower and change before heading to LSI head-quarters, he turned his playlist to her Celtic band and smiled. He thought of how his mother would have loved the music.

Now, on a second cup of coffee as the others came in, he once again hid his yawn behind his hand.

"So, did she forgive you?" Tate asked, clapping Clay on the shoulder as he slid into the seat next to him.

"Yeah, it ended fine. I felt like an ass because she had to take a cab all the way back to Portland for her symphony practice, but I was waiting for her when she got home, and we talked."

"Good," Babs said. "I have no idea what you did to

upset her, but I'm glad to hear you worked it out. I really like her."

"Just take it easy on her, Babs. And tell the others, also. She's not used to our way of life."

Sylvie scoffed. "And you think we were? Well, maybe Babs. But not the rest of us. I assure you, before I met Mace, my life was normal. Boring."

"I beg to differ," Mace reported, turning toward his wife with his hands on his hips. "I got called in when David witnessed a murder. That happened before you ever met me."

Sylvie winced and said, "You know what I mean. The same goes for Helena, Julie, Sara, Nora—"

"You can't count Claire," Levi interjected. "She was being chased when I came along."

"He's got you there, Sylvie," Babs laughed.

"I still stick to saying that most of us were leading boring lives," Sylvie said.

Mace walked over and kissed her forehead. "Yes, but you've always said it takes a special woman to be with a Keeper."

As the others continued to debate, Clay thought about Mace's statement. Christina *was* special. And the last thing he wanted was to see if she could handle herself in the middle of a dangerous situation.

The group settled, and Levi began his report. "The FBI said that what we found in the packages was pure heroin. Street value is easily over half a million dollars, maybe more."

"Any fingerprints?" Clay asked.

"No. They must've worn gloves because there were

no fingerprints on the papers, plastic wraps, containers, or tape. The tape they used can be found in any store anywhere. Same for the plastic wrap."

"So, they were heading north at night, and whoever was steering the boat didn't know their way, so they ended up on the rocks."

"That's what it looks like. They were probably afraid they wouldn't have time to get away if they tried to deal with the bricks of heroin, so they took weights from the boat and dropped them into the water. They probably hoped to go back today or tonight to retrieve them."

"Was any evidence found on the rocks near the wreckage?"

"There was no physical evidence left at the scene. Again, dealing with professionals."

Drew snorted. "Professional drug dealers, but amateur boaters."

"They're lucky they didn't burst open the heroin packages when they landed on the rocks. Inhaling that shit would've killed them."

Clay asked, "Is the Bureau watching the area today in case someone goes back?"

Levi nodded. "Yeah, they've got it under surveillance, but the Minotaurs questioned will go back and alert the others. I doubt anyone goes looking."

"How the hell is Jerry Kincaid not being questioned about this?"

Mace sighed. "No evidence. No way to trace this back to him other than a phone message which he didn't reply to. He can always say it wasn't meant for him. If they go to him now, they tip their hand that he's being watched."

Clay nodded, hating that Mace was right.

Josh added, "He travels a lot, but when in Maine, he mostly stays at Congressman Bennett's guesthouse."

"And always alone, right?" Cobb asked. He looked around at the others, then added, "I'm sure what Josh has found is that when Jerry has a date, he'll entertain them in his condo. It's important for him to keep his personal life private from the eyes and ears of those on the Bennett estate."

"He's right," Josh said. "And his dates are all above board. No prostitutes, strippers, drug kingpin daughters."

The others laughed, but Clay watched as Cobb shifted in his seat. "You get this, don't you?"

Nodding, Cobb replied, "Yeah, politics is a world unto its own. There are rules to follow if you want to get where you're going. Break them, and you'd better hope it stays out of the press. Although, I gotta admit, things are changing from past times. Nowadays, politicians can get away with all kinds of shit that in my father and grandfather's time would have had them ousted from their political careers quicker than you can blink."

"That strict?" Bray asked.

"People fucked up back then, but there was a code to keep quiet. Keep it away from your political enemies. Keep it away from the press. Hell, even in my prep school upbringing, I knew to keep quiet. Try being a quarter Hispanic, a quarter Native American, and only half Caucasian in a mostly white prep school." He looked around, then shook his head. "My take on Jerry? He'll do what he can to protect the congressman."

"So, if Jerry's trying to keep whatever he's doing away from Bennett, then would it make sense for him to use the boathouse as a possible stopgap for moving drugs?" Clay asked.

"I know it sounds risky, but sometimes keeping things close to home means you can control the prying eyes. Marinas and harbors have too much traffic and security. But a private boathouse on the congressman's estate? It could just be exactly what he needs to help move things along."

Josh shook his head and said, "So far, with surveillance on the boathouse, I haven't seen anything untoward. Certainly nothing that would tie him into the stash of heroin that was found yesterday, although he spends a lot of time on that top floor of the guest-house. The one that has windows on every side and looks out over the estate, the main house, and the water." He looked back toward his screens. "Holy shit." He leaned closer to the screen. "What the fuck?" Flipping on the audio, the sound of violins filled the main LSI room.

Clay's eyes jerked toward the surveillance feed that Josh was staring at. He immediately recognized Jerry's guesthouse. And there, dancing around on the first floor, were two women. One with a violin that was tucked under her arm as she grinned widely at the other woman playing. *Christina? What the hell?*

Christina twirled several times while playing, smiling as Amelia Bennett clapped and danced. Finally coming to the end of the song, she stopped and plopped into one of the chairs.

"Oh, Ms. Monroe, that's exactly what I want to do!"

"Amelia, I'm not sure that's what your parents had in mind when they hired me. Plus, they want you in the high school orchestra, not twirling around in the talent show."

"The orchestra is so dull, and what you just did was exciting. It made me want to jump up and twirl with you, clap and stomp, and... and... it made me want to practice the violin so that I can do exactly what you did!"

"Well, the practicing part is good." She leaned back in the chair and lifted her gaze. "This place is amazing. This huge room that goes up three levels with the glass windows on one side has incredible acoustics," Christina admitted.

"I told you so! I discovered this quite by accident. My mom was having a group of ladies over for tea, but I knew I needed to practice because we were having tryouts at school. I didn't want to be upstairs where everyone could hear me, and I knew that Mr. Kincaid was gone. I came here just to find a private place to work, then discovered the acoustics made even me sound good!"

"Who's Mr. Kincaid?"

"Jerry Kincaid. He's my dad's closest friend. They've been friends forever. He also runs Dad's campaigns."

"He lives here?"

Amelia nodded. "Yeah, he used to have a place in town, I think, but he was always over with my parents or staying late talking to Dad. We had this place, so Dad just told him he could move in here."

Eyes wide, Christina sat up straight. "So, we're literally trespassing in someone else's house right now?"

"Ms. Monroe, this is just part of my parents' estate. I mean, yeah, Mr. Kincaid stays here, but it's owned by my parents." She laughed and added, "And by default, owned by me as well."

"Well, I suppose that since this place *belongs to you*, then it's okay for us to be here." Holding the young teenager's gaze, she asked, "How about your parents? Do they know that you come here?"

Amelia scrunched her nose. "No, not really. I mean, I've never been told *not* to come, but I don't announce that I'm doing it. I'm always sure that Mr. Kincaid is gone when I pop in." She shrugged, then her eyes brightened. "Ms. Monroe, you should check out the top floor! You can see everything!" She jumped up from her chair and waved her over. "Come on, I'll show you."

Christina followed Amelia up the stairs to the second floor. One side of the hall looked down over the great room, and the other had doors leading off, probably to bedrooms. Amelia continued to jog up the next flight of stairs, and Christine followed more slowly. "I don't have your youth or stamina!"

Amelia stopped on the stairs and looked over her

shoulder, rolling her eyes. "Don't give me that, Ms. Monroe! If you can dance around for a full concert the way you were downstairs, I know you have stamina." She turned and continued to bounce up the staircase.

By the time Christina made it to the third floor, she was awestruck by the large room, complete with windows on all four walls. Looking out over the water, she said, "Oh, my goodness! This is gorgeous!"

Amelia plopped onto her knees on the sofa and leaned over the back, her eyes trained toward the water. "I can see why Mr. Kincaid has a couple of telescopes up here. I'll bet he can see all kinds of ships from here."

Christina walked around and peered out of each side of the observatory. "Is that a boathouse next door?"

"Yeah. Mom and Dad don't do a lot of sailing, but they have a few boats there. Nothing really big. I haven't even been in there in a while. In fact, since Dad was elected, he and Mom never go out anymore."

"Wow, you can even see all the way up to the main house from here."

"You know what you should do? You should play your violin as you walk back down the steps," Amelia said. "I did that once just to hear the different acoustics on the different floors. It was really cool."

"That's an interesting idea. Why don't you do it with me?"

The two of them walked to the top of the stairs and, descending carefully, began to play a simple tune. With Amelia taking the easier music, Christina added the more difficult melody. Amelia was right, as the sounds reverberated throughout the great room, they resonated differently the closer they got to the bottom. As soon as their feet touched the floor, the sound of clapping met their ears.

Whirling around, Christina stared at a handsome man standing by one of the sofas. His hair was styled, his suit was impeccable, and his smile was wide. Shocked, she stood with her mouth open for a few seconds as Amelia cried out her greeting.

"Mr. Kincaid! I didn't know you'd be back so early!"

Realizing they just been caught in the man's house, Christina's face heated. "I'm so very sorry. Amelia said it would be fine for us to practice here."

He stepped forward, his smile still firmly on his face as he held her gaze. Turning slightly, he said, "Amelia, you're really getting much better. And this beautiful woman must be your teacher."

"Yes, I'm Christina Monroe. Again, please, accept my apologies for—"

"No apologies are needed," he assured, reaching out to take her hand. "I'm Jerry Kincaid. It's very nice to make your acquaintance. It's not often that I come home to find beautiful women creating beautiful music. In fact, that's never happened before."

Amelia laughed, and Christina knew her teenage mind was unable to comprehend the embarrassment of the situation. Extracting her hand from his, she turned to her student. "Amelia, our lesson is definitely over for today." Looking toward Jerry, she murmured, "Let me get my violin case, and we'll be out of your way."

"More's the pity," he said. "Ms. Monroe, I certainly hope I get to hear you play again."

Amelia piped up, "She plays for the Philharmonic Orchestra. And she plays for the Celtic band, Amhrán M'anama. You should hear them sometime, she's fabulous! She plays the fiddle and dances all over the stage at the same time! They even go to festivals all over, even Canada."

"I'm not sure it's quite as exciting as Amelia thinks—"

"And I'm equally as sure that as beautiful as you are and as exquisitely as you were playing earlier, it would be very exciting."

Inclining her head, she placed her violin into her case and turned to make sure she and Amelia had not left anything behind. Ushering her young charge in front of her, she said, "Even though you said it was no imposition, I thank you for the use of your house. Amelia was showing me the acoustics in this great room, and I have to admit they are impressive."

"Then I hope that any time you and Amelia want to use this, please, feel free."

He escorted them to the door and then took her hand once again, holding it for longer than the shake. She glanced down at his smooth move but felt no tingle or excitement in the least. Certainly not like when Clay touched her.

"I hope to see you again very soon, Ms. Monroe. Very soon."

Offering a weak smile, she extracted her hand and hurried after Amelia as they walked back toward the main house.

13

"Get him."

Clay was already out of his chair, stalking toward the exit of the LSI main room, heading to the elevator when Mace's firm command met his ears. Drew and Walker jumped in front of him, their hands up.

"You do not want to keep me in here," he growled. He felt a hand on his shoulder and whirled around, seeing Tate. "I need to go, and I need to go now."

"No."

The one word came from Mace, and he turned, offering a hard stare toward his boss. "I just see my woman in the presence of a man we're investigating for drug running, and you're telling me no?"

"I know this is hard, but right now, she can't be told anything."

Fists on his hip, he cocked his head to the side. "Excuse me?"

"Christina is not cleared for any information. You go

out there pissed as hell, and you could compromise our investigation."

"You've got to be shittin' me. We were just talking about all the women you guys have ended up with, and they sure as fuck knew what was going on."

"Yes, because each and every one of them was involved in the mission. None of the Keepers were telling their girlfriends about a mission. They had to know what was going on with them because they were actively in danger. Christina? She was simply at the wrong place and happened to meet someone we're investigating. But she's not involved. She doesn't know anything about Jerry Kincaid, so she can't know about our mission."

White-hot anger speared through him, burning deep inside. He dropped his chin and stared at his boots, aware that he needed to pull his shit together while wanting to lose it at the same time.

"I know this is hard for you," Mace said, standing closer, his voice low. "But—"

"I get it."

No one said anything for a long moment. The cavernous room that would normally echo sounds remained silent as no one moved. With his fists still planted on his hips, he lifted his head. Holding Mace's gaze, he repeated, "I get it. I don't fuckin' like it, but I get it."

He could hear a collective sigh of relief but ignored it, turning and stalking through the room past his coworkers. Heading to the gym, glad that no one followed him, he took his frustration out on the heavy bag. Thirty minutes later, Tate and Cobb walked in. By then, he was a sweaty mess and was unwrapping his knuckles. Even with the protection, they were swollen and red.

"Look, Clay, I'm not going to begin to say that I understand how you feel. I know you said it was easier to have a relationship with Christina because she wasn't involved in anything, but you've got to see, that's still true. She may have been in the Bennett guesthouse where Kincaid lives, but she just met him. There's no reason to believe that she'll ever see him again. She doesn't know he's being investigated and doesn't know that you're part of that. So, it's just a poor fuckin' coincidence."

He growled, "We're doing the FBI's dirty work for them because someone high up doesn't want anything connected to Congressman Bennett. So we have to keep it all quiet for now."

Tate sucked in a quick breath and shook his head slowly. "I know, and it sucks."

Voice still shaking with rage, he said, "I watched that asshole take Christina's hand. I watched him hang on to her fingers. You tell me if he did that to Nora, you wouldn't care?" Another quick inhalation was his answer.

"Look, Clay," Cobb said. "We're stepping things up. We started with just surveillance, but Levi's already on a secure line with his liaison. The FBI may be stalling this guy's investigation, but Mace has clearance from the DOJ."

Tate added in, "Just be cool with Christina. She

won't see him anymore, and we can get who we need. The last thing you want to do is freak her out."

Nodding, he said, "I know. You're right. She just managed to be in the wrong place, that's all."

"What about the daughter's violin lessons? Does Christina usually go to the estate?"

"Honestly, I have no idea. I know she gives private lessons, but I never had a reason to ask her who her students were or where she met them."

"Well, if you do bring it up, remember—"

"Seriously? Don't go there. I don't need a lecture on how to maintain mission security."

Clapping him on the shoulder, Tate said, "I know, sorry, man. Come on, I'll buy you lunch."

As he walked back through the cavernous room, he was glad the others were all involved in their work. Most looked up, gave him a chin lift in support, then went back to their duties. He knew they had his back, and it felt good. It also felt good that they trusted him to do what had to be done. *Now, if I can just trust myself not to strangle Jerry Kincaid.*

———

Clay opened his door, his smile wide as he ushered Christina inside. When she'd called to say that she had a full day off with no practice, no concerts, and her private student had canceled, he jumped at the chance to be with her. He had offered to drive to Portland, but she said she was dying to get out of the city and would love to come to him. No way was he going to turn down a chance for her to be at his house again.

Now, standing in his living room, he stared at her, torn between wanting to pull her into his arms and kiss her and grouse because she'd been in Jerry Kincaid's house. He jolted when she placed her hand on his arm.

"Are you okay, Clay?"

"Sorry, sorry! Got some stuff from work on my mind." He opened his arms, and as she stepped forward, he enveloped her in his embrace, pulling her close to his chest. With her low heels, she once again was tucked under his chin. Her hair was down, flowing around her shoulders, and he kissed the top of her head.

She leaned back, held his gaze, and smiled. He took her lips in a slow-burn kiss. Nips and nibbles, soft and gentle. No matter what kind of kiss they shared, his cock rose to attention. With her plastered close to him, his arousal pressed against her stomach.

"Are we going to eat first or play first?"

Laughing, he said, "I'll be a gentleman, and we'll eat first."

She scrunched her nose and laughed along with him, then they walked into the kitchen. "Wow, that smells good. I didn't know you could cook."

"I'm not a gourmet, but I can fix more than mac and cheese. Although, I have a mac and cheese recipe that's amazing."

"As a starving musician, I've had plenty of mac and cheese, ramen noodles, and peanut butter and jelly sandwiches. Believe me, anything over that is wonderful."

He checked on the lasagna in the oven, glad she opened the conversation to her life as a musician, giving him a chance to dive in for more information. "As much as you work, it's hard to imagine you being a starving musician."

She poured some wine and sat on the stool, taking a sip. "I'm not really, not anymore. I was lucky that my parents paid for my college education as long as I paid for my room and board. But as soon as I could, I got out of New York City. I would have to sell a kidney just to have a tiny room in a tiny, shared apartment. I also never wanted to use my parents' reputation or name to get ahead. I looked at Boston but then tried out for a position with the Portland Orchestra and discovered that I really loved Maine. The symphony salary is decent, but not great. My private students help, and I have to admit the money I get from Amhrán M'anama with the gigs we play makes a huge difference."

While he was curious about the band, he wanted to focus on her private students, and once again she'd provided the opening. "How many students do you teach?"

"It varies. Twice a year, I'll teach a class to very young children. The symphony actually pays me for that. I usually keep about six to ten private students, but to be honest, ten is a lot. Right now, I have eight."

"Do you like teaching one on one?"

She smiled, and his heart squeezed. *Damn the investigation.* What he really wanted was to just know about her. What made her happy or sad, frightened or excited. He wanted to know how she spent her days.

"I really do love it! The little kids are great, but I have to admit there's something about tutoring a teenager. I know a lot of people don't like working with teens, and if I had students that really weren't into it and were only doing it because their parents wanted them to, I'd hate that. I've had a few of those, but I try to weed those out early. One of the first questions I now ask before taking on a new student is whose idea it was. If they tell me it was all the parent, then I tell them to call me when it's their own idea. When I get a young person who loves to practice, really cares about what they're doing, then it's so exciting."

Seeing the smile on her face, he leaned over the counter to kiss her lightly. Taking the lasagna out of the oven and sliding in the garlic bread slices, he looked over his shoulder. "I'll bet you're a fabulous teacher."

"I find that even young people can teach me things. There's a lot of accomplished musicians who think there's nothing they can learn from someone younger, but I always want to be open."

"So, what have you learned recently?"

Clapping her hands together, she replied, "It actually happened yesterday. One of my students lives on a rather large estate. Normally, she comes to one of the practice rooms at the concert hall, but she didn't have a way to get there, so I drove to her house. Her mom was having a social get together, and we didn't want to make a lot of noise in the main house. My student told me they had a guesthouse with really cool acoustics. Well, you can imagine I was intrigued."

He grinned at her enthusiasm. "And you couldn't wait to check it out, could you?"

"Oh, you know it! I thought it was going to be this little guesthouse, and it turned out to be a three-story massive building. I mean, only somebody rich would call it a guesthouse! Anyway, when you first enter, there's a great room that goes all the way up three levels with stairs and other rooms on the backside. So we started playing violins, and she was right! The acoustics were amazing."

Keeping his expression neutral, he continued to probe. "Do you just teach classical or do you ever teach the Gaelic music?"

Eyes wide, she said, "That's so weird that you asked! I've been focusing on symphonic pieces because that's what her parents wanted, but she really wanted to learn some of the Gaelic music. So, the next thing I know, I'm playing and dancing around this great room, the acoustics were tantalizing, and then we went all the way up to the third floor. You should have seen the view... I could see the whole estate and even out over the water!"

"So, you gave a free concert to whoever was staying in the guesthouse."

Her brow scrunched and she shook her head. "No, we were alone. Well, at least at first. Amelia explained that there was someone living in the guesthouse, but he wasn't present at the time." Rolling her eyes, she added, "Of course, by the time we are ready to leave, the man showed up. I was so embarrassed."

"Was he upset that someone was in his house?"

She smiled and shook her head. He wished Jerry was

in the room so he could punch him for putting a smile on Christina's face. Maintaining a blank expression, he waited for her reply even though the image of them on the camera ran through his mind.

"Well, technically, he was staying in the guesthouse that Amelia's parents own. But no, he wasn't upset. Mr. Kincaid was very charming and nice and said that he really liked our music."

Turning back to the oven, he pulled out the lightly browned garlic toast. "He'd have to be an idiot to not like your music or appreciate a beautiful woman showing up in his house." After setting the plates on the table, he poured their wine. "I'm curious... who did the estate belong to?"

"Congressman Bennett."

"I've met him and his wife. Do you know him or just his daughter?" He held his breath, afraid she would recognize being questioned, but she was too interested in the food.

Diving into her meal, she moaned in delight. "This is delicious!" Taking another sip of wine, she added, "I'd only met the congressman a couple of times. Usually, his wife drops Amelia off for her lesson. But I know the congressman has been fabulous for being a benefactor of the symphony orchestra. Oh, and by a stroke of luck, he's now going to be a benefactor of the band as well."

At that last bit of information, Clay's fork stopped on the way to his mouth. "The band. Amhrán M'anama?"

"Yeah. Amelia must have told him about us because Steven called today to thank me, saying that he was contacted by Mr. Kincaid to say that he was interested in helping an indie band. I guess he's handling things for the congressman."

"So, the congressman hasn't seen the band?"

"No," she laughed. "I can't see Dunk and the congressman together."

"Speaking of Dunk, is he always as drunk as he was at the festival?"

Her gaze darted up to his quickly, and she chewed slowly before swallowing, seeming to carefully consider her words. "I know you're not a cop, Clay, so what's the interest in Dunk?"

Setting his fork down, he leaned his weight on his forearms, moving closer. "Christina, babe, you're important to me. The drummer I saw the other day might be your friend, but he was also drunk. I assume the band never lets him drive like that?"

Sighing, she nodded. "I'm sorry. I guess I just get defensive about them. The guys have been really good to me, and they were doing fine on their own but said that with the addition of me, my fiddle, my energy, not to mention my short skirt, they get more money at the bars we play." Shrugging, she said, "I'd like to think it's more my fiddle than my legs!"

"I'd like to think so, too. I hate the idea of having to beat up too many guys who stare at your legs."

She barked out a laugh. "Don't worry, I'm always perfectly safe. Actually, the band is really protective. I know Dunk has issues, and he definitely drinks too much. Jamie and Mike usually make sure he gets home safely. Steven gets frustrated and says that if Duncan wasn't such a good drummer, he'd fire his ass. But they're good friends, too. And no, he never drives us."

He loved learning more about her, but as the meal drew to a close, he decided to forgo any more questions. *I can always do some digging on my own... especially why Kincaid was now interested in her band.* Leaning back in his seat, he smiled. "So, now that I've fed you..."

"Then let's play!"

Grabbing her hand, he grinned. "Best idea I've heard all day."

14

"Fuckin' hell."

Josh looked over at Clay. "What are you working on?"

"I'm just looking to see who Christina is involved with."

"Using company resources to scope out your new girlfriend?" Cobb asked, a grin on his face. Throwing his hands up as Clay glared at him, he added, "Hey, I'm not judging."

"No. It's just that she was talking yesterday, and it seemed she's now involved with some who are linked in ways I hadn't thought about."

Levi looked up from his desk. "The Kincaid case?"

"Sort of. In a roundabout way."

Levi closed the file on his desk and rolled his chair closer. Looking around, Clay saw he had the attention of several of the other Keepers.

"I wanted to find out more from her perspective about Kincaid. Now, before anybody gives me grief, I also just wanted to know more about her. So, I specifically asked about her private students. You can imagine the conversation rolled around to Congressman Bennett's daughter."

"I'm not sure it's real smart for you to be questioning her," Tate said.

"I wasn't questioning her! I mean, I was, but just because I want to know more about her." Seeing the expressions on some of his friends' faces, he huffed. "Yeah, I wanted to hear her side of the story about meeting with Kincaid, but I'm interested in everything about her."

"Ignore them. Keep going," Josh said. "What did you find out?"

"She normally doesn't go to the Bennett estate. She teaches her private lessons somewhere else. But the daughter didn't have a ride and her mom was giving some sort of party. The daughter suggested they go down to the guesthouse. She also mentioned that the man who was staying in the guesthouse showed up."

"So, she'd never met Kincaid before?" Mace asked.

He shook his head. "No. But then she mentioned Congressman Bennett. She said he and his wife were benefactors of the orchestra that she plays in—"

"That's hardly a surprise," Cobb threw out. "A lot of politicians attend functions like that and give donations. It's a tax write off."

"Yeah, I know, but then she mentioned that they got a call about donations for the band."

"The Celtic band?" Walker asked. "I mean, they're

great, but I don't really see that being something that the congressman would donate to."

Clay leaned back in his seat and scrubbed his hand over his face. "She indicated that he gives money to indie artists."

"That's probably true, too. Honestly, that doesn't seem like anything to worry about," Cobb said. "Christina just happens to be on the periphery of the investigation, not in it in any way."

Sighing heavily, Clay said, "Yeah, I know, but then I started looking at her band. The drummer? Duncan Byrne. He goes by Dunk, but his other nickname is Drunken Duncan. He's been picked up for public intoxication and disorderly conduct quite a few times. And then there's Mike, one of the bagpipe guys. He had a few arrests when he was younger."

"Clay, listen to yourself. You know that being high on a college campus or being picked up a couple times for being drunk is not a big deal," Tate said. "I'm not trying to downplay any of this, but a lot of college students smoke pot, drink alcohol, and even play around with a few stronger drugs. I'm not saying all musicians do it, but it's not that uncommon, either. The most important thing is that Christina is clean."

"Well, what about being arrested for distribution? That one was laid on Mike, but the charge was thrown out."

"So, what's the problem?" Rank asked.

Jerking his gaze around, he said, "You can't seriously be asking me that! I'm telling you that my girlfriend is closely involved with a group of people and most have alcohol or drug use in their history. Now, I know that Congressman Bennett isn't tied into the drugs, but since he's going to give money to the band, it makes me wonder if Kincaid isn't the one handling it. Seems like any money coming from the congressman would have to go through Kincaid anyway."

"If you want to know something about a politician, follow the money trail," Cobb agreed.

The group became quiet, each seeming to think about his words.

"There's something else you're not telling us," Mace said, causing Clay to stare at his boss.

He ground his teeth together before admitting, "The band's been to Canada. Not often, but to several festivals. And when I looked at a few of the pictures on the internet, I saw members of the Minotaurs were in attendance."

"Shit," came the expletive from the rest of the Keepers.

Mace finally said, "Keep looking into this angle because we all want to know everything that Kincaid is doing, especially if it involves the Minotaurs. Just be smart and keep Christina out of this. She's not going to like having her friends investigated or find out that you were questioning her for more than just getting to know her."

He nodded as he turned back to his computer. *No worries... that's the last thing I want her to know I was doing.*

With her fingers creating the vibrato, the bow slid across the strings and the familiar vibrations of the violin underneath her chin moved throughout her as the music swelled all around. Completely focused on the final piece of the evening, Christina's eyes moved between the music and the conductor, making sure each note coming from her instrument was perfect. Considering the same professionalism resided in all the members of the orchestra, she had no doubt that they'd given the patrons their money's worth tonight.

With a final note resounding throughout the concert hall, the conductor made his grand, circular movement and silence hit the room for only a few seconds before the thunderous applause rained down upon them.

Smiling, she glanced toward the other musicians around her, then directed her gaze to the other side where she met Amy's wide grin and waggling eyebrows. She knew exactly who Amy had spotted. Twisting her head slightly, she could see Clay in the audience. She was surprised to see Cobb sitting next to him.

As soon as they were able, she met Amy in the back room as they put their instruments away before moving to the reception in the lobby.

"Holy moly, Christina, your boyfriend is gorgeous. And nice. And dedicated to the arts. And devoted to you—"

"I get it, I get it! You're right, he's fantastic." Accepting a hug from Amy, she said, "I know I'm really lucky."

Amy leaned back and shook her head. "You're not

the only one. He's very lucky to have you. Now, let's go get some champagne."

They made their way to the lobby quicker than normal, her gaze searching for the tall, gorgeous man that was already holding her heart. Knowing that he might have gotten caught behind some slower patrons, she turned when she heard her name called out.

"Ms. Monroe!"

Recognizing Amelia's voice, she watched as Amelia and her parents approached. Nodding politely, she greeted, "Congressman Bennett, Mrs. Bennett, it's nice to see you." Turning to Amelia, she asked, "Did you enjoy the concert?"

Before Amelia had a chance to answer, the man from the guesthouse, Jerry Kincaid, stepped up. A beautiful woman clung to his arm. Tall, cool, blonde, in an elegant gown, she towered over Christina, cast her gaze over her, and obviously decided she was no competition if the bored, somewhat smug expression on her face was anything to go by. Turning her attention back to the Bennetts, Christina smiled.

"I thought the concert was wonderful," Amelia said.

"Your solo was exquisite," Congressman Bennett said, his smile warm as he wrapped his arms around his wife and his daughter.

"Amelia tells us that you play in a string quartet. I'd love to have you perform at one of our gatherings," Mrs. Bennett said. "Would you ever consider that?"

"If it fits into my schedule, I'd be honored."

The congressman turned toward Jerry and said, "Make sure to get Ms. Monroe's information from my wife, and I'll let you arrange her performance for our next gathering."

Amelia and her parents said their goodbyes and moved on. Christina snuck a look at Jerry's date, who eyed the champagne table while tugging on his sleeve, huffing loudly.

"Ms. Monroe," Jerry greeted, his voice smooth as he reached out to take her hand. "It seems we are destined to meet again."

"I'm not sure it's destiny, Mr. Kincaid. You know I play in the symphony, so if you're here, you will certainly find me." She glanced toward the cool blonde who had now stepped away.

His gaze followed hers, and he chuckled as he turned back. He leaned closer, his lips near her ear. "It seems that someone prefers their alcohol over meeting the musicians. I assure you that is not the case with me."

Her smile was dutiful, but she slid her hand away from his. A man flirting when he had a date made her feel uncomfortable. "I need to mingle, but it was nice to see you again."

"I hope that you'll come back to the guesthouse anytime you like. The invitation extends to you, even when you aren't giving Miss Bennett a lesson."

Not replying, she inclined her head and moved back into the crowd, running into Amy.

"Who's that? He's handsome… in a devilish way," Amy asked, peering around Christina's shoulder.

"He's here with Congressman Bennett. I met him last week."

Amy looked around. "So, where's Clay?"

"I haven't found him yet—"

Arms encircled her as Clay made it to her side. Beaming up at him, she was surprised when his arm banded around her waist and he pulled her close.

"Glad you're here, Clay," Amy said, grinning. "I thought another man was going to swoop in and carry Christina off to his lair."

"Oh, hush," Christina said, rolling her eyes. "Ignore her... she's imaging things."

"That man may have had a date, but he was seriously looking like he wanted to start at your fingertips and kiss all the way up your arm," Amy retorted, winking at Clay before moving to another group of musicians.

"What's she talking about?" Clay asked.

"Oh, just someone with the congressman. Actually, it's the man who lives in the guesthouse I was telling you about. Mr. Kincaid."

A muscle in his jaw twitched. "Do I need to be worried?" He lifted his head and appeared to search the room.

Laughing, she shook her head. "No, of course not! He had his own date who was my exact opposite... tall, long-legged, blonde. He was just being polite because the Bennetts want him to arrange for my quartet to play at one of their events."

He smiled down at her, but for a second, she could have sworn a dark flash moved through his eyes. Blinking, the specter was gone. "Um... did Cobb leave?"

"Yes, he said to give you his congratulations on the performance."

She stifled a yawn. "I think I've mingled enough. I'll

get my violin and we can leave."

Waving toward the guard outside the practice room where their instruments were kept, she was surprised to see that most of the orchestra members had already collected their belongings. Not having to push through a crowd, she quickly checked her violin case, grabbed her music satchel, and headed back into the lobby.

Clay usually waited for her next to the stage door, but not seeing him, she walked toward the front door leading outside. Even as short as she was, she could see him standing to the side of the lobby, head bent in deep discussion with Cobb.

She scooted between people, finding him alone once she reached his side. He smiled down at her, and she asked, "I thought Cobb had already left."

"He did."

"But you were just standing here talking to him."

He took her jacket and held it as she slid her arms in. "I thought he'd left earlier but actually saw him as he was leaving and had a chance to say goodbye."

She opened her mouth to say that their conversation looked rather deep for two people saying goodbye but snapped her mouth shut. *They're friends and coworkers, working in the security business. They probably have a lot to discuss, none of which I should ask about.* Instead, she turned, looped her arm through his, and winked. "You ready to take me home?"

A wolfish grin spread across Clay's face as he pulled her close. Laughing, they walked out into the cool night air that didn't come close to putting out the fire building between them.

15

Clay sat at a high-top table in the bar, his back next to the wall. A few of the other Keepers and their women were at the table as well, but his eyes were glued to the small stage at the back.

When he'd first sat down, a faint scent of cigarette smoke wafted from the walls, a holdover from the days when smoky bars were the norm. But now, the music reverberated against the wood, filling the space. Considering that much of the crowd was clapping and stomping in time to the music, he was glad that they'd chosen to sit close to the stage so that he could hear the music and keep his eyes on Christina.

Watching her dance and twirl while playing the fiddle in her high-heeled boots, she looked and sounded amazing. It might be fanciful, but he could almost imagine her doing the same out in the woods, appearing like an ancient Celt sprite.

"You may not like the rest of her band members

much, but you've got to admit their music is fuckin' awesome."

He glanced over at Drew and nodded before shooting a grin toward Babs as she bounced her head in time to the music.

Turning back to the stage, he watched Christina's long hair tossing back and forth as she twirled. He wondered how it did not catch in the strings or bow, but she was in control of every movement even if she appeared to be completely free-spirited. Her arms and fingers flew as she fiddled, blending perfectly with the bagpipes, drums, and Steven's vocals.

Her heeled boots only made her legs appear longer and her black tank top made her curves more pronounced.

His gaze reluctantly left her and scanned the bar, knowing other men were just as enraptured at her performance. He was surprised that jealousy didn't spear through him, but instead, he felt immense pride in her talent. When the song came to an end, the room erupted into more stomping and applause.

Christina lowered her fiddle and bow, a smile on her face. Her eyes drifted over the crowd calling out for 'Tiny', seemingly oblivious to all the other men as her gaze settled on Clay, brightening as soon as she found him. A light sheen of sweat dotted her brow, and the tendrils of hair next to her face curled with the dampness.

Their show was over, and Steven grabbed a water bottle and drank deeply. Considering the top had already been off when he came on stage, Clay wondered what was actually in the bottle. Mike was doing the same, but Dunk and Jamie were downing another beer. Shadows were visible underneath her kohl-lined eyes that occasionally darted over to Dunk. As patrons gathered closely to the stage, Clay stood, ready to move in if necessary.

"It just looks like they want the band members to sign their T-shirts," Cobb said. "It's smart that they had some merchandise to sell."

"She says that Steven comes up with ideas for them to make money and get their name out there."

Babs leaned over, her lips tight. "Jerry Kincaid is on the other side of the room."

Clay stiffened as he watched Jerry make his way through the crowd toward the stage. Christina reacted with surprise at seeing him but laughed when she shook his outstretched hand. Clay started to stand, but Cobb stopped him with a hand on his shoulder. "Wait."

Forcing air in and out of his lungs, he watched as Babs darted through the crowd, making her way to the stage. She managed to maneuver right next to Jerry.

Christina hugged her, turning away from Jerry. Babs leaned in closely and whispered something that made Christina nod and place her fiddle on the stool behind her near Steven's microphone. The two women walked toward the bathroom in the hall behind the bar.

Whipping his head around, he stared as Jerry watched Christina leave and then moved toward the others. He shook hands with the group, and they all chatted a moment before he moved to Steven. Leaning closer, Jerry talked to just Steven. Jerry maneuvered the two of them around so that he was able to keep an eye on the hall where Christina had gone.

"Their drummer is so stoned I can't imagine him understanding anything Jerry said to him," Cobb commented.

"Yeah, I've had my eye on him all night. Christina says they never let him drive anywhere but the man makes me nervous."

"Damn, I should have had Babs stay near Jerry. What do you think he's talking to him about?" Drew said.

"I don't know, but I'm glad Babs got Christina away from the man. I don't like the way he looks at her."

"You mean different from the way most of these men in this room look at her?" Drew laughed. Clay shot him a narrowed-eyed glare, and Drew threw his hands up in supplication. "Hey, just stating the truth."

Clay looked back toward the stage, noting Jerry was now walking out of the bar. Sighing, he said, "Yeah, I can deal with the other men. Plain old lust and awe, I get. Jerry? I don't know what his game is when it comes to the band. Is he just a lackey for Congressman Bennett or is he working his own angle?"

Swinging his head around, he grinned as Christina and Babs approached. Babs hopped up on the chair next to Drew, and Christina moved directly to Clay as he slid from his barstool. Wrapping his arms around her, he said, "Great show, babe."

She beamed, then stood on tiptoe to meet his lips in

a quick kiss, wrapping her arms around his waist and squeezing. "Thanks."

The others in their group threw out their appreciation for the performance as well. She continued smiling, accepting the bottle of cold water Clay had ready for her. She fit in so well with his friends, a fact that meant a lot to him. He now understood what his fellow Keepers meant when they found women that suited not only them but meshed with the group.

Twisting her head around to the stage, she appeared to be taking stock of the band. "I need to get back up and help take things down. I especially need to get my fiddle. As much as I love those guys, I don't trust them!"

"I'll go with you," he offered, earning another wide grin. As they pushed their way through the crowd, he kept one arm protectively around her and used the other as a block to keep people from bumping into her.

"You know, I'm used to getting run over most of the time," she joked.

"Babe, get used to someone making sure you're taken care of." Holding her hand, he gave her a boost up onto the stage. She maneuvered around the small platform, deftly stepping over wires and cords as Jamie and Mike unplugged and packed the amplifiers. The bagpipes had already been safely stowed in their cases, and Dunk staggered in from the back after having taken part of his drum set out to their vehicle.

Dunk approached Christina and grabbed her by the waist, lifting her up. "Great show, Tiny."

"Put me down, you big oaf!" she complained.

Just as Clay was ready to come to her rescue, Dunk

set her feet back on the stage and swayed slightly as he moved back to his drums. She looked at Clay and rolled her eyes, shaking her head.

"He's a good percussionist. And friend," came a comment from behind.

Clay swung his head around at that comment, seeing Steven standing close by. Having been so focused on Christina, he hadn't noticed the man approach. Glancing down, he saw Steven shoving an envelope in his coat pocket.

Offering an explanation to Clay's unasked question, Steven tapped his pocket and said, "The bar owner gives us a cut of the evening's cover charge. Gotta admit that amount has grown larger since Christina joined us. People like her music, but let's face it... men like having a pretty face to stare at while they're drinking."

Clay wanted to argue but knew Steven was right. "I just hope she's appreciated for her musical talent more than the sex appeal you're trying to bring to the group."

Lifting his hands up in front of him, Steven replied, "Hey, we all have the utmost respect for her musical talent. Hell, our fans do, too. They might like having someone pretty to look at, but the way she plays her violin while moving to the music is pure magic."

He nodded, unable to deny Steven's assessment.

"We just hope she sticks with us as we get bigger."

Clay's gaze moved from Christina to Steven. Cocking his head to the side, he waited to see what else the other man had to say.

Steven shrugged slightly, then exclaimed, "It's taken us a while, but we've got an agent. Well, a part-time agent. Someone who likes the demo we made and says he can take us further. Of course, he'd take his cut, so we're not ready to sign with him yet."

"That's smart. There's a lot of unscrupulous people in the entertainment industry."

"You're preaching to the choir, man. I grew up in this business." At Clay's raised eyebrow, Steven chuckled. "My grandfather had a garage band back in the '60s. He was sure he was going to make it big but never did. My dad played guitar for a small-time metal band in the 80s. My first few years were spent being dragged around from city to city. Looking back, the band had a real chance, but they kept putting their faith in one asshole agent after another, having most of their money stolen."

Clay had looked into each of the band members but now regretted that he had not done a full background check. Continuing to keep his eye on Christina as she chatted with Jamie and Mike, he asked, "Is there a reason you're telling me this?"

"I've never seen Christina with someone," Steven said, jamming his hands into his coat pockets. "She's never had anyone come to our concerts. I don't have any illusions that the band's goals are just to go around and play in some bars. We've had our eye on getting on a much larger stage—national, international. We're already a hit in the northeast and getting a name in a few places in Canada. As far as I'm concerned, the sky's the limit."

Turning so that his body now fully faced Steven, he eyed the man with a hard stare. "And Christina being front and center is a big part of where you want to go."

"Told you, I respect her talent. Hell, if I just wanted a short skirt and legs, I can get that anywhere. But the whole package that's her gives Amhrán M'anama a chance to make it big."

"Including the fact that she gave the band its name."

Steven sucked in a quick breath, then narrowed his eyes. "Yeah... the name is hers."

"What about the Portland Orchestra?"

Snorting, Steven shook his head. "I get that she loves that gig, but she's never going to make a name for herself being one of many violins sitting in an orchestra that's not internationally known."

"So, you think she'll choose the band over the orchestra if it comes down to having to make a choice?"

"Absolutely. What musician wouldn't go for the money and the recognition? The question is would she choose the band over you?"

Hands on his hips, he looked down at Steven and steadied his breathing in an effort to keep from planting his fist in the other man's face. "And now we come to the crux of your approach. What? You gonna threaten me to stay away? Find out what my motives are with her?"

"Just letting you know where things stand. The band is going to do everything we can to convince her that when we make it big, she's right there with us. It would be nice to think that you care enough about her to want her to be successful."

"I want what's best for her. I want her to make that decision, and then I'll support her any way I can."

Steven held his gaze for a long moment, then grinned and nodded. "Well, all right." A loud crash drew their attention back to the stage, and Steven cursed under his breath. "Fuckin' Dunk." He jumped up onto the stage and headed to the percussion that Dunk was stumbling over.

Clay swung his gaze back to Christina. She was staring pinch-lipped while the other band members laughed with Dunk.

"I'm heading out," she called to the others. "You all okay?"

The other men offered their assurances and good-byes, and she gave a long look over the stage that was now mostly clear. Sighing, she turned back toward Clay, her face brightening as soon as her eyes landed on him. That smile bolted straight through him, and he returned it with one of his own. Lifting his arms toward her she walked to the edge of the stage, he wrapped his hands around her waist as she held onto her violin case and music. Lifting her easily to the floor, he bent and kissed her lightly.

With his arm around her, he glanced back to the stage and saw Steven staring at the two of them. Offering a chin lift, he turned and escorted her out of the bar. Steven's words rang through his mind as they walked to his vehicle. He had never asked Christina what her professional goals for the future were. He had never asked her if she had to make a choice between the orchestra and the Celtic band what her decision would be. He had also never asked her if she had the opportunity to become a national or international musician would she leave Maine to do so.

He glanced to the side as they drove home in silence, her eyes closed in fatigue and her steady breathing indicating that she was sleeping. Gripping the steering wheel a little tighter, a dull ache began in his heart. He was falling for the beautiful musician but had no idea if they had a future.

16

Clay rolled to his back on the cool sheets, scrubbing his hand over his face. His large frame covered most of the space in Christina's small bed, but sleeping curled around each other felt so right. They had made it home before Amy the night before and immediately headed to bed. Making love with soft words and whispered endearments, his body moved over hers, each reverent thrust filled with meaning.

Now, she'd slipped from bed to make him breakfast before he needed to leave. Guilt speared through him over her unselfish action. He could feel the silent questions pouring from her, knowing his taciturn mood had invaded the bedroom. But he had no answers and found conversation to be difficult when so much was swirling in his mind.

Smart enough to know his silence was born and bred from his childhood, he lacked the knowledge to move past his reticence. Having witnessed his parents' angry arguments and nasty insults hurled toward each other, neither willing to give an inch, he would fall into silence, hiding when a child and leaving the house when a teen. Avoidance seemed to be the best course of action. *And here I am, taking the chickenshit way out instead of talking to her.*

He envied Drew and Rank's ability to throw out witty comments no matter what mood they were in. Snorting, he also knew that Babs and Helena could see straight through their men's attempts at deflecting.

Glancing at his watch, he threw the covers back and quickly dressed in the clothes he'd worn to the bar the previous night. No answers were forthcoming, and he needed to hit the road for his drive home. Heading to the kitchen, he was greeted with Christina's wide smile but concerned eyes. Walking straight to her, he pulled her into his embrace and kissed her soundly. "You didn't have to do this, babe, but thanks for breakfast."

She kept her smile firmly in place as she set two plates on the counter, and they slid onto side-by-side stools. Eating mostly in silence, she walked him to the door as he readied to leave. Encircling his waist with her arms, she leaned back and held his gaze. "Are you sure you're okay, Clay?"

Pulling her in close, he kissed her deeply. "Absolutely." Feeling the need to offer some kind of explanation, he added, "I know I've been poor company. I just have a case on my mind. I'm sorry."

"Honey, you never have to apologize. I know the work you do is important and stressful. I also know you can't talk about the cases you're working on, so all I can do is just try to support you."

Another round of guilt hit him, and he bent to kiss her once again. "That means everything, babe."

She hesitated, then said, "I don't have a lot of violin practices this week since the symphony's season is almost over. But I need to let you know that I'll be in Ottawa Wednesday night. The band will head up that morning and be back the next day."

"Ottawa?"

Shrugging, she nodded. "We play some gigs in Canada a few times each year, more in the summer. Steven sprung this on us. He said that Mr. Kincaid arranged it."

"The man from the congressman's guesthouse?"

"Yeah, it seems he has some contacts. He and Steven have hit it off, and he really wants to help get more exposure for the band."

He nodded but didn't reply. She huffed slightly, then added, "Are you sure you're okay?"

"Yes," he said, his voice definitive as his arm squeezed her again. "I just don't know what I've got going on this week either."

She cupped his jaw. "Look, Clay, I know our schedules conflict a lot but—"

"But we make it work, sweetheart. You're important to me, so we'll do what we have to do to make it work."

Her smile was almost blinding, causing his breath to hitch. Kissing her once again, he headed down to her apartment parking lot. During the two-hour drive home, his mind continually rolled over the case with Jerry Kincaid's association with the band, her upcoming trip to Canada, and how the whole investigation was going to impact Christina. The feeling that things were about to get messy continued to invade his thoughts.

"Jerry Kincaid has arranged for Christina's band to play in Ottawa Wednesday night." Clay glanced around the table at the other Keepers as he made his pronouncement.

"Fuck," Mace cursed. "It's a connection and a complication we didn't expect, but we've got to investigate what his game is as well as the band."

"Jerry is not just a lackey for the congressman," Rank said. "He's making his way in the drug trade."

Cobb leaned forward and said, "He can still play the lackey. Often, a politician's campaign manager will move into other positions once the politician is elected. Granted, as soon as they're elected, they start thinking about the next election. Considering that Bennett and Jerry's friendship goes back to childhood, it's not unusual for Jerry to take whatever position comes up. In this case, assisting the Bennetts in any way he can just solidifies their need for him. It's a smart move on his part. He becomes indispensable, trusted explicitly, and not watched carefully."

Clay listened to the comments coming from the others, his mind racing through possibilities. "I can see how a man like Jerry would want more power and money coming from the cartels, especially if he feels like his career is subservient to the congressman. What I can't figure out is if he's the only one in it or if the congressman is part of their drug smuggling. And if Jerry is in bed with the Minotaurs, I can't figure out what he's doing with a local indie band. That really doesn't make any sense to me."

"You, like a good investigator, hate unanswered questions," Mace said.

He held his boss' gaze, then nodded his agreement.

"Levi, keep working with the FBI to see if they have anything on the drugs that were found and how they think they're being moved. There's more going into the pipeline than are in some of the small boats in the area. Clay, take a deeper look at the band. See if you can dig up more of a connection between Steven and Jerry."

"I appreciate that, Mace." He hesitated for a few seconds, then added, "I'd like to follow the band to Ottawa. On my own time, of course—"

"No, you'll do it *on* company time." Before he had a chance to protest, Mace continued, "Look, Clay, this is all part of our investigation and Jerry Kincaid. So, you keep up with time, travel, and expenses, and get them turned into Sylvie. No argument. And let's face it, most of us have worked on cases where we needed LSI resources to help with something that one of our women was involved in. We all jumped in to do that, no questions asked. This is the same. We know that Christina is not part of this investigation, but she's on the periphery. We all want to make sure she's safe as well as find out what the fuck Jerry Kincaid is up to."

He let out an audible sigh, relief flooding him. Nodding again, he offered his thanks.

Mace looked around. "Who's going with him?"

Every Keeper in the room shouted their acquiescence. Eyes wide, Clay grinned.

"Just as I thought," Mace chuckled. "Drew, you and Blay have to finish the security job. Josh, we'll need you here, especially if they can get monitoring equipment near the Minotaurs and Steven. Tate, Rank, and Walker are needed for the Simmons case they just started on. Levi is here with the FBI part of this investigation. Blake is in the middle of the Westmoreland security detail."

"Well, damn, boys. Guess that means I'm heading to Canada," Cobb laughed, throwing his palm up for a high-five with Clay.

Glad to be planning and not just worrying, Clay nodded. "Let's get to it."

While Cobb talked to Babs to arrange their travel, Clay settled at the computer station next to Josh. "I want to see if I can follow a money trail with the band. Are you still searching on Jerry?"

"Yes, but he's slippery. I'm digging through his finances. Hell, I'm even digging through the congressman's finances. I'm also looking at the campaign finances, but I'm not sure what I'll find out there. Those have to go through political committees, but that doesn't mean there isn't wrongdoing. I've also got Bray looking into Jerry's friendships and political associates. You want to take on the band members, go for it."

Twisting around, he began tapping on the keyboard, beginning with basic information on Duncan Byrne, Michael Kelley, James Iversen, and Steven McPherson. All four had extensive social media accounts, both individually and under the band's name. Searching through those gave evidence they exhibited no restraint when it came to posting drunk pictures, bar life after their band's gigs, or a multitude of women vying for the camera while hanging on to the men. Going back several years, he discerned that Michael and Jamie had met in high school, both part of a youth bagpipe band. It appeared Duncan had been playing percussion since he was very young. Steven had been a singer in a number of garage bands from the time he was a teenager, finally pulling the other three together. Not finding any evidence of Jerry, he began digging deeper.

Agreeing with Cobb's advice to look at the money, he discovered Mike and Jamie with very modest bank accounts. Mike's full-time job was working in the supply distribution department of a local company and was recently promoted to manager. Jamie was employed as a master mechanic. Duncan worked part-time in a restaurant, but interestingly enough, had more money in the bank than either Mike or Jamie. Cash deposits. Not an excessive amount at any one time, but the frequency indicated it was more than just earned tips. And the total was adding up.

Duncan had already landed on Clay's suspicion list, now justifiably. Checking Steven's account, he could see that he not only had a comfortable savings account, but he also was in charge of the band's money. Not surprisingly, he worked for a local accounting firm as a billing assistant. His paycheck was slightly higher than either Mike's or Jamie's but not enough to account for the extra money in his account. Now curious to see how he was handling the books for the band, Clay dug deeper.

An hour later, a frustrated groan left his lips as he leaned back in his chair. Seeing Josh's gaze land on him, he twisted around to see the remaining Keepers' attention on him as well.

"Steven McPherson, the vocalist and leader for Amhrán M'anama, works as a billing assistant in an accounting firm. He's also handling the books for the band, and they're a fuckin' mess."

"Well, he's an assistant, not an accountant," Walker said.

Sylvie looked over at the group and said, "Yes, but he works for an accounting firm. He would easily be able to get help with the band's books. He could probably even get a discount or have one of the accountants help on the side."

"Exactly," Clay said. "It makes me wonder what he's hiding."

"Or what money might be laundered through the band."

At that statement, everyone looked toward Sylvie. She glanced at Mace, then smiled and shrugged. "Just a thought," she added in a singsong voice.

"Shit, I never thought about that," Clay said, his words being echoed by the others. Turning back to his computer, he continued to maneuver through the financial records. Feeling a hand on his shoulder, he twisted his head around and looked up.

"I spent some time going through financial records in my former job," Sylvie said. "Granted, I'm not an accountant and certainly wouldn't be able to look through a multimillion-dollar corporation's finances. But if you want some help looking through what Steven is keeping on the band, I'll be glad to do that."

Thanking her, he shot a look toward Mace, gaining a nod. Looking back up toward Sylvie, he said, "Looks like the boss says it's okay, so I'll take all the help I can get."

Laughing, she patted his shoulder and pulled the records he'd sent to the printer. Hearing a sigh of frustration coming from Walker, he looked across the room. "This must be the day for all of us to run into roadblocks."

"I've been scanning the security screen on the Bennett estate, paying particular attention to the boathouse. Other than a few friends coming and going, all easily identifiable, there is nothing untoward happening at the boathouse. Jerry occasionally goes in empty-handed and comes out empty-handed. But he doesn't do that very often. So far, the Bennetts haven't used the boathouse."

"We've got nothing else on Jerry that ties him to any other harbor, marina, or boathouse. Whatever is going on with moving drugs through the area, it has to be there," Tate huffed.

Clay looked over toward Mace. "Boss, we didn't add surveillance to the inside because the FBI said they were monitoring the boating activity."

"The FBI have it on their radar. I've gotten no indication from them that they've seen any unusual activity," Levi threw out.

Mace nodded. "Maybe we should even add a wider scope of visuals in case Jerry is using someone else from the household to facilitate the transfer of drugs."

So deep in thought, Clay didn't notice Walker had asked a question until his name was called the second time. Jerking his head around, he said, "Sorry. What did you say?"

"I asked what the fuck you were thinking about so hard. Why do I get a feeling it's not just the case?"

His hand rubbed over his head, squeezing the back of his neck corded with tension as a headache had built. "It's Christina. Or rather, the fact that I'm investigating her friends in the band and their finances."

"Oh, man, the relationship guilt is setting in," Walker said.

"Huh?"

Tate replied, "You're the first one of us that had a relationship that wasn't part of an investigation, something I know you value. And who the hell knew it was going to happen, but you're now entangled with the woman you care about while subsequently investigating things that are going on in her life."

"Yeah, and she knows nothing about it."

"That's the way it's gotta be," Walker said. "Look, it's not much different than if you were still on active duty. There are married special ops, and their spouses understand they can't know everything about a mission."

Rank added, "Just think about it like a police detective. Same kind of thing. They can't talk about what they do with their spouses."

"So, how do you deal when the investigation

involves the person you're with and you can't tell them?"

Barking out a rueful laugh, Rank added, "You're missing the other question. How do you deal when they do find out what you *are* doing?"

"Shit," he cursed on exhalation. "I can't believe the man we're investigating is somehow tied up into the band she plays with. I gotta watch out for her without telling her what's going on. And then, when all the shit blows up, she's gonna know."

"All relationships have their challenges," Tate said. "Keepers just seem to have special challenges."

"I didn't want relationship challenges. I wanted easy. I wanted simple. I wanted to meet someone, develop a relationship, have feelings for each other, and move forward. I wanted everyone to be happy and get along."

"Hate to tell you, man, but just like Tate said, all relationships have challenges," Walker said. "Thinking a relationship was going to be completely drama-free was pretty naïve. And Clay, you don't strike me as naïve."

Sighing, he nodded, thinking about his parents. They certainly never cared what each of them thought about the other. Maybe that's why they couldn't get along. *Christina and I are different. We started by really caring about each other.* As much as he hated what her reaction would be when she found out she was part of his investigation, he hated the thought of her not being in his life even more.

17

The plane dipped and so did Christina's stomach. She hated cheap, crowded flights. It wasn't that she was a travel snob but flying always made her nauseous. And traveling with the band didn't make it better. She'd managed to acquire a seat away from the others, knowing she was going to be with them for the next twenty-four hours, she wanted as much space between her and them now as she possibly could have.

Landing in Ottawa, they moved through customs and she slipped into a different line so that she wouldn't have to hear Dunk's attempts at being a witty smartass and Steven trying to make sure they all got into the country with their instruments without being arrested. Sometimes, she wondered if being with the band was the right thing to do. She loved the music. Loved the act. But couldn't imagine doing this more than a couple of times a year. *And traveling all over the country or world? Hell no!*

Meeting with the others once they were through

customs, she walked toward them as Steven got on his phone to locate the transportation that would take them to the Ottawa Celtic Festival venue.

Dunk threw his arm around her and said, "As usual, you managed to disappear. If I didn't know better, I'd think you were ashamed of us."

Rolling her eyes, her lips quirked upward in spite of her efforts to appear stern. "There are times, Dunk, when you are absolutely adorable. But arguing with someone in customs when you know we have a concert to get to is not one of them. And I, for one, refused to be part of that."

"Damn, I think your new boyfriend has made you stuck up."

"Leave her alone," Jamie said, knocking Dunk's arm from Christina's shoulders.

Dunk simply grinned, twirled his ever-present drumsticks between his fingers, and walked over to the van that just parked near them. Steven was talking to the driver and Dunk stood near his percussion cases.

"Don't mind him. You know how he is."

She looked between Mike and Jamie as they flanked her, walking toward the van. She sighed. "I know. I'm sorry, guys. I'm really not trying to be a bitch, but I just recently decided that being his babysitter is not what I want to do."

"We don't expect you to be his babysitter. Anyway, I think Dunk's drunkenness is more of an act than a real problem," Mike said.

Cocking an eyebrow toward him, she jerked her chin back. "Seriously?"

Mike shrugged. "I don't know. I think he likes the persona of being Drunk Dunk."

Before she had a chance to ask more questions, Steven hustled them into the van and gave directions to the driver. Still feeling queasy, she sipped on water as the driver zipped in and out of traffic from the airport, through part of town, and finally out to the rolling hills and green pastures.

Once they were through the gates of the festival where the entertainers, food trucks, athletes, and vendors could park, they began unloading their equipment. The van driver assisted, and she noticed he didn't leave immediately.

"Is he staying?" she asked, making sure to carry her violin.

Steven grinned and nodded. "Yeah, he's paid to spend the day of the festival with us. He's going to help with our equipment and then get us back to the hotel tonight when the festival is over."

"And how much is that going to cost? If we pay him all that money, that means we hardly made anything on this gig."

Steven put his arm around her shoulders and squeezed. "Don't worry about it. I told you that I've been working on an angle, and the guy who's helping with an agent said he'd foot the bill."

She opened her mouth to question him further, but Steven turned and walked away, directing the move of their equipment to the back of the stage at the entertainment tent.

"Hey, don't look a gift horse in the mouth," Jamie

said. "I like having somebody to schlep all our equipment around."

Though the band did not have a lot to move, it was true that the couple of amplifiers and Dunk's percussion weren't easy to transport. She only had her violin and always tried to help the others, but between the band members and the driver, they made quick work of their equipment.

Settling into chairs behind the stage area, they listened to the other musicians. She could not help but think of the last Celtic festival where Clay discovered her playing in the band. She smiled, that being one of her favorite memories. After a while, she stood and walked to the doorway of the entertainment tent. The scent of food from the food trucks and the shouts of spectators at the stadium where the heavy athletics were competing had her longing for Clay's companionship and she wished he was there so they could enjoy the entire festival. Looking over her shoulder, she asked, "How much longer before we go on?"

"About an hour and a half," Steven said, looking up at her. "Why?"

"I'll be back. I just want to grab something to drink and take a look at the vendors."

"You never do that," Dunk said, his eyes closed as he leaned back in the chair with his feet stretched out in front of him, boots crossed.

"Yeah, well, maybe it's time I got out a little more." She slipped out the back of the entertainment tent. Buying bottled water and a Scotch egg at one of the food trucks, she bit into the fried goodness, once again thinking of Clay. Finishing her snack, she wiped her fingers and tossed her napkin into a nearby trashcan before wandering through the vendors, admiring the hats, leather purses, kilts, soft wool scarves, and silver jewelry.

Immediately heading to the men's jewelry, her gaze snagged on a pendant hanging from a thick, silver chain. The design was a silver lighthouse nestled in a Celtic circle. *Perfect!* Refusing to look at the price tag dangling from the chain, she handed it to the shop-keeper. Pulling out her credit card, she could barely contain the grin as he rang up the sale and placed it into a small box. She dropped it into her purse, thrilled with her purchase.

As she turned around, a large man to the side caught her attention, tanned complexion with a heavy black mustache and reflector sunglasses hiding his eyes. A ball cap was pulled low on his head. He looked like so many of the others at the festival, and yet she could swear he'd been watching her. Unnerved, she quickly retraced her steps through the crowd and made her way back to the entertainment tent.

Stepping to the side so that another band could leave, she waited as they moved their equipment out of the tent. Taking a sip of her water, she heard Steven's voice and turned to glance toward another small tent nearby, seeing him chatting with several heavily tatted, rough-looking men. They sported leather vests that appeared worn with age and covered in insignia patches. The festivals always attracted bikers, many of whom loved Amhrán M'anama's sound. She never felt afraid, but then she'd always been up on stage when they were around. But these men gave off a scary vibe that made her more curious as to why Steven was talking so intensely to them.

She hesitated, uncertain what to do. *Maybe if I just get Steven's attention, he'll come back over. It's got to be near time for us to go onstage.* She took several tentative steps toward the tent for a better look when one of the men glanced over Steven's shoulder. His scowl morphed as his lips curved upward. His leer caused her to halt her progress, a snake of fear slithering through her.

Steven still had not noticed her, but now that she had attracted the attention of several of the large men, she opened her mouth to call out to him. Suddenly, she was jostled from the side and her water spilled over her skirt and down her leg. Hearing a mumbled apology, she jerked her head up as another large man with a ball cap pulled over his long ponytail walked past. With his long, somewhat dirty beard and sunglasses, she decided it was in her best interest to simply glare at his back as he walked away.

One of the men outside the tent laughed and she turned quickly, no longer caring what Steven was up to. Hurrying inside, she groused as she looked down at the water droplets falling from her skirt, streaming down her leg, and landing on her boots. Forgetting Steven and whoever he was talking to, she rushed over to where her band was now standing.

"What happened to you?" Jamie asked, his brow furrowed as his gaze dropped to her legs.

"Someone bumped into me, and I spilled my water. Is there a towel around?"

"Here you go," Jamie said, tossing her a wad of paper towels. "Just be glad it was water and not beer."

She looked at him and nodded. "Yeah, you're right. By the way, who the hell is Steven talking to? It looks like he's out there mingling with a bunch of bikers."

"He stepped out right after you left. Who the fuck knows what he's doing?" Dunk replied, taking another long drag from his beer.

"Yeah, I saw him. Looks like a rough group he's talking to," Jamie said, his attention now back to his bagpipes.

Mike looked up from tuning his pipes. "I think it was some guys from another band. At least, that's what Mr. Kincaid said."

Halting in the middle of wiping off the water, she stared at him. "Mr. Kincaid is here?"

"No, he called Steven. Wanted to make sure we were okay and had everything we needed."

Before she had a chance to ask more questions, Steven suddenly walked in quickly, a big smile on his face. Rubbing his hands together, he said, "Okay, let's get ready."

"Who were you talking to out there?" she demanded, her hand planted on her hips.

Steven's smile dropped slightly before he tapped her on the nose and said, "Don't worry your pretty head about it. Just meeting some guys that will help us get our name out there for bigger gigs."

She started to retort, but he grabbed her shoulders,

whirled her around, and gave her a nudge toward the stage. "We're up, Tiny. Get going."

The next fifteen minutes were spent in a rush as they loaded their equipment onto the stage, and she had a chance to look out at the crowd. The entertainment tent was large, filled to capacity, and the side walls were rolled up so that people could spill out in every direction. The energy was vibrating over the crowd and she sucked in a deep breath.

Quickly tuning, she looked toward Steven and caught his wide smile. As irritated as she could get at the band, this was the moment she always waited for. The crowd was anticipating the first notes. Dunk was twirling his drumsticks in his fingers. Mike and Jamie were already starting to blow on the bagpipes.

Steven winked at her, stepped up to the microphone, and called out, "Are you ready for Amhrán M'anama?"

The crowd erupted into applause as Steven began to clap and Dunk pounded the beat on his drums. The whine from the bagpipes began and their sound resonated. With her fiddle tucked underneath her chin and her bow dancing across the strings, she began to play, losing herself in the music.

While Cobb stayed near Christina when she left the entertainment tent, Clay wasn't far away. He watched as she wandered casually, seeming to take in the festival. A tightness in his chest hit as he remembered being with her after discovering her as Tiny with the Celtic band.

His fingers clenched as he battled the desire to go over and take her hand. *Looking like this, I'd scare the hell outta her.*

Long, dirty hair pulled back into a low ponytail. Long, dirty beard. Reflector sunglasses. Heavy jacket. Motorcycle boots. Of course, glancing around, he blended in with the eclectic crowd at the festival. The difference was the earpiece receivers and transmitters on the collars of the jackets they both wore.

He'd kept an eye on the Minotaurs motorcycle gang. They had taken over a small tent where they gathered, posting three men outside as guards.

"You need me to start a diversion?" he asked.

"I got it," came Cobb's response.

A large group of people heading into the entertainment tent passed nearby, and Cobb tripped one, causing him to fall onto the side of the Minotaur's tent. As the guards stepped over to shove the bystander along, Cobb reached up and attached a listening device to the side of the tent. Undetected, Josh would now be able to listen to what was being said while back in the LSI headquarters.

Their plan had been to stay close, but suddenly, Christina appeared and walked to the food trucks. Inclining his head toward her, he said, "Follow." He watched as Cobb nodded and headed after her. Unable to stay away, Clay wandered at a distance, keeping her in his sights.

It was when she shopped at the Celtic jewelers that Cobb moved closer. She lifted her head and stared right at Cobb, and Clay held his breath, sure that she would see through his disguise. When she dropped her purchase into her purse and hurried away, he breathed a sigh of relief.

He followed her back to the entertainment tent while Cobb moved to a position so that he could observe the Minotaurs. Seeing Steven talking to the gang members, Clay's anger ratcheted up at the danger Amhrán M'anama's leader was placing on the other band members. So focused on Steven, he almost missed seeing Christina making the same observation. As she turned to walk toward Steven, one of the Minotaur guards grinned, his gaze devouring her. Lust raced across the man's face, and Clay reacted instinctively, bumping into her, making sure to hit her open bottle of water, causing it to pour down her front.

Fighting the urge to throw her over his shoulder and race away, he simply mumbled an apology and continued on his way. She hurried back inside the entertainment tent, and he turned to look at Cobb.

"Shit, man, that was close," Cobb whispered.

Heart pounding in his chest, he stared at the tent flap where she'd disappeared, torn between wanting to go to her and knowing he needed to keep an eye on Steven and the gang he was meeting with.

Soon, Steven jogged back to the tent and disappeared inside. It appeared the Minotaurs were breaking up their gathering, and he and Cobb wandered to the parking lot, easily finding the motorcycles. Walking past, they clapped two miniature devices onto two of the cycles, giving LSI and the International Drug Task Force a chance to see where they were going as well.

Circling back inside, they pressed into the crowd, not surprised when others moved for the two large, rough-looking men. Leaning against a pole, he stared enraptured as she danced, twirled, and entertained with her fiddle.

"I gotta admit, your girl has got it going on."

Clay looked over at Cobb and shook his head. "I know it. Every time I hear her play, whether it's a symphony, Gaelic music, or just something for fun, I'm amazed at her talent."

"Man, she scared the shit outta me when she looked at me at the festival. I know you wanted me closer to her so that she wouldn't recognize you, but I swear she looked right at me, and I was afraid she was going to call out my name!"

"Hell, I don't know how. With your disguise and the sunglasses, she couldn't have known."

"I know, but she's a smart cookie."

Frowning, Clay said, "Normally, I'd agree with you, but when I saw her start to head toward Steven and that group of Minotaurs he was talking to, I could've throttled her."

Cobb laughed and leaned back in his chair, his feet propped up on the coffee table. "I was standing off to the side, ready to intervene if I had to, when you slammed into her, spilling her water. You walked away, but man, you should've seen the glare she shot toward your back!"

Clay laughed, but he'd been on edge the whole day. An untold number of missions in his careers, but he'd never been as nervous as he was today trying to keep up with where she was, what she was doing, and if she was safe. Wanting to protect her was the only thing he could think of. "I know we were supposed to be watching the band and seeing what happened with Steven, but damn, Cobb. I went into protection mode, and I've never done that before."

"Look, whether you want to be or not, you're involved with a woman that's now part of our mission. It didn't start out that way, but that's the way it is. So that protective instinct is going to kick in."

Scrubbing his hand over his face, he nodded. He and Cobb had managed to check into the cheap hotel near the airport that Christina and the band were in. Just down the hall from them, they ordered room service so they could avoid being seen. He knew the band members had gone down to the bar earlier, and Cobb had followed to observe. Not surprised when Cobb returned to report that Steven met outside with a few more of the Minotaurs, he was still angry, nonetheless. Cobb had watched as Steven accepted an envelope from one of the gang members and they alerted Josh to keep an eye on Steven and the band's bank accounts.

Clay stayed in the room, keeping an eye on Christina's door. He wasn't surprised that she'd also ordered room service and stayed in. Looking over at Cobb, he asked, "So, what did we learn?"

"Josh logged a phone call from a burner phone to Steven. It wasn't from Jerry's number, but he's got

Steven's phone tapped and recorded the call, so he knows it was Jerry's voice. At first, Jerry just checked to see if Steven had the money to pay the driver and if everything was going okay. Steven gushed his thanks, and then Jerry casually mentioned that there were people Steven needed to meet with."

"And he told him where to meet them?"

Nodding, Cobb said, "Told him to wait outside the tent. That's all. Yeah, Jerry is a slick-shit. So, Steven goes outside and then is called over to another smaller tent."

Clay shook his head. "What an idiot."

"Yeah, it was the Minotaurs. I mean, most people would shit a brick if they saw a gang of big, ugly, rough guys... but no, Steven hurried right over."

"I couldn't get too close without raising suspicions, but I couldn't see a transfer of any packages or money. My guess was it was a chance to make a connection. The payoff didn't happen until tonight outside the hotel. Josh will be able to tell us more."

"I thought maybe Jerry was going to use the band to transport drugs," Clay said, standing and stretching his arms above his head, trying to ease the tension he felt in his back.

"The amount of drugs that the band could try to sneak over the border would be pennies compared to what Jerry's dealing with. I still think that he's using the band to launder money, and he's going to keep Steven in line by making sure Steven knows what'll happen to him if he breaks rank."

A little later, Cobb headed into the connecting room, and Clay climbed into bed. He was determined to make sure Christina got to the airport safely the next morning, then he and Cobb would take another flight back to Portland.

Lying in bed, he wished he could slip across the hall to be with Christina. Rolling over on his back, he threw his forearm across his brow and stared at the ceiling. Nothing about this case was easy. Not the connection Jerry had with the Bennetts, or the band, or—by default —Christina. She might be angry when she found out what was going on, but he had to take that chance. He'd fallen for the beautiful violinist, and keeping her safe was the only thing that mattered.

18

Clay paced on his front porch, waiting for Christina to arrive. It had been almost a week since he'd seen her last and he found that he couldn't wait until she was in his arms again. He'd discovered a few videos of the band playing, taken by fans and uploaded to the Internet. While the quality was not perfect, he watched them over and over, never tiring of the music she made and the heartfelt performance she created.

As she turned into his drive and her eyes landed on him, she greeted him with a wide smile. By the time she parked and climbed from her car, his long legs had eaten the distance, and he moved directly into her space, standing toe to toe. Wrapping his arms around her, he kissed her, loving the way she melted against him as her arms slid around his neck.

"I like your greeting!" she enthused.

"If you think that was a proper greeting, let me get you inside, and I'll really show how glad I am to see you."

She laughed and gently pushed against his shoulders. "Let me grab my things—"

"I've got them, babe." Opening the back door, he saw her overnight bag and her violin. Taking the bag, he looked over his shoulder and said, "I'll let you take your violin."

She placed her hand on her waist as she cocked her hip. "Are you afraid of my violin?"

"I'm terrified. Terrified of dropping it. Terrified of breaking it. It's such an extension of you, and I'd feel a whole lot better if you carried it."

Smiling, she pushed past him and reached into the car to snag her violin case. His gaze dropped to her delectable ass, then shot up as she turned around. Looping her arm through his, they walked up the front steps and into his home.

She set her case just inside the door and he placed her overnight bag on the table. Turning, he said, "I thought we might do something different if you're game."

"I've missed you so much, sweetie, I'm up for anything you want to do."

"How about we take the canoe out on the water."

She clapped her hands, her eyes wide. "Really?" Suddenly, her smile dropped. "Uh... do you have a life jacket? I can swim, but not very well—"

He linked fingers with her, pulling her close. "Of course, we'll have life jackets. Babe, your safety is my top priority."

"Your top priority?" she cooed, lifting on her toes for a kiss.

"Well, on the water it is. But once we get back here, I'll show you another priority." He wiggled his eyebrows and she laughed as he led her out the back and down toward the water.

Soon, she was seated in his canoe, her hands gripping the sides, her knuckles white. He looked over as he pushed them away from the pier and dug the paddle into the water. "You okay?"

"Yes, once I get used to the rocking motion," she assured. Soon her hands relaxed, and she was pointing out the sights along the wide creek that led to one of the bays. "Are we going out to the ocean?"

"No, we'll stay where the water is calmer."

As they glided past the thick green shoreline, she dragged her fingers through the water and inhaled deeply. "Wow, it feels as though I can really breathe out here."

"I love it," he admitted.

"I never asked where you grew up."

"I was born in Oklahoma. Little town."

She cocked her head to the side. "You don't sound like you liked it very much. Was it because of your parents?"

Nodding, he said, "Yeah, I guess. Not really the town's fault, but it was small. Everyone knew everything about each other. And believe me, my parents' reputation for fighting nasty was well known."

"You were embarrassed," she stated, her voice soft.

He nodded, holding her gaze, seeing concern in her beautiful aqua eyes. She looked down and smiled, pointing to the other paddle.

"Can I use that?"

"Absolutely." He handed it to her and offered simple instructions. She was a fast learner and they were soon gliding faster through the water. Laughing as they disturbed waterfowl, they watched the birds take flight nearby. Occasionally, a fish would leap from the water, splashing back down, causing more ripples. The sun rose high in the sky and Christina's back was reddening. "We need to head back before you get sunburned. I should have thought of that."

"This was amazing, Clay. And now that I'm an expert paddler, I hope you'll take me out again."

He had gone out many times on his own or with the other Keepers near the lighthouse, but he had never enjoyed his time on the water as much as he did with her. *Everything with her is better.*

Once back at the house, they walked into the kitchen and he asked, "Are you hungry?"

His words were cut off as she leapt forward, and he barely caught her in time as her body slammed into his. Wrapping her legs around his waist, she grabbed his jaw and kissed him. Lust shot straight to his cock, and he twisted, pressing her back against the wall, erasing any space between their bodies. Heads moving back and forth, he thrust his tongue into her mouth, gliding it over every crevice, loving the velvet feel of her tongue on his and the sweet mint from the gum she'd obviously been chewing.

He was so focused on the electricity moving between his mouth and his cock, he almost missed her sliding her hands in between them, her fingers working the buttons on the front of his shirt. Having no idea how she managed it, he felt her tugging the material over his shoulders. Hating to lose their contact, he debated taking her against the door, bending her over the sofa, or heading down the hall to the bedroom. His brain short-circuited as he tried to decide, and as though she could read his mind, she simply said, "Now."

Letting her feet slide to the floor, he stepped back just enough to jerk his shirt off, tossing it to the side. Her fingers went to his belt buckle then she lifted her hands into the air as he divested her of her shirt. Grabbing a condom from his wallet, he shucked his pants as she jerked her jeans and panties down her legs, kicking them to the side.

She looked up and held his gaze, her smile spread across her beautiful face. He wasn't opposed to wall sex but wasn't sure how comfortable that would be. Her eyes cut to the living room, and he scooped her up, stalking toward the sofa. With a tug on the cord, he made sure the blinds were closed as she flipped around with her knees on the cushions and her hands on the back. Wiggling her ass, she glanced over her shoulder.

He reached his hands around and palmed her rosy-tipped breasts, tugging lightly on her nipples. Bending forward, he kissed her neck, over the fluttering pulse, and down her back. Lowering to his knees, he licked her slick folds, inhaling deeply the musky scent of her arousal.

The globes of her ass beckoned, and he kissed first one and then the other, ending on a nibble that elicited a squeal. "Jesus, babe, you're beautiful. Every fuckin' inch of you is beautiful."

"Now," she begged.

Laughing, he asked, "Is that the only word you can say?"

Looking over her shoulder, she glared. "If you don't get on with it, the only word I'll say is goodbye!"

Palm on her ass, he tapped it lightly. "Don't threaten to leave, babe, before I have a chance to worship this body."

"At the risk of being mocked again, please... I need you now."

Leaning his body over her back, he slid a finger deep inside her core, moving it in rhythm as he tugged on first one nipple and then the other. He could feel her body shiver, and soon she cried out as her orgasm rocked through her. Holding her tightly until her body eased, he slid his hand up to his mouth, licking her juices off his finger. Standing, he noticed her delectable body was at the perfect height and angle. His hands almost shaking, he rolled the condom onto his eager cock, settled his large hands on her hips, lined his cock up to her entrance, and thrust forward.

She gasped, bolting forward slightly, her fingers grabbing tightly onto the back of the sofa. He stopped, filled with concern. "Was that too much? Are you okay?"

"Yes!" she rasped. "Keep going."

Rocking back and forth, his gaze drifted down the perfect line of her spine, the way her waist curved in before flaring out to her hips. Her ass filled his hands, and he felt her press backward as though seeking more contact. Bending his front over her back, his hands slid up to her breasts, tweaking her nipples once again.

She lifted her head, and he pressed his cheek against hers. They turned toward each other at the same time, their lips meeting. He kissed along her jaw, shifted her hair over her shoulder, and trailed his lips along her soft skin. Her breathing hitched, and he recognized she was close. Grabbing her hips again, he increased his rhythm, plunging deeply until she flung her head back, crying out his name. He allowed her inner core to milk his cock until finally, the fire rolled through him, his fingers dug into her flesh, and through gritted teeth, he roared out his own release.

After the last drop left his body, he gasped in a ragged breath, falling forward so that he was curved over her back. His legs felt weak, and he could not remember ever having an orgasm that rocked him so deeply. Awareness slowly crept over him as his cock slid from her warmth. He eased the grip on her hips, now fearful that her tender flesh would bear bruises.

He reached for her shoulders, turning her gently toward him, then pulling her body tightly flush against his. "Holy shit, babe, that was intense."

She shifted slightly, peering up at him, a smile curving her lips. He leaned over and pressed his mouth to hers, the kiss full of meaning and promises.

The room had grown darker, and Clay winced. "I was going to feed you as soon as you got here but jumped you instead."

Her laughter was musical as she smiled, her eyes

twinkling. "I believe it was me who kept demanding 'now.'"

"You're right! That was you who was climbing all over me." He wiggled his eyebrows.

Her top teeth landed on her bottom lip, her breath rushing from her lungs. "Well, I was hungry, but not for food."

"And now?"

Laughing again, she nodded. "Yes, now, I'm hungry for food!"

They rolled from the sofa and stood. He headed into the bathroom and took care of the condom. By the time he walked back into the room, she had slipped on her bra and panties and was just zipping her jeans. He kissed her quickly, then pulled on his boxers and jeans as she settled her shirt over her breasts. He snatched his shirt from the floor but only fastened the bottom buttons. Linking fingers, he led her into the kitchen, assisting her onto one of his stools.

He pulled the chops from the oven and dumped a store-bought salad into a bowl. Warm, buttered, garlic toast and glasses of wine were placed on the table. After the fun of the canoe trip and the incredible sex, he knew he needed to find out about her trip. Unable to figure out how to bring the conversation around, he simply blurted, "How was your trip to Ottawa? I know we talked on the phone, but I'd love to hear more about it."

Scrunching her nose, she said, "It was okay. I was going to say that it was like all the other festivals we've played at, but all I could think of was wanting you to be there with me."

"Really?"

"Since I had experienced the festival with you, I walked around outside the entertainment tent. I got something to eat from the food trucks and looked at the vendors. It was really nice, but I would've much preferred you'd have been there with me."

"And the band?"

Shaking her head, she rolled her eyes. "About the same as always. Dunk was being his usual self, and I was certain he was going to get arrested in the airport. Steven was weird."

"Weird?" The idea that subterfuge was easier with someone he wasn't in a relationship with hit him. Keeping his face blank, he lifted his brows while attempting to adopt a casual interest.

She scrunched her nose. "Yeah. Usually, he gets us to a venue, then plops down, easy as can be until it's time for us to set up. He left and ended up in some random tent with a bunch of scary-looking bikers!"

"Wow, what was he doing?"

"Who knows? I was peeved... well, at first, I was curious. I started to go to him—"

"What were you thinking?" he bit out.

Her head jerked back slightly at his harsh tone. "Uh... I wanted to see what he was up to."

"And you were going to walk straight into a den of bikers?"

Huffing, she argued, "Well, Steven was there... I didn't think it was dangerous—"

"It doesn't sound like you were thinking!"

"Clay, you weren't there! You can't possibly know

what I was doing. It was daylight. A lot of people were around. I wasn't waltzing into the lion's den, I was just going to call to Steven to see what he was doing." Pinching her lips, she continued, "But it didn't matter anyway. Some jerk ran into me and spilled my water all over the place. My skirt, legs, and boots were soaked."

Clay's stomach clenched, and he hated the way their voices rose with each statement. Forcing his breathing to steady, he watched her carefully, noticing that she was irritated but not screaming obscenities or hurling accusations. *I'm not my parents... it's possible to not agree but not devolve into a raging maniac.* Holding her gaze, he watched as her face softened, the tight lines diminishing.

Unable to stop himself, he blurted, "You were beautiful."

She blinked, her head tilting slightly to the side. "Were?"

"No... uh... no, I said 'are'. You *are* beautiful." He held his breath for a second, then his heart lightened as a smile curved her lips and a blush tinged her cheeks.

"I'm sorry that I lost my temper," she admitted, sighing softly. "You're right. Walking toward those guys wasn't very smart. I have no idea what Steven was doing, but it's not my job to babysit the band." She leaned toward him and offered her mouth, a gift he was never going to refuse. The meal was forgotten for a moment as they kissed. Finally, pulling back, he stared into her hooded eyes and kiss-puffed lips. "Eat up, babe. We've got the whole weekend for kissing."

"Is that what we're going to be doing all weekend? Kissing?" Her eyes twinkled as she stared up at him.

"Hell, if you agree, I don't know that we'll get out of bed."

"It is our first whole weekend together."

"I've waited for this for a long time," he said. Standing, he collected their empty plates as she gathered the glasses. They stood side-by-side at the sink as he rinsed them and placed them in the dishwasher. He opened the refrigerator door and pulled out two plastic-wrapped saucers, each containing a large slice of cheesecake topped with raspberry sauce.

"Oh, my goodness! You even have dessert!"

"What's dinner without dessert?" he asked, handing one of the saucers to her. "I'll grab two forks, and we can go into the living room."

A moment later, settled on the sofa, he was once again distracted by the moans of delight coming from her. Forcing his cock to behave, he finished his slice and then set the dishes on the coffee table. Pulling her into his arms, he shifted their bodies so his back was propped against the padded arm of the sofa, his long legs stretched out on the cushions, and she was draped next to him, her head on his chest and her arm wrapped around his waist. She pulled off her glasses and tossed them gently to the coffee table.

"So," she began, "what have you got planned for the rest of the weekend? Or are we really going to spend the whole weekend in bed?"

"Would that be a problem?" he teased.

She hummed as her fingers traced a pattern over his

abs. "Not a problem with me. I've been so excited about us having so much time together."

"Well, as much as I would love to stay in bed with you the whole time, we've been roped into a Lighthouse get-together tomorrow."

She shifted around and held his gaze. "What exactly does a Lighthouse get-together entail?"

"Blake and Sara have a great house about twenty minutes from here. They have a huge kitchen that flows into a massive deck overlooking the woods and the water. Everyone will meet there, bring some food, grill out, and just have a good time." He twisted slightly so that he could look into her eyes. "Is that okay?"

She nodded, her soft hair tickling his chin. "Absolutely. It sounds like fun, and I'm honored to be invited."

"The honor is mine, Christina." He kissed her lightly again and repeated, "Having you with me... being with me... the honor is all mine."

They kissed again and all sense of time was lost as they pressed together, devouring each other. Finally, he lifted his head and somehow managed to get to his feet with her in his arms. With her carefully tucked into his embrace, he stalked down the hall toward the bedroom.

19

Christina walked into Blake and Sara's kitchen to grab another plate from the counter. Clay had been right—their house was amazing. The water views were spectacular. The kitchen and deck layout were perfect for entertaining. She felt as though she were with old friends even though she'd only been around all the Keepers and their wives and fiancées at the Celtic festival. The camaraderie among the gathering was palpable, and it was not lost on her how comfortable she felt with them.

There were two new men she hadn't met, and Clay had explained they were visiting while on leave from their military service. Rick was Rank's brother and Knox was Drew's brother. While Clay had not said more, she had a feeling those two men would one day work for Mace as well. A few of the men were single, but it appeared most had settled into loving relationships.

"Are you okay? Finding everything you need?"

She jumped, startled. Jerking her head around, she saw Sara standing nearby. "Oh! Sorry, I was lost in thought."

Smiling, Sara stepped closer and glanced out toward the deck. "I'm sure we're a lot to take in."

"It is a bit overwhelming, but to be honest, I was thinking how comfortable it felt being here." Turning, she held Sara's gaze. "Does that sound strange?"

Sara continued to smile as she shook her head slowly. "That doesn't sound strange at all. I knew that you'd fit in."

She stared at the other woman, not understanding her comment. Unasked questions must have moved over her face, because Sara said, "One of the things that the men don't do is bring someone to a gathering that they're not serious about. In other words, there are no casual flings, one-night stands, friends-with-benefits, or any other women that would fall into those categories brought to a company get-together. I have no idea if it's something that Mace actually declared or if it's just the respect the men have for each other and the women." She patted Christina's arm. "I have a feeling it's the respect that they have for each other and us."

The two women smiled, then turned and looked out the wide kitchen windows as the large group of people milled about, talking and laughing.

"I know this might sound strange, but what you just said seems to add a little bit of pressure to me. Or maybe to me and Clay." She chewed on her bottom lip for a few seconds before continuing. "We haven't been dating very long. In fact, this is our first full weekend spent together."

Sara laughed and shrugged. "You've just described almost all of our relationships." They were silent for another moment before Sara added, "Clay has introduced you to us because you're special to him. Very special. And because you are, you fit in very well with the rest of us. There's no pressure, Christina. Just a heartfelt welcome."

"Can I ask you a question?"

"Absolutely."

"How did you meet Blake? I know that might seem impertinent but I—"

Laughing, Sara shook her head. "Oh, Christina, we truly have no secrets around here. I'm an interpreter and was in French Guiana at a conference. Blake was there as a bodyguard for one of the men. On the last morning, I was simply in the wrong place at the wrong time and was kidnapped right in front of Blake. I could have been lost forever, but he wouldn't let that happen. I was taken deep into the jungle, and he found me, rescued me, and brought me back. We've been together ever since."

Christina blinked rapidly, and her mouth dropped open. "Uh... I... uh..."

Sara laughed again and said, "I know, sweetie. It sounds horrible and it was. But it all ended well."

Christina's gaze shot out the window again, and Sara must have understood her unasked question.

"Babs works at LSI, but she'd taken a cruise and ended up stranded on an island. She and Drew had liked each other for a long time, and he flew out to help her when she had a run-in with modern-day pirates out to kill her. I'd like to say he went to save her, but Babs is pretty good at taking care of herself. Sylvie's son witnessed a murder and was in danger, and that's how Mace and she became involved. When they married, he adopted David." She laughed again and added, "Rank was working undercover, and Helena dropped on top of him right when he was getting ready to gain some information in a back alley. From what I understand, they had a very auspicious beginning to their relationship!"

"I don't even know what to say to all of that."

"Julie was in the jungles of Mexico chaperoning some teenagers on a trip, including a senator's daughter. When an earthquake hit and they couldn't get back, Walker went down to rescue them to make sure they were safe from drug runners. The girls got out easily, but he and Julie had to spend some time down there." Wiggling her eyebrows, Sara said, "That seems to be a theme with us. Although, with Tate and Nora, they'd been in a relationship many years ago. They broke up and were separated for almost a decade. When she was kidnapped by some meth-heads, Tate was right there to rescue her as well. And the last of the couples is Levi and Claire. She was being chased by embezzlers, and he managed to save her."

Christina remained quiet, and Sara pulled her into a hug. "Christina, if you feel like you don't fit in, you do. Believe me, you don't have to be in dire straits, kidnapped, or a witness to a crime to be in a relationship with a Keeper. Personally, I think you and Clay are perfect."

Leaning back, Christina held her gaze and saw nothing but honesty in the other woman's eyes. Her lips curved, and she said, "Well, I hope you don't take this the wrong way, but I'm thrilled that Clay and I met over nothing more than a love of music."

Smiling, Sara grabbed a platter, handed it to Christina while she carried another, and the two women walked back outside.

As soon as Clay's gaze landed on her, he left the group he'd been conversing with and made his way directly to her. Setting the platter on the table, he wrapped his arms around her, pulled her in close, and kissed the top of her head. "You okay, sweetheart? If you're tired or if this is too much, we can leave."

She leaned back and smiled. "As much as I want to spend more time alone with you, I'm not ready to leave." She lifted on her toes and kissed his jaw. "I really like your friends." A little sigh slipped from her lips. "Actually, it's really nice to see such a large group of people who work together and their significant others get along so well."

He lifted a finger and rubbed it along her jawline, the touch comforting. "It sounds like there's more behind that statement than what you're saying."

She blinked and gave her head a little shake. "Let's enjoy your friends for now." Settling on her heels, she led him over to the group he'd been talking with, noting how the others shifted to the side, easily welcoming them into their conversation. She had a camaraderie with the band but not like this. Often, the band was more like herding cats.

And as much as she respected her fellow orchestra members, other than Amy, she couldn't say they were true friends. That thought was depressing, but she pushed it down. Today was for enjoyment, and she was determined to make the most of it.

Still full from lunch, that evening she drank a glass of milk while Clay fixed a sandwich for himself. He worried that she would be hungry, but she assured him that she couldn't eat another bite. As they sat on the sofa, her thoughts drifted.

"Did you have a good time today?"

Glancing at his plate, she realized her mind had wandered while Clay finished his huge sandwich. Looking up at him, she saw worry in his eyes. Rushing to assure, she nodded emphatically. "I had a wonderful time today."

"You just seem a little down."

She shifted on the cushions so that her leg was tucked under her and she was facing him. He had placed his plate on the coffee table and settled into a position so that he was facing her as well. "Maybe a little melancholy seeing how wonderful all your friends are together, but that's all."

Their fingers linked, and he gently rubbed her knuckles. "Melancholy?"

"My life is so busy, so full. I enjoy being around people, and yet I don't have a lot of people in my life that I could call true friends. Watching all of you today made me realize that I'm envious. Glad for you, but a little envious."

"What about in the orchestra?"

She blew out a breath, puffing her cheeks as she thought of her response. "The musicians are wonderful, and I enjoy the hard work we put in to create a beautiful musical experience for others. It's competitive, so while you have to work together, there's also the feeling of making sure your musical skills are on par or better than the person next to you. Honestly? Other than Amy, I can't say that I have any really good friends in the orchestra. Lots of friendly coworkers, but not true friends."

They were quiet for a moment before he asked, "And the band?"

An indelicate snort slipped out, making her giggle. "I love the music that the five of us create. Jamie and Mike on the bagpipes are fabulous. Those are not easy instruments to play, and they're phenomenal. But other than the band practices and gigs, we don't hang out. Other than our music, I don't think we have a lot in common. Dunk? He's a big goof, but I'm afraid his personal problems would always get in the way of us being friends. Bandmates? Yes. A sometimes babysitter? Yes. Friends? Not so much."

"And Steven?"

She sucked in her lips and thought for a moment. "That's a little harder. I like Steven. He's got a great voice, and he's a good organizer. If it wasn't for him, the group would completely fall apart. And he handles our money, so I have a lot of trust in him." She felt Clay jerk ever so slightly, and her gaze shot from their intertwined hands to his face. Something flashed through his eyes, but she had no idea how to interpret it. And almost as soon as it came, it left. *Maybe it was jealousy.* Wanting to allay any concerns, she rushed, "I have no feelings for Steven other than just professional admiration. Like the others, I can't even say that we're true friends. While my experience with the band is a lot more fun than the orchestra, it still has its own share of headaches."

"That sounds a little lonely," he said, his hands still holding hers tightly.

His voice held concern, and the quip on her lips faded away. She nodded very slowly and admitted, "I'm surrounded by people, but unlike your group of friends today, I don't have that kind of camaraderie."

"And if the band goes national? International? Will you stay with them?"

His question seemed simple, and yet there was a heavy undercurrent flowing between them, an uncertainty if Clay was simply asking out of curiosity or if his reason had to do with them as a couple. Licking her lips, she decided she could only answer him from the heart, not worry about his reasons or reactions. "I know the idea of making it big has a certain appeal to someone in this business. To break away and have a name that's recognizable. To have record deals and travel all around filling concert halls. But somewhere along that road, there's a great risk of losing yourself."

He cocked his head slightly to the side, and her lips curved at the corners. "My parents love being at the top of their field, but they also want to work in the environment of an orchestra, not a solo career. I derive great pleasure from creating beauty with my instrument. I don't crave fame or recognition or a huge bank account. While I don't mind some travel to perform, I don't want to spend months on end simply going from one city to another. I know Steven is talking to an agent, but I have no idea if my goals will fit in with the others." She hefted her shoulders in a little shrug and added, "If not, then I'll leave the band."

"Do you see Dunk being able to handle that lifestyle?"

She winced, the thought making her sad. "No, I think he would burn out very quickly."

"So, you'd just stay with the orchestra and your students?"

"I have no desire to leave Maine. I don't even see myself like my parents where I would want to pick up and go with a more prestigious orchestra. I love teaching and would continue to have students. And if Amhrán M'anama disperses or goes international without me, then I might find a few other like-minded Celtic musicians to play with."

Clay remained quiet, and she could not help but wonder his thoughts. *Do I seem too complacent? Not having long-range, lofty goals?* Unable to stand the silence, she blurted, "What do you think?"

Surprise crossed his face, and he reared back. "Think?"

She huffed and pushed her glasses up on her nose. "You're the one who asked me what my goals were, and

I told you. I know you don't have to have an immediate reaction, but I can't help but wonder if you're disappointed in my answers."

"Disappointed? Jesus, Christina, I'd never be disappointed in you."

Now, it was her time to stay silent, giving him a chance to pull his thoughts together. He didn't make her wait long.

"I asked because I truly wanted to know where you saw your future leading," he began. "I'd never want to hold you back from your dreams of fame or fortune, concerts all over the world, the chance to spread your music everywhere." He shifted in his seat, appearing uncomfortable. "I know, though, if that was what you truly wanted, I'd be your biggest supporter. But I also know that it would make it hard."

"Hard? For us?"

"That makes me sound like an ass, doesn't it? Even if it was hard, I'd still want to do everything I could to be with you," he confessed.

She smiled, relief flooding her. "Whew! I want to be with you, too."

A smile curved his lips, and he leaned forward, brushing his mouth against hers. "I loved the sound of your band, babe, but those guys make me a little nervous. You say you babysit them, but that's not your job. And I know you try to keep Dunk out of trouble, but that's not your job either. I just want to make sure that while the five of you are making music, you're not being taken advantage of."

"You're sweet, Clay. Honestly, I think Steven has a

harder job. He handles the band, he handles the schedule, he handles the money, and is working on getting an agent." She scrunched her nose. "Although, I think Mr. Kincaid is helping him out. They were talking the other night, and I only caught a few words, but I think he's offering to help Steven with an agent. I thought he was just Congressman Bennett's employee, but I guess he wants to do something besides politics." She twisted to look at him. "You know, I just remembered what one of the guys said about Steven when he was meeting with the biker dudes."

"Dudes. Seriously, Christina... dudes." Giving his head a little shake, he asked, "What was said?"

"That Mr. Kincaid had told Steven to meet up with some others and we thought they were musicians. But I've got to tell you that I've never seen a group like them!"

"I can't figure out what makes me more nuts... you think it's your job to babysit the band a-fuckin-gain or being so reckless that you'd walk up to *scary dudes* in motorcycle jackets," he growled.

She opened her mouth to defend herself, but he wasn't finished.

"I've seen the kind of guys you were talking about. I've had to take down the kind of guys you were talking about. And believe me, they'd have no problem dragging you in that tent, gagging you, tying you up, and doing whatever the fuck they felt like doing, not giving a shit who was practically five feet away on the outside of the tent."

His gaze was so intense and his voice so harsh, she

swallowed deeply, blinking back the tears. Unsuccessful, one rolled down her cheek. His face fell, and his arms snatched out to pull her close. With her face buried against his chest, he murmured against her hair. "Damn, Christina, I'm sorry. I'm sorry, babe. I never meant... I didn't want to upset you, but I just... I just... shit."

She sniffled against the soft material of his shirt and said, "I know what the other women would've done."

At that proclamation, he shifted so that her face was no longer buried but instead held his gaze once again. "What the other women would've done?"

"Sara told me. I know that you said that the others met during intense situations or missions, but I didn't really understand. Sara didn't go into a lot of detail, but I have to admit I was stunned to find out exactly how they met. As dumb as it sounds, I think I told you about the bikers tonight so that you wouldn't feel like you were the only one with a wimp."

His large hands cupped her face and his thumbs swept under her eyes, wiping away any traces of tears. "Christina, I've gotten to know you, the real you, and believe me, you're not a wimp. I've fallen for exactly the woman you are... strong, smart, dedicated, talented, hard-working, kind. You don't have to prove anything to me. And you especially do not need to put yourself in danger thinking that's the kind of excitement I need in my life. I want you. Safe, sound, and whole."

She licked her lips, the warmth of his hands seeping deep inside of her, curling around her heart. "You've fallen for me?" she asked, her voice barely above a whisper.

A slow smile spread across his face. "Yeah. I've fallen in love with you. Christina. Tiny. The whole package."

Her fingers clutched his shoulders, her short nails digging in slightly as she moved to where their lips were only a breath apart. "I love you, too." Before she had a chance to close the distance, he stood with her in his arms. A surprised squeak accompanied her arms wrapping around his neck as he stalked down the hall to the bedroom. As his lips melded with hers, thoughts of forever moved through her mind.

20

"How are you doing?"

Hearing Blake's question, Clay leaned back in his chair and scrubbed his hand over his face. Looking around, he spied not only Blake but several of the other Keepers nearby, eyes on him, waiting for his answer.

"I can't fuckin' believe that we have a mission involving an FBI-suspected drug runner, and somehow the woman I'm seeing is innocently tangled in this mess."

With sympathy in his eyes, Blake shook his head. "I know you never wanted to meet someone on a mission—"

"I didn't meet Christina on a mission. I started a relationship with her that didn't have anything to do with this. But she's now firmly in the middle of all these players and yet not part of it. I'm worried about her. Worried about her ending up in Jerry's sights, worried that Steven will figure out that she knows something's up, and worried about how all this will play out for us."

"Damn, for a man who didn't want any drama in his relationship, looks like you've got it," Drew said.

Clay's stinging retort died on his lips as soon as he looked at Drew and saw concern, not a smirk on his friend's face. He sighed again and rubbed the back of his neck where another tension headache was setting up residence.

"Break it down. What have we got?" Mace asked.

Levi said, "The good news is that the International Drug Task Force, while already having their eyes and ears on the Minotaurs, had not been following the small group in Ottawa that Clay and Cobb watched. I've forwarded the recording from their conversations inside the tent at the festival, and they are now tracking that group as they move back and forth from the Canadian and U.S. border. They'd focused their attention on Montréal and Quebec City, so they've now expanded their range of surveillance."

Clay added, "The cartels might be sophisticated, but the Minotaurs aren't. What they are is efficient and dangerous as fuck. I can't believe Steven walked into that group."

"They move drugs around, and they're big on selling what comes to them," Blay said. "But no way are they the brains behind any of this. They answer to the cartels."

"And Steven?" Mace asked. "What do we know about him?"

"Sorry," Josh said, shaking his head. "I wish I could give you more. He didn't mention Jerry by name to them. The part of the conversation that I recorded with the Minotaurs was he knew he was supposed to meet someone that would pass along the message."

"And the message?"

"He claimed that he's a middleman. He claimed that money that goes through him won't be traced."

Clay shook his head. "Steven isn't stupid but isn't very smart, either. He handles the band's money, but I don't think he's smart enough to figure out a money-laundering scheme."

"No way," Sylvie piped up. "It's got to be Jerry behind that, too." The others turned to look at her, and she shrugged. "I'm still looking. Steven does a piss-poor job of keeping the band's books clean. Clay, my guess would be you should delve deeper into any other account that's associated with his name. Or the band's name."

"Does Christina's band have any more trips to Canada coming up?" Mace asked.

"She mentioned that Steven wants them to go to New Brunswick. He said that Jerry has told him it's a way to make easy money since they don't have to fly. They can drive like they have before."

Tate asked, "They've been there for concerts before?"

"Yeah, from what she's said, that was the first place they started playing Canadian festivals."

Cobb shook his head. "There's got to be other places Jerry is laundering his money. Christina's band just isn't big enough."

Suddenly, Clay jerked, looking around. "Christina mentioned that Congressman Bennett and his wife supported indie artists. What if her band isn't the only one where Jerry launders money?"

"That actually makes sense," Babs said. "Most indie bands aren't going to have an entourage of people keeping up with their money, schedule, or resources. Plus, they usually want more visibility, and if someone's willing to help them travel and pay expenses, they'd be perfect."

Nodding toward Mace, Clay said, "On it." An hour later, he leaned back in frustration. Glancing toward Josh, he said, "I can't find any trace of Jerry being involved with musicians or bands. Whatever he's doing, he's making sure to stay off the radar. I know he went to the bar where Christina's band was playing because I saw him, but he's not tagged at all."

"See if you can dig in through the congressman. Find out who he supports and then take a look at their money. It's a backdoor way of seeing if we can tie Jerry in."

It didn't take long for Clay to tap into the donation list of Congressman Bennett. What surprised him was seeing Mrs. Bennett's donation list. It appeared most of the money the couple gave to indie musicians came from her. Sliding down another rabbit hole, he spent another hour poring through the digital surveillance on the Bennett estate, unable to find a time when Mrs. Bennett spent time alone with Jerry. Snorting, he glanced toward Josh and said, "One fuckin' thing leads to another. I just spent an hour trying to see if the congressman's wife and Jerry had a thing going on since it looks like she's the one who deals mostly with the donations to musicians."

"I take it you didn't find a connection?"

Shaking his head, he said, "Not at all. No phone records and no private assignations on the estate." Twisting his head and looking to the others, he added, "And I'm not seeing any boats coming or going from the Bennetts' boathouse. How the hell are those drugs being moved?" Clay growled, dragging his hand over his face.

Just as he was going back in to investigate further, Sylvie called out to the group, "Marge just called down. She said Horace just got back from the grocery and hit the deli. She's got a ton of fresh meat and has made homemade bread. She's ordering everyone upstairs for lunch."

The Keepers didn't hesitate. When Marge called, they answered. And considering she was a phenomenal cook, they had no problem taking orders from her.

The house at the base of the lighthouse boasted a large dining room with a massive table. Marge had lined the kitchen counter with platters of roast beef, chicken, ham, turkey, and bacon, as well as lettuce, tomatoes, olives, and onions. The Keepers elbowed each other for position, finally settling into a semblance of order as they made their way down the counter. She sliced long, freshly-baked rolls and put them on a plate so the others could fill them with whatever they wanted. Condiments and bowls of chips were at the end.

Manners counted when Marge was in charge, and

they waited until everyone was seated before diving in. Babs glanced at Sylvie and rolled her eyes before quipping, "You all eat like a pack of wolves that have gone starving all winter."

"Did you know that Portland, Maine, claims to be the birthplace of the Italian sandwich?" Horace wiped his mouth before taking a sip of iced tea.

"We always called them hoagies when I was growing up," Rank said.

Horace dipped his chin as he stared at Rank over the top of his glasses. "That term came from Philadelphia. The Italians working in the shipyards were in an area known as Hog Island. Therefore, their sandwiches became known as hoagies."

Walker shook his head. "I thought they were called hero sandwiches."

"Some people think the term hero sandwich came from the original Greek gyro, but that would've been in more modern times," Horace replied.

Drew burst out laughing. "What I want to know is how did you become the king of sandwich knowledge?"

Horace sat up straight and said, "Grinder. Another name for the sandwich that comes from the Italian-American slang for a dockworker. Those sandwiches had a hard crust, though, and required a lot of chewing." He cut his eyes toward Marge and smiled. "*Your* bread is perfect."

By now, the group was all laughing but their attention was focused on Horace.

"Wedge. That's from the country sections of New

York and Connecticut. They'd cut the sandwich into wedges. Oh, and then there's always Spukie."

Clay snorted, almost spitting out his tea. "Spukie?"

"That's from Boston and comes from the Italian word that means long roll. But, of course, most people just know them as subs since the bread is in the shape of the submarine."

Clay jolted, his gaze darting around the table. The thought that had slammed into him must have hit others considering the electric vibration moving about the room. "Submarine... that's how the cartel is moving drugs."

The Keepers leapt from their seats, shoving down last bites of sandwiches and chips, draining the dregs of iced tea from their glasses before rushing from the room to head back downstairs. Marge and Horace's laughter rang out behind them.

"Midget submarines or submersibles. We trained with these when I was a SEAL but didn't use one until I was with the CIA," Mace said. "Several of you were on a couple of those missions with me."

Clay had not participated in any of those missions, so he read the information sent to their tablets with great interest. "You can get an entry-level, winged submersible without a pressurized cabin for about a million dollars."

"That's chicken feed to the cartels," Walker said.

Nodding, he continued, "Two-million will get a

pressurized, two-person submarine." He looked toward Mace. "Are these just for short range?"

"Some of them have a battery life of twelve hours. Considering they can leave from the north coast of Maine and travel less than fifty miles to be in a remote area of New Brunswick, this would be the perfect way to transport drugs. If the cartels have some of the Minotaurs on the receiving end, that makes it easy."

"We've seen no evidence of refueling in the Bennetts' boathouse, so what about replenishment of power?" Cobb asked.

"No fuel, just charging. It says here that the charging time is only five to seven hours," Clay responded. "Jerry doesn't have to do anything. He doesn't even have to be present. There just has to be a power source for whoever's manning the submersible to recharge before making the last jump, carrying the drugs up to New Brunswick."

"You want to go back in?" Mace asked.

"I think it makes sense," Clay said, looking around and seeing nods of agreement from the others.

"Okay, let's figure out Jerry and the Bennetts' schedule and make it happen," Mace said.

It didn't take long for Clay to discover that Jerry was in Washington D.C. "I can get into the boathouse tonight."

That night, hours after checking in with Christina to see how her day went, he buried deep the uncomfortable feeling of investigating the band and their finances. Moving in the night with Tate, Cobb, and Walker, he once again made his way over the Bennett estate, this time slipping into the boathouse.

Inside the large wood and steel structure, they found six docking areas, each with their own custom-made boat hoist. He recognized a sports boat, two fishing boats, and a luxury wooden boat that appeared to be a refurbished antique.

Two of the docks were empty. "The charger won't have to be very large," he said, looking around while the others set up security cameras covering the doors and all angles on the boat docks. Checking with Josh to make sure the equipment worked properly, he turned toward Tate and watched as he made his way slowly around the two empty docks. "Whatcha got?"

"Trying to discern if anything was here recently. Josh said that there haven't been any vessels coming or going in the last three days, and yet there's water splashed all around the decks."

"Could that indicate a submersible came in under the door and was lifted here?"

"I don't know. But we haven't had any rough weather in the past week, so I can't see any reason why normal tides or oceanic wave patterns would make this area so wet considering the boathouse doors were down."

Clay deftly unlocked several lockers and containers in the area, finding a total of three battery chargers. "Don't know if these are the right ones, but with the surveillance cameras in place, we'll be able to see what they might be used for."

Slipping back out, he glanced at the clock, knowing Christina should be finishing up her gig. He hated that he missed it but knew he wouldn't be able to see all of her shows. He had tried to figure out how they could take their relationship to the next level and move in together. *But we live two hours apart...* Sighing, he pulled out his phone, hoping to catch her as she drove to her apartment.

21

Christina danced and played, twirled and smiled as the crowd clapped and stomped, often calling out, 'Tiny!' But instead of coming from her soul, tonight's performance was definitely an act. Fatigue made it difficult to feel any enthusiasm, relying on years of professionalism and practice to make the experience worthwhile for the audience.

The orchestra conductor had decided for the last concert of the season to add a new piece, forcing several long practice sessions. Tonight, Amhrán M'anama was playing to a packed crowd in a bar they'd performed in before. The spectators were loud and enthusiastic but easy to please. She wished she could say the same for the other members of the band.

Dunk had been drinking steadily since before they took the stage. Every time he downed another shot, the crowd roared, and she grimaced. Steven had been in a piss-poor mood all evening. As usual, picking up on everyone else's mood, Mike and Jamie avoided Dunk and Steven, keeping to themselves while leaving her feeling very much alone. It didn't help that Clay had been unable to come tonight. It was ridiculous, but she'd already become used to having him in her life more and more. They had even started making the trip to spend the night in each other's homes as often as possible.

Now, the final set was over, and all she wanted to do was pack up, load up, and drive home. Some of the crowd pushed forward to get the band members to sign T-shirts. Steven was calling out, reminding people to check their YouTube channel. "We're all over social media. Make sure to like and follow!"

"Jesus, what's got him all hyped?" Mike asked. "I'm glad people are enthusiastic, but I'm ready to go home."

She nodded, murmuring, "Yeah, me too." Keeping a smile plastered on her face, she accepted the accolades on the band's performance, making sure to thank each fan. Finally, they were able to start packing up. A man she didn't recognize was on the stage and picked up her violin. Rushing forward, she cried out, "No! Don't touch that!"

He turned around, surprise on his face before his eyes cut over to Steven.

"Chill, Tiny!" Steven said. "This is Will. He's been hired to help."

"Hired to help? Is this another one of Mr. Kincaid's ways to spend our money?"

"You don't have a clue about our money," Steven bit back. "Mr. Kincaid is making sure that we're fine and can focus on the band. Fuck, you act like we're never going to go anywhere."

She pinched her lips together, then turned to Will. "I'm sorry, I spoke sharply since we haven't been introduced. But I prefer to be the only one to handle my violin."

"No problem, ma'am."

"Don't *ma'am* her," Dunk laughed, swaying slightly. "She's just Tiny."

She turned her back on the rest of the band as she placed her violin in its case. Fatigue warred with fury, but she was determined to get out of the bar as soon as she could.

While Mike and Jamie placed their bagpipes in the cases, Will and Steven unplugged the equipment and amplifiers, taking them back and forth to the van Steven had driven. Dunk stumbled around several times before Steven finally told him to step aside and let Will take the percussion to the van.

As they walked outside, Mike slung his arm around Christina's shoulders. "I can tell you're tense, but Steven is just trying to take this band as far as it can go."

Twisting her head up to look at him, she asked, "And are you along for the ride? All the way?"

He ducked his head and shrugged. "I've got to admit, the fame sounds intriguing, but I don't know." His voice trailed off, and she followed his line of sight to where Jamie was trying to pull Dunk along.

"He did nothing but drink all night," she said.

"I used to think it was mostly an act, but I'm not sure anymore," Mike admitted.

"Are we done so we can get out of here?" Steven asked.

"Who pissed in your beer?" Mike groused. "You've been barking orders all night."

Deciding she'd had enough, Christina said, "Okay, look, everyone. We're all tired and grumpy. Why don't we just go home, have a couple of days to rest, and then get back together?"

"Best thing you said all night," Steven quipped before turning and walking to the van.

Ready to get away, she was glad she'd driven her own car. Carefully placing her violin on the back seat, she left the driver's door open as she sat with her legs sticking out of the automobile. Pulling off her tall, heeled boots, she wiggled her toes for a moment, wishing Clay was there to offer a foot massage. Reaching behind her, she grabbed her sneakers from the passenger seat and slid them on. The comfortable footwear made her the happiest she'd been all evening.

Just then, her phone vibrated, and she looked at the caller ID, seeing Clay's name. "Oh, my God, you must've known I was thinking about you!"

"Are you all finished for the night, babe?" Clay asked.

"Yes! Finished for the night and finished for the week! I'm sick of these guys and ready for a break!"

"I'm actually not too far from your place. I know we didn't settle anything for sure, but would you like some company tonight?"

"I can't think of anything I'd like better—"

"You can't drive!" came a shout from nearby. Jerking her head up, she saw Will and Steven inside the van, but

Mike was standing outside of Dunk's truck, arguing. "You're drunk! Unlock the door, and I'll drive you home."

Dunk laughed, wiggled his fingers, and shouted, "Fuck off, man!"

Clay's voice came over the phone. "Are you still there?"

"Oh, Jesus! Dunk drank too much, and now he's trying to drive out of the parking lot. Mike's trying to get him to stop, but I don't think he's going to."

"Babe, stay away from them. If Mike can't get Dunk to stay put, then I don't want you on the road with him driving around."

She heard Dunk's truck engine race, expecting him to peel out of the parking lot. Instead, he threw it into reverse instead of drive, and she watched in horror as his truck lurched backward, heading directly toward her. She barely had time to jerk her feet inside at the last second before the back of his truck slammed into the driver's side of her car.

The sound of crunching metal filled her ears as her car scooted sideways, and her body was propelled backward. Screaming, her heart raced as she tried to scramble toward the passenger side, covered in shattered glass.

"Christina? Christina! What the hell happened? Are you okay?"

Her phone had been tossed to the floorboard, and all she could do was cry out, "He hit my car! He hit my car!" She reached for her phone as Jamie and Mike pulled open her passenger door.

"Shit, Tiny! You're bleeding!" Mike exclaimed as the two men reached in, taking her arms and gently pulling her out of her car.

Her legs were shaky, threatening to give out from underneath her as they escorted her away from the vehicles. She looked to the side to see Steven and Will tugging Dunk from the driver seat of his truck. Jamie was on the phone calling 9-1-1, and she was barely aware that Mike took her phone from her hand.

"This is Mike. Who's this?"

"You've got Clay. What the fuck is going on? Is Christina okay?" Clay barked so loudly that Christina heard him even though her phone was pressed to Mike's ear.

"Yeah, yeah, man. She's fine. There's been a... a... accident. Fuck, but she's okay—"

"I'm coming. Tell her I'll be there in just a few minutes."

Mike looked down at Christina, and she plopped her bottom down to the pavement, no longer willing her legs to hold her up.

"That was Clay. He said that he'll be here—"

"I heard," she said, lifting her hand to wipe the moisture from her cheek. Glancing down, she saw the blood on her fingers. "Dunk... is he okay?"

"Unconscious, but I think he's just drunk," Jamie said, bending over, his face filled with concern. Squatting in front of her, he asked, "How are you?"

"Check on my violin. Please, get it out of the backseat of my car."

With a shake of his head in a rueful grin, Mike

looked at Jamie. "Beat to hell, and she's worried about her violin. That's our Tiny."

The sounds of sirens were heard in the distance, and soon flashing lights filled the parking lot. An ambulance pulled close to her, paramedics immediately rushing over. She lifted her shaking hand. "I'm fine, honest I'm fine."

"Let's check you out, ma'am," the paramedic said.

"But what about Dunk, the man who was in the truck—"

"Fuck him, Tiny," Mike groused. "Don't worry about him. The police are dealing with him."

Before she had a chance to respond, the squeal of tires sounded nearby, and she looked up to see Clay stalking toward her. The image of an avenging angel swooping went through her mind, and she wondered if she'd hit her head. She had never seen Clay angry, but at that moment, rage poured from him and the air vibrated with his fury. When he reached her, he lifted his hand, and with a gentle touch, placed his finger on her cheek where the small bandage had been taped.

"I'm fine," she said, wondering how many times she was going to say that phrase this evening even as she heard the shakiness in her voice.

"You're going to be fine," he amended. "But right now you're not fine." He turned to the paramedic. "How is she? Should she go to the hospital?"

The paramedic glanced toward her and asked, "Ma'am, is it okay for me to talk to him?"

She nodded, and the paramedic said, "Her blood pressure and heart rate are elevated, but that's to be expected. She says she didn't hit her head, and the cuts are superficial."

She thanked him as they packed up their equipment but jolted as Clay's voice barked to the others. "What the fuck happened?"

"It was an accident—" Steven said, walking over.

"The fuck it was!" Mike bit out. "Dunk was drunk. And he was going to drive home, and you were going to fuckin' let him."

"I don't have control over him."

Mike looked toward Christina, his face pale and his voice shaky. "Jesus, fuck, Tiny. You barely got your feet inside the door of your car before he hit you. If you hadn't, your legs would have been amputated right here in the parking lot."

She sucked in a quick breath, his description not erroneous but slamming into her. Clay swung around, his eyes wide and filled with fury. Lightheaded, she feared he would spend the night in jail for assault if she couldn't calm him. She grabbed his arm and said, "Honey, I'm fine—"

"Babe, swear to God, if you don't stop saying you're fine, I'm gonna lose my fuckin' mind." His gaze cut toward Steven, and he added, "And you're the one I'm coming for right after Dunk."

"Me?" Steven squeaked.

Mike stepped forward and said, "Clay, please, take her home."

He sucked in a deep breath and let it out slowly, the inward battle visible in the muscle tick of his jaw and the tension radiating from his body. He nodded, then pulled out his phone. "Need a favor. Got a wrecked car in the parking lot of the Irish pub on Bellweather Street and Chaps Drive. Haul it in, and I'll call tomorrow to see what needs to be done." Softening his voice, he asked, "Sweetheart, is there anything in there you need to get?"

Jamie answered for her. "I've got her purse, boots, and violin. I didn't see anything else in there."

"Okay, let's go, sweetheart. I'll take you home."

She nodded, the fatigue from earlier now slamming into her with full force.

Steven stepped closer but halted as a growl emitted from Clay. Glancing between them, he settled his gaze on her and said, "I'm sorry, Tiny. I should've kept a better handle on Dunk. I never meant for anything like this to happen, and I sure as hell don't want anything to happen to you. You're the best out of all of us."

"It's nobody's fault except Dunk's. He's the one who's responsible. No one else."

"Will and I'll get everything back to my place. Go home, rest, and take care of yourself."

She nodded and watched as Steven jogged over to the van where Will was waiting. Jamie and Mike both moved directly to her, pulling her into a hug before they headed to their vehicles as well. As they drove away, she turned and looked back at her car, the smashed driver's door making it useless. Swallowing deeply, she sighed. "My car is so old, I'm sure it's going to be totaled. And I have no clue if Duncan even has insurance, so this may all fall on me."

"It's a good thing the police have already carted him

off," he said. With his hands on her shoulders, he gently guided her toward his SUV. With great care, he scooped her up and settled her inside. Closing her door, he jogged around the front and climbed behind the wheel.

"Steven will bail him out tomorrow once Dunk has had a chance to sober up."

As they drove down the road, Clay said, "Steven is not going to bail him out. Dunk needs to spend some time behind bars to learn his lesson. I'm looking into all of them and not liking what I find."

"What do you mean you're looking at all of them? You're looking at the band?"

He scrubbed his hand over his face and sighed. "Look, Christina, I care about you. So yeah, I'm going to investigate the people that are around you."

"Wait, wait, wait. I can't quite get past where you're investigating the people around me."

"I don't trust Steven, okay? You say he handles the money for the band, but how do I know he's doing things the right way? And who the hell was that guy with him tonight?"

"That's Will. Somebody that Mr. Kincaid hired to help us out. And I don't even know why I'm telling you this because it's not your business!"

"If it has to do with you, it is my business."

She knew she should stay quiet and face things with the band tomorrow. Instead, frustration had her picking a fight with Clay. Twisting slightly to face him, she huffed. "Why would you be investigating the band? Don't you have cases to work on and do great, big government stuff?" Her head was beginning to pound and anger was making everything worse.

"Mr. Kincaid—a politician's right-hand man—has hired somebody to help your dinky band around," Clay said. "Doesn't that strike you as weird?"

"Dinky?" she screeched, wincing at the sound of her own voice.

"Hell, you once even said that your band was dinky."

"Piddly. I said the band was piddly, not dinky. There's a difference!" She crossed her arms over her chest and said, "You know what? I'm going home. Let me out here, and I'm going to call for a taxi."

"No, you're not."

Suddenly, unable to keep the tears at bay, exhaustion won over anger. He pulled to the side of the road and put the SUV in park. Shifting toward her, he wrapped his arms around her, tucking her into his embrace. She began to sob despite her best efforts to appear completely in charge of her emotions.

"Babe, I'm so sorry."

She didn't respond but continued to sniffle and then wiped her nose on his shirt, unable to care about the messy gesture.

"Do you have practice tomorrow?"

She shook her head, still sniffling.

"Okay, I'm taking you to my house. I know it will be a little bit of a drive, so I want you to settle in and try to sleep. I'll wake you up when we get there." She lifted her head to peer at him through watery eyes, but he rushed, "Please, let me take care of you, Christina. You need to rest, and I want to make sure you truly are fine. Let's not talk anymore about the band tonight, and tomor-row, things will seem better."

Tired of arguing, she nodded. "Okay," she said, heaving a great sigh. "That sounds good."

He grabbed a soft jacket from the back seat and settled it next to her so that she had a place to lay her head. It didn't take long for the gentle lull of the drive to send her into a deep sleep.

22

The morning light peeked through the blinds in Clay's bedroom. He had slipped from the bed earlier and called Mace, letting him know what had happened. Taking the day off, he then slid back under the covers, curled his body around Christina's, and held her tightly.

She was fast asleep by the time they'd gotten to his house, and he carried her in without her waking. He had managed to get her tank top, bra, and skirt off, pulling a large, soft T-shirt over her head when she finally roused awake. After guiding her to the bathroom and pressing a toothbrush into her hand, he'd walked out to give her some privacy. As soon as she stumbled back into the bedroom, he'd led her to bed and tucked her in. Her head had barely touched the pillow when she fell sound asleep. Glad that she was able to rest, it had taken him much longer.

Standing in the parking lot seeing her crumpled car, shards of glass still in her hair, blood drops on her chest, and the bandage on her cheek, he'd become so angry at the thought of her being hurt that he'd almost blurted his suspicions. Glad that he hadn't, not wanting to place her in danger, he knew they needed to talk later that day. He just hadn't figured out what he needed to say.

But one thing was certain—he now truly understood that two people who loved each other could disagree and work through their anger and issues without handling things the way his parents did.

His arms tightened and she stirred, blinking as her beautiful eyes focused on him. Neither spoke as their gazes held each other. They lifted their hands at the same time, his to brush her soft hair back from her face and hers to rest on his jaw.

"I'm okay," she stated softly.

"I know, but that doesn't keep me from being scared about what happened or terrified about what could have happened."

"I'm sorry we argued." Her fingers traced his morning stubble.

"I was just thinking that you've taught me a valuable lesson." Seeing her lifted brows, he explained, "My parents' nasty arguments were the only thing I knew about a couple's disagreements. Name-calling, belittling, screaming, door slamming, throwing things. When you and I first became angry, honest to God, I felt ill. More nervous than any mission I've ever been on. But you've shown me that we can stick to the issue, express our opinions and concerns, and come out stronger on the other side."

They held each other, soft kisses and murmured words of comfort moving between them until the sunlight brightened the room a little more. Finally, her stomach growled, and she blushed.

"I need to feed you, babe," he said, his eyes dropping to her breasts as she stretched. He then tamped down the lust that always speared through him at the sight of her body. "Hell, I need to feed both of us."

"I don't want you to do everything, but I'm desperate for a shower. Will you wait and let me help with breakfast after I get cleaned up?"

"How about we shower together?"

She inhaled quickly and her eyes flared. "Oh, yeah..."

By the time they had stripped, the water in the shower had heated. She had peeled off the small bandage, exposing her cheek. The cut was small but combined with several other tiny cuts dotting the side of her neck and shoulder, and he hated each one.

Ignoring his body's response to her beautiful nudity, he lathered the body wash in his hands and gently smoothed it over her shoulders, back, and legs before turning her gently and sudsing her neck. As his hands glided down her chest and around her breasts, her eyes closed and her head fell back. A smile curved her lips as she clung to his shoulders, and he continued to lap her breasts, his thumb sweeping over her nipples.

Determined to finish his task without distraction, his hands glided over her tummy. Suddenly, her fingers tightened, and her eyes flew open. Gasping in air amidst a giggle, she squirmed backward.

"How did I not know you were ticklish?"

"Because you've never done that before!" She had nowhere to go in the shower, and as his hands moved forward again, her eyes widened.

"I'll avoid your tummy—for now." He continued to wash her arms, letting the warm water from the shower help soothe her tight muscles. Well acquainted with adrenaline rushes, he knew they could make someone feel invincible, and then later the aches and pains would come slamming in full-force.

By now, her head tilted back and her hair was slicked away from her face. Taking the shampoo, he carefully lathered her long tresses, making sure there were no tiny shards of glass hiding in the thick strands. Lastly, his thumb swept over her cheeks, wiping away the last vestiges of dried blood drops. "If you want to go ahead and step out and start drying, I'll be out in a minute," he offered.

Her blue-green eyes stared up at him, and her lips curved into a smile again. Shaking her head, she said, "No way I'm leaving you. You have me feeling wonderful. Now it's your turn."

Before he could claim that she didn't need to wash him, she leaned forward and kissed the middle of his chest. The delicate touch shot straight to his cock.

His gaze zeroed in on the cut on her cheek and it was as though he'd been doused in cold water. "While I'm tempted to take you in here, shower sex is for when you're feeling your best, not recovering from an accident."

With that proclamation, he flipped off the now-cooling water and carried her to the thick, warm floor mat. Grabbing a towel, he began to dry her body carefully.

She lifted her head and peered at him, a smile on her face. He kissed her soundly, his tongue gliding over hers, his fingers running through her wet hair. Finally, mumbling against her lips, he asked "Are you okay, babe?"

"Yeah," she breathed, still smiling. "Now, you can feed me."

He barked out a laugh. "I'll get right on that." He quickly showered and walked out of the bathroom to find her in his large T-shirt once again. She'd snagged her panties, and the thought hit him that she needed to start leaving some clothes at his place. Deciding to wait until later to bring that up, he pulled on his boxers and jeans.

Once in the kitchen, they worked together scrambling eggs, frying bacon, and cooking french toast. The scent of coffee filled the air, and they soon settled at his table to eat.

The only sounds heard for a few minutes were the click of the forks on the plates and the "mmm" sounds emitted from Christina. "You remembered this is my favorite," she said, wiping the syrup from the French toast off her lips.

He tried to tell his cock that she was enthusiastic about breakfast but the reminder of the little sounds she made during sex was a distraction. Looking down at his now-empty plate, he wasn't sure he remembered actually tasting his food.

Pushing her plate back, she captured his gaze and cocked her head to the side. "We need to talk, sweetie. The band? Investigating? I know things were intense last night, but Clay, I want to know what's going on." Before he had a chance to speak, she threw her hand up and quickly added, "And don't give me any *Lighthouse-I-can't-talk-about-it* lines. Maybe the other women can deal, but I can't. You've got to at least explain what's going on that affects me."

"Okay."

She blinked, her head still cocked to the side. "Okay?"

"Yeah, okay. You're right, I won't talk about missions that don't have anything to do with you. But since some recent developments have come to light and you're involved on the periphery, I will at least explain what I can."

She slumped back in her chair, seeming surprised at his acquiescence. He stood and picked up the plates, setting them in the sink. Returning to the table, he held out his hand, pleased when she placed hers in his. He guided them to the sofa, settling them on the cushions, wanting her to be comfortable. In truth, it also gave him a chance to organize his thoughts.

He reached across and held her hand, linking their fingers, craving the simplest physical connection with her. Lifting his gaze to her face, he beheld her trust and his chest eased slightly. Taking a deep breath, he began.

"When I first saw you playing with Amhrán M'anama, I was totally captivated by you. Your dancing, your music, your talent... everything about you.

As good as the band was, you were the song of *my* soul."

Her fingers flexed and her breath hitched, but she remained quiet.

"I wanted to make sure you were safe, but I didn't worry about the others until…" The inner battle was real, still grappling with how much to tell her. Closing his eyes for a second, he pulled on his memories of Mace and the other Keepers when working to keep their loved ones safe. Sucking in a deep breath through his nose, he let it out slowly, opening his eyes, allowing his gaze to fixate on Christina's beautiful face. "Until the band ended up on the periphery of one of my investigations."

Her brow crinkled as she cocked her head slightly to the side, continuing to hold his gaze. She sucked in her lips, confusion mixed with interest on her face. She continued her silence, offering him the chance to explain without argument, for which he was grateful. Something he could never remember his parents offering to each other.

"Without giving away more than I should, let's just say that someone Steven has allowed to become involved with the band is not someone I trust. And because of that association, I've now had to include your bandmates and the finances that Steven controls in my investigation." Having no idea what her response was going to be, her startled reaction surprised him.

"It's Mr. Kincaid, isn't it?" Her gaze snapped, and she snorted when he didn't answer immediately. "I know it is! He's the only one who's been around lately." She released Clay's hand as she leapt to her feet, pacing to the other side of the room. Whirling around, she threw her arms out to the side. "Suddenly, Steven's been 'Mr. Kincaid this' and 'Mr. Kincaid that!' I thought it was weird! I mean, he's like an assistant or something for Congressman Bennett. Why would he suddenly want to practically manage a small-time Celtic band? I mean, even if we were superstars, the niche is small, and we'd hardly bring in a ton of money for him." Her hands that had been waving wildly suddenly slapped against her thighs, and she stared back at him. "And of all the dumb luck... I ended up in his house! That crazy-ass, huge house. And then he shows up at the concert." She stopped pacing and quieted. "This isn't just about him, though, is it? You're talking about the band as well."

He stood and reached his hand out. "Please, sweetheart, come back over and sit with me. I'll explain what I can, but I want you to be calm and comfortable."

Her breath left her lungs in a whoosh, and her shoulders slumped. She reached out her delicate hand, and he wrapped his much larger one around it, drawing her near. Settling her once again on the sofa, this time much closer, he kept hold of her hand with his other arm wrapped around her shoulders.

"I have no idea what his interest in the band is at this time. Maybe he just really likes the music. Maybe he just really wants to help. I don't know, Christina. But what I do know, I don't like. My fear is that Steven is so enamored with the idea of the band making it big, he's liable to make decisions that aren't wise. On top of that, I know that Dunk has a drinking problem, and even

238

Mike had a brush with the law. All of this combined makes me concerned for you."

She twisted her head around so that she could face him and lifted her free hand to cup his jaw. Her gentle touch soothed him, and he prayed his words struck a chord deep inside her.

"I know you can't talk about your investigations, so I know you can't talk about Mr. Kincaid." Scrunching her nose, she added, "I guess it's all politically motivated since he works with the congressman."

His chest eased slightly when she didn't question him further and accepted that there were things he couldn't divulge. He reached inside his pocket and said, "I bought you something." Hesitating, he added, "Actually, I bought it the day I first heard you play with the band." He opened his hand and there, resting in his palm, was a beautiful, silver, Celtic cross necklace. "I saw you looking at the jewelry and wanted you to have this, but I've carried it around for all this time, trying to figure out the right time to give it to you."

Her eyes widened before she smiled and clapped her hands together. "Oh, my goodness! Clay, this is beautiful!" She lifted her hair, and he draped the necklace around her neck, settling the cross at the top of her breasts. Touching it gently, he slid his knuckle to her chin and kissed her deeply.

"We're still getting to know each other, and I don't want you to feel weird about me giving you the necklace," he said.

"I'm sorry you had to be concerned," she said. Her eyes sparkled and she laughed. "I have something for you, too. You won't believe it!" She jumped up and hurried to her purse still sitting on the counter. Rummaging through it, she pulled out a small bag. Walking to the sofa, she sat down next to him again. "I bought this for you when the band was in Ottawa."

He had forgotten the purchase she'd made when Cobb was keeping an eye on her. Taking the bag, he pulled out a small box. Lifting the lid, his eyes widened at the sight of the heavy silver chain with the lighthouse within a Celtic circle. "Oh, wow, babe, this is perfect."

"You don't have to wear it—"

His actions stopped her words as he slipped it over his head and settled the lighthouse pendant on his muscular chest.

Her thumb swept over the stubble on his face, and she leaned in, kissing his breastbone just above the silver, then slid her lips up over his jaw, finally landing on the corner of his mouth. "I love you," she mumbled against his lips.

He took over the kiss as it flamed hotter, threatening to singe both of them with its intensity. All semblance of finesse flew out the window as noses and teeth bumped, tongues danced against each other, and she squirmed until she was straddling his lap, her breasts pressed against his chest.

There was more he was sure he meant to say, but all rational thought flew out of his mind. Even the ability to make it to the bedroom seemed impossible. His hands skimmed over her bare thighs, up under the bottom of the large T-shirt, and he whipped it over her head, their lips separating just enough for the material to pass between them. Falling over to the side, he took her with him, his hips nestled between her open thighs.

Words no longer mattered. Speaking with whispers and touches, nuzzles and nips, licks and kisses, they spoke their own language of love with their bodies.

2 3

Christina waved goodbye after another long, wet kiss while standing in the open door of her apartment. Clay had driven her home, and much to her surprise, a rental car was sitting in her parking space. When she expressed concern that he had spent money to not only get her car towed but that a rental car was there for her use, he simply stated that he wanted her safe. He'd explained he had a mechanic friend who ran a garage and would handle everything with her car and insurance. He also said she had use of the rental until she received the insurance check and was ready to buy a new car.

She almost argued with his handling of her situation but snapped her mouth closed. That would be foolish. He cared about her, and she certainly didn't have money for a car right now, so she would gratefully accept his help. Grinning as he drove away, she had to admit she felt loved.

She had left his house with her short skirt and tank

top but added one of his button-up shirts around her top and tied at the waist. Ready to change clothes, she almost ran into Amy as her roommate was heading out the door. Amy halted long enough to get the details from the previous evening, including a few of the details from the morning.

"Honey, I love your band members, but I'm so pissed at Dunk," Amy groused. "He could have killed you! Or maimed you! I hope he sits in jail for days!"

"To be honest, I'm not in the mood to see him, either. Last night, I was full of shock and anger, but now I really need to think about the band situation."

Amy cocked her head to the side, and asked, "The band?"

"Yeah." She sighed and ran her fingers through her hair, pulling it away from her face before securing the tresses into a sloppy bun with a pencil lying on the counter. "The band's future. And more specifically, my future with the band."

Amy put her hand on Christina's arm and squeezed. "Oh, honey, I'm so sorry you're having to go through this." She glanced at the clock on the stove and added, "Are you going to be okay? I've got to run to a sectional practice, but I hate leaving you."

"No, no, please, go on. I need to do some thinking. Plus, I might even take a nap."

Nodding with enthusiasm, Amy said, "Definitely, a cup of tea and a nap sounds perfect."

After Amy left, Christina did exactly that, and several hours later woke refreshed and ready to get some answers. She grabbed the new car keys that had been left on the kitchen counter and headed out.

Twenty minutes later, she arrived at Steven's house. Parking in the front, she walked to his door and knocked. He threw it open, his wide-eyed expression showing his surprise. Reaching out, he grabbed her in a hug, squeezing tightly.

"Oh, my God, Tiny. I was so fuckin' scared last night. Are you okay?" With his hands on her upper arms, he pushed her away just enough so that he could stare into her face, his gaze landing on her cheek. "Shit, I can't believe that happened."

"I'm okay, I really am," she assured. His greeting warmed her, reminding her of the friendship they'd had bonding over music before the recent strained times. She glanced past him and asked, "Can I come in?"

"Of course, of course, come on," he said, ushering her into the living room.

As usual, his house was clean if not a little messy. Sheets of music were scattered across the coffee table as well as the piano in the corner, and near one of his chairs, a guitar was propped in a stand. "Are you writing new material?"

He glanced around and shrugged. "Not really. I was trying to get my mind off the horror of last night, but I wasn't able to get out of my head long enough to put anything decent on paper." He waved a hand toward the sofa and asked, "Can I get you some water or soda? I've even got orange juice."

Smiling, she shook her head. "No, thanks. I'm good." She sat on the sofa, but instead of sinking into the soft cushions, she perched on the edge, her hands clasped in her lap.

"You look like you've got something on your mind, and your posture tells me I'm not going to like what you're thinking," he said, his words soft and sounding a little sad.

She held his gaze and smiled. "No, it's not bad. It's just… well… I've got some thinking to do. And maybe I need some answers while I'm doing that."

He sat in the chair near the guitar and leaned forward, placing his forearms on his knees. "You got it. Tell me what I can do."

"I suppose, first of all, we need to talk about Dunk—"

"He's still in jail."

She blinked at Steven's rapid-fire response. "Oh, okay… uh…"

"I know I've bailed him out of trouble before, but not this time," he said. He let out a long breath and slumped back in his seat. "I thought I was taking care of him by always covering for him. He's a talented percussionist and always brought a great vibe to our performances. Pounding out the beat, shouting encouragement to us and the crowd, downing whiskeys… The audience loved him, and we all gave him a wide berth to just keep being Dunk. Even Drunken Duncan was a stupid moniker. I see that now. He had a problem, and I didn't recognize it in time, and it could've got you killed."

"Steven, I'm not here to cast blame. Certainly not in your direction. What I said last night is true—this is all on Duncan. We may not have stepped in and recognized the problem, and that's on all of us. But he made the decision to get behind the wheel of his truck last night. And I'm not sorry that you've left him in jail. While there he needs to learn, either by jail time or being forced into a program. I don't know if either will work, but something's got to change."

They were silent for a moment, then Steven said, "I get that there's more here than just Dunk and what happened last night."

"I want you to know that I'm not rushing a decision. I'm still thinking and pondering my options. I'm just not sure that I'm going in the same direction that Amhrán M'anama is going."

"Tiny, you're a huge part of our success, and I don't want to lose you. Honest to God, honey, if it comes down to choosing between you and Dunk, Dunk is out."

Her hands flew up as she shook her head back and forth. "No, no, Steven. I'm not asking you to choose between Dunk and me. It's just lately, I feel as though you've been pushing for us to grow beyond my comfort zone. I know that Mr. Kincaid has had more and more say over what we're doing, and I'm not sure I'm comfortable with that direction."

Steven sighed heavily and nodded. "You know, I understand what you're saying, but it's really my fault that I haven't gone about things the right way. I was so excited when Mr. Kincaid approached me about wanting to help the band move onward and upward that I took his suggestions and just ran with them. He loves the idea of you front and center with me. Let's face it, Tiny, it gives us balance."

"Balance?" Her brow crinkled as she tried to understand his meaning.

"Our music's great, everyone knows that. Mike and Jamie on the pipes, decked out in kilts and boots. Same with me. Dunk is the hard-core, out-of-control drummer. And when you start playing and dancing, you can bring the house down with your talent and sex appeal."

"And that's what Mr. Kincaid wants to focus on? Our personas more than our talent?"

"I feel like I'm saying this all wrong and at the wrong time. I should have taken the time to sit down with all of you and explain what I was thinking and what we were doing. I'm sorry, Tiny. I really am."

His acquiescence surprised her, having braced for arguments and deflections. Uncertain how to proceed, she sucked her lips in, her brow furrowing as she thought. Finally, she said, "Perhaps that's the best way to move forward. I think whatever is said needs to include Jamie and Mike as well. We each have our own musical goals as well as the band's. If Mr. Kincaid is sincere in his desire, the rest of us need to see that. And we each have to decide if the band's future is where we need to be."

Steven nodded and said, "I think that's a good idea, Tiny... uh... Christina." He grimaced as he stood. "I'm so glad you came, and I really hate to cut this short. I'm not bailing Dunk out, but I did promise that I would check on him today."

Quickly coming to her feet, she apologized. "I'm

sorry for just stopping by. And as frustrated with Dunk as I am, I'm glad you have a chance to see him. When you arrange something with Mr. Kincaid, just let me know. The symphony's season is almost at a close, and I'll have more time."

"Let me grab a couple of things from the back, and we can walk out together."

She watched as he walked down the hall and entered the bathroom. Just then, his phone vibrated on the coffee table and she glanced down, seeing an incoming text from JK.

The money is now in your account. Keep D in line and out of sight from the others until you hear from me.

She heard the toilet flush and moved quickly. By the time Steven walked back into the room, she was standing at the piano, looking through the music with a wide smile on her face. "I hope you don't mind, but I couldn't stay away from the music. This looks really good, Steven."

"Thanks, that's an honor coming from you." He grabbed his phone and shoved it into his pocket before escorting her out to her vehicle.

She waved as she drove down the street, her fake smile now gone. Blowing out a shaky breath, she had no idea what was happening with the band, but Steven was lying to her if he was working with Jerry Kincaid to bail out Dunk. *Whatever they're planning with the band is going to impact all of us.* She feared her days as a member of Amhrán M'anama were numbered.

By the time he got back from dropping Christina off at her apartment, it crossed Clay's mind for about two seconds to go home. But his work ethic kicked in, and he wanted to check to see what the others were working on, so he drove straight to LSI. He knew Mace had told the others about Christina's accident and wasn't surprised when Horace and Marge both asked about her. Assuring them she was fine, he hoped his words would sink into his own head, still filled with the image of her in the parking lot, tearful and bleeding. Blowing out a deep breath, he headed down to the main compound room deep in the caverns.

Again, stepping into the vast area, he was met with a barrage of questions coming from all directions. Figuring it would be easier to explain all at once, he gave a quick synopsis of what had happened in the parking lot, assuring them she was not seriously injured. When he described how she jerked her legs inside her car just before Dunk's truck hit, they all gasped.

Suddenly, as though the vision of her legs being crushed hit him, his own legs buckled and he plopped into a chair. "Christ," he muttered. A hand landed on his shoulder and he twisted around to look up at Tate's angry visage.

"I can't fuckin' believe that guy did that," Tate barked.

Nodding, he said, "I know, I know. Right now, his

ass is in jail, and while I'm sure he feels remorse, I don't want him around her."

He sighed, then looked at Mace. "I need to let you know that I gave some information to Christina. If it was the wrong thing to do, I'll take the consequences, but I'm going to come clean right now." He relayed what he had said to her that morning and received assurances from Mace and the others that he had not violated any LSI confidential information or compromised the investigation.

Swiping his hand over his face, he said, "I wanted to give her enough information to keep her safe but not do the wrong thing. How the hell did you all do this?"

Babs stepped up and plopped her fists on her hips, lifted an eyebrow, and held his gaze. "How did she handle it?"

Piqued, he defended, "She handled it great. She seemed to know instinctively that I was talking about Jerry Kincaid and even said he'd given her a bad feeling. I didn't tell her anything else about him or the investigation, just that I wasn't overly happy with his involvement with the band. She knows I have a job to do and that I want her safe at the same time."

Babs laughed, her demeanor now eased. "I knew she'd be fine. She's definitely one of us... worthy of a Keeper."

He hadn't thought of Christina in those terms, never before understanding what the others meant. But now, he knew Babs was right. Christina was smart, intuitive, and hadn't fallen apart. Instead, she'd accepted that he had an investigation, wasn't going to stand in his way, and understood that he had a desire to protect her. Giving his head a little shake, he looked over to the wide screen on the wall to see what the others were working on. There were several photographs of small two and four-person submersibles with information next to each of them. Standing, he walked over and asked, "What have you found out?"

Levi reported, "The FBI was glad for this line of inquiry to follow. They hadn't considered submersibles as a way that the cartels might be moving drugs. Even a small two-person submersible would have plenty of room for one person and a significant load of drugs to transport. They would easily be able to make several hundred miles at a time, resurfacing to charge somewhere innocuous, and then be on their way again, out of sight, out of suspicion."

"I suppose it's too much to ask if Kincaid has had any recent purchases of million-dollar submersibles," he joked.

The others chuckled and shook their heads. "If only it was that easy," Levi said.

Cobb piped up, "But I've been looking at the money trail along with Sylvie. It's a convoluted trail, but we're finding evidence that Kincaid has been siphoning money from Congressman Bennett's campaign funds. Not a lot, just a little. I've also managed to find two offshore accounts that are tied into him. One of them, surprisingly, is for a corporation he calls M'anama."

"You're fuckin' kidding me?" Clay growled. "He's using part of the band's Celtic name as a company front?"

"Yep. The feds can't get into what's inside those offshore accounts, but I," Cobb wiggled his fingers and added, "and Josh, have the magic touch."

"And?"

"We're still working on it, but we can see where almost half a million has gone in. My guess right now is those are the cartel's payoffs."

Walker added, "One of the things we're wondering about is how the cartel got their claws into him."

"Any ideas?"

Nodding, Walker continued, "If he was embezzling money from the congressman's funds and someone found out, that would be leverage to blackmail him into working for them. And with the money behind the cartels, it's easy to keep him in line."

"How can we find out about a submersible?"

"About the best thing we can hope for right now is to keep an eye on the security cameras that we have inside the boathouse near Kincaid's residence. Now that we know what we're looking for, we don't have to waste our time on the outside. Let the FBI do that. We just have to look at the inside and see what pops up into one of the empty docks."

Mace moved closer to the center of the room and said, "If I can have everyone's attention." Instantly, the chatter in the room quieted and everyone turned their gaze toward him. Mace grinned toward Rank. "You all have met Richard, Rank's brother, and know that he's been interested in becoming a Keeper. Rick and I have been in discussions, and he's just received his honorable discharge from the Navy. He was stationed at Little

Creek in Virginia Beach, spent the last week in North Carolina with their parents, and is moving in with Rank and Helena until he can find a place. I've offered him a position with LSI, and he wants to start immediately. So, immediately begins tomorrow."

This was met with a rousing cheer and applause from everyone.

"Sylvie will have forms for him to fill out, he'll have to get acclimated to how we do things, and one of the first jobs I was going to hand him was looking through the security feed, watching for a submersible coming into the boathouse near Kincaid's place. Boring as fuck job, but I figure he'll be glad to do it."

Always glad to have someone else join their team, Clay offered his congratulations to Rank before moving to the chair next to Cobb. "Okay, let me help look at these financial documents. Maybe we can piece more together. Anything to bury Kincaid."

24

"I know you've got something to say, so you might as well go ahead and say it," Christina said, looking toward Amy. She had taken it easy for several days, even going so far as to cancel a few of her private lessons. Now, she felt ready to get back into the full swing of things, which was good considering the symphony had just completed its final, long practice before the last symphony of the season at the end of the week. Steven, Mike, and Jamie had all called to check on her. She hadn't asked about Dunk, and Steven didn't mention him.

Amy was driving them home from their practice and had been glancing nervously to the side the entire time. Scrunching her nose, Amy said, "It's just that I have some news, and I don't know how to tell you."

Hearing the seriousness of Amy's voice, she said, "Now, you've got me worried. Please, just go ahead and tell me."

"It's not anything to worry about... well, not

exactly. You know my grandmother lives about an hour north of Portland. She's gotten to a point where she could use a little bit of help. My parents have asked me to consider moving in with my grandmother. They understand I'd have to travel back to Portland during the symphony's season and practices. But they said they'd make sure any living and travel expenses were paid for because it would save on having to get someone outside the family to stay with my grandmother at night. Plus, I'd save on rent and utilities."

"Oh, Amy, of course, you've got to do it," she agreed.

"Yes, but that would leave you without a roommate. And you're my best friend, and I hate that we wouldn't be living together."

Christina sighed and nodded slowly. "Yeah, you're right. I'll miss you like crazy. We'll still see each other for practices and symphony nights, but I totally understand what you need to do."

Amy glanced to the side again as she pulled into their apartment parking lot. "Can I ask about Clay? I wondered if maybe you two were ready to move in together."

"I don't know," she shrugged. "We haven't talked about it, but we both mentioned that it's a real pain to have to go back and forth. In fact, Clay even suggested I keep some clothes at his place."

"Would you consider moving to his house?"

"He lives close to his work, but it's almost two hours to get from his place into downtown Portland where the concerts are. Even though our apartment is north of the city, the thirty-minute commute to downtown has been nice."

"Maybe he'd consider moving a little south so that you'd have less of a commute."

She nibbled on her bottom lip, remembering when he told her the house he lived in now was not his forever home. "Maybe. We just haven't had a chance to talk about anything like that. I suppose, for now, I'll finish up the lease in our apartment even if you're not there."

She and Amy shared a late lunch, then she received a call from Amelia.

"Ms. Monroe? Can you come out to my house for my lesson this afternoon? My parents have gone out of town, and we were going to have our housekeeper bring me, but I thought maybe you'd like to come here instead."

"Sure, there's no reason for your housekeeper to drive you into town. It's actually closer for me to just come to your parents' place." Since the Bennett estate was also on the north side of town, she quickly calculated that if she threw an overnight bag in her car, she could spend the night at Clay's house.

Telling Amy what her plans were, she packed a bag, grabbed her violin and music satchel, and headed down to her rental car. The day was beautiful and all during the drive she pondered her living situation. She didn't want Amy to feel bad for the move to help her grandmother, but considering they'd been roommates for several years, she would miss her. Sighing heavily, she thought about the changes in her life that seemed to be hitting her all at once. *Am I ready to move in with Clay?* She sat at a red light, a wide grin spread over her face. Glancing to the side, she realized the driver next to her probably wondered why she had such a huge smile. *If they had a man like I do, they'd be smiling too!*

Pulling through the gate of the Bennett estate, she spied the large home sitting on a green hill surrounded by carefully planted trees with water in the distance. Her gaze drifted to the guesthouse, and she sucked in a quick breath, thoughts of Jerry Kincaid hitting her. It had been obvious Clay battled with how much to tell her. While she had no idea why Jerry was being scrutinized, she trusted Clay explicitly and was glad he'd confided his concerns.

Once parked outside the large home, the housekeeper stepped onto the front veranda. Greeting her, she followed the housekeeper's instructions and walked up the grand staircase to the family wing, making her way into Amelia's room. It was large and bright with windows that overlooked the gardens leading down to the water. Amelia's bedroom was as large as Christina's entire apartment, and she grinned at the teenage decor. Bright-colored bedspread. Eclectic framed posters that ranged from vintage rock to the London Philharmonic Orchestra.

Amelia was seated at her desk, books piled around her laptop. Twisting her head around, she called out, "Hi, Ms. Monroe!"

Smiling at the enthusiastic greeting she received, she asked, "Wow, what do I owe this reception?"

Laughing, Amelia said, "My parents are gone for the

week, but Mom said that I could have a few friends over tomorrow if I get all my homework done, my English Lit paper close to being finished, and have my violin lesson." Throwing her arms out to the side, she said, "That's why I thought it would be better to have you come here. It saves me time to finish the paper!"

"Having friends over when your parents are gone is definitely motivation," she grinned.

Amelia looped her arm through Christina's. "Oh, you know I love you, Ms. Monroe. I'd be glad to see you even if it wasn't a means to an end!" Glancing out the window, she added, "How would you like to go down to the guesthouse again for our lesson?"

"The last time we did that, the resident showed up!" Christina kept a smile on her face, but the idea of running into Jerry Kincaid held no appeal after knowing there was something fishy about him.

"Oh, there's no chance of that. My parents are in New York City for some political event." Amelia shrugged and added, "Mr. Kincaid, Mom's secretary, and some of Dad's aides went with them. I don't mind, though, it's kind of nice to have the house to myself occasionally."

Christina barked out a laugh. "As big as your house is, I'd think you could get lost even if it was filled with people."

"You're right," Amelia nodded. Her brow lowered. "That was a very elitist thing to say, wasn't it?"

"It's fine, Amelia. Actually, you're incredibly down to earth considering your family's heritage."

"Mom and Dad always insist that I understand the

advantages I have that aren't offered to many. I know a lot of people think teenagers are young and silly, especially those who have privilege, but I try not to be."

Staring at the beautiful teenager in front of her, Christina's affection for her was real. "If you'd like to go to the guesthouse for practice, that's fine with me. I have to admit, playing the violin in that beautiful space with the water just outside is very uplifting."

She smiled as Amelia picked up her violin case, music, and her phone. Blushing, she looked up at Christina and said, "I know that normally I have my phone turned off, but Mom said she'd call sometime this afternoon. She wants to check on the progress of my English Lit paper, and of course, to check with the housekeeper about the friends I'm having over tomorrow."

The two hurried down the path that wandered through the lush gardens toward the guesthouse. Once inside, they quickly got to work, Christina aware that they'd spent extra time chatting and walking instead of practicing. Amelia was always motivated but today even more so. The lesson flew by, and Christina praised her pupil's accomplishments.

Amelia's phone vibrated, and she said, "Oh, this call is Mom!"

"Of course, go ahead and take it. Tell your mother I said hello."

Amelia darted outside the guesthouse and began walking up the path. Christina followed slowly to give the teenager some privacy. She turned to look back over the estate, breathing deeply the fresh air. The grass was already green, and the trees were budding. The water-front at the edge of the estate was crystal blue, reflecting the cloudless sky. She thought for a moment about Clay's house. He'd told her that several of the Keepers had residences near the water, if not directly on it like Blake and Sara's house. *I wonder if that's what he'd like... to continue to live near the water.*

Her mind filled with the idea of a house near the water that she and Clay could share. At that thought, she smiled, her heart feeling lighter. *Maybe the time is right for us... or at least close.*

"Ms. Monroe!"

She startled out of her musings and looked at Amelia shouting from the other side of the garden.

"I forgot my music! Would you mind getting it for me?"

Chuckling, she waved her acquiescence and turned back toward the guesthouse. She found the small satchel of music on the coffee table and turned to walk back out. A movement in the distance caught her eye and she peered out the window. Jerry Kincaid was walking rapidly around the back corner of the guesthouse, disappearing inside the adjacent boathouse. *Amelia said he was in New York City with her parents.* Suspicion snaked through her, and she sucked in her lips, curious as to why he was back on the estate. Glancing around, she saw no one else outside, and Amelia had disap-peared into the main house.

Suddenly, the thoughts of everything Steven told her came slamming back and her anger rose. *How dare he try to walk in and change everything with the band!* Deciding it was time she had a few words with him, she marched forward, determination on her face.

Clay walked over and clapped his hand on the shoulder of the newest Keeper. Rick was similar in looks and build to his brother, Rank. Also filled with confidence, eager to learn, and not overly cocky, that made him the perfect match for the rest of the Keepers. Mace insisted that egos had no place at LSI. "How's it going?"

"I've been staring at this damn monitor for three days, going back over the feeds," Rick said. "I've stared at it so much that I feel like I'm starting to see things. A few minutes ago, it looked like there were ripples in the water and then nothing."

"I know we don't have any idea how often these drug runs are made, and my assumption—since the submersibles run on a simple charge—could be anytime day or night."

Rick twisted his head up and looked at Clay. "Have you ever been in one of these?"

Shaking his head, he replied, "Not me."

Walker looked over and added, "I was pulling up fuckin' YouTube videos of what it's like in one of these two-person submersibles. They say some of them can go really deep, but the idea of doing that wouldn't make me comfortable."

"It makes me think of the movie Titanic."

That comment had everyone swinging their heads around toward Sylvie. She looked up and blushed.

"You know, the James Cameron movie, Titanic? At the beginning, they had the submersibles that were going around and looking at the Titanic wreckage." The men in the room gave her a blank stare, and she rolled her eyes. "You all need to expand your horizons!"

"The only thing I know about that movie is if I heard Celine Dion singing My Heart Will Go On one more time, I was going to shoot the radio," Walker said. Looking around, he hastened to add, "My sister had it on all the time."

Clay looked up at the screen that Josh was now showing and watched a video of a two-person submersible. Turning to Josh, he asked, "Is the Coast Guard able to track any of this with sonar?"

"Yeah, they have the equipment but too much of an area to cover," Josh replied.

"What about us? Anything from a satellite we can ping?"

Josh twisted in his seat and grinned. "I've already been looking, and if I have an idea where they are, then yes, we could follow them. The problem is, like the Coast Guard, the area is too big unless they can pinpoint where you're looking."

"So, for example, if we can see them in the boathouse near Kincaid, then you can follow them?"

"Absolutely. If we were unable to apprehend them where they are, then I'd be able to follow them and give directions to someone on a boat."

"Shit, there's more than ripples in the water!" Rick called out, drawing everyone's attention to his side of the room. With a quick tap, Josh pulled up the video to the wide screen on the wall.

A glass-domed bubble rose from the surface, and they watched as the hatch on top was pushed open. A single man climbed out and hopped to the dock, securing the submersible. It only took a moment for him to move to a cabinet, pull out a key, and open it, retrieving the charger.

"Do I call it in now?" Levi asked. "My FBI contact is standing by."

"Wait until we're sure," Mace said.

Movement was visible from the side, and Clay watched with the others as a man walked into the boathouse from a side door. As he turned, his face became visible. "Kincaid... it's Kincaid. Get the volume up."

"His itinerary has him in New York with the congressman," Babs called out as Josh brought the sound from inside the boathouse to a volume they could all hear.

"Obviously, he's had a change of plans," Clay said. "Can we get an ID on the man from the submersible?"

"On it," Josh said.

Clay sat down quickly, tapping on his keyboard. "I'll take the international database."

"His tats are Minotaur," Rank identified.

The submersible driver walked through a door and Tate said, "Bathroom," as an explanation to the other Keepers. They continued to watch as Jerry moved over to the submersible and squatted, appearing to check the charger.

The door to the outside opened again, and they watched as Jerry leapt to his feet, turning quickly. Another figure walked in, and to Clay's horror, he heard Christina's voice.

"Mr. Kincaid? I didn't know you would be here today, but since you are, we need to talk."

"Talk? Talk about what?"

"Amhrán M'anama. And quite frankly, what I consider to be your interference with the band."

"Ms. Monroe, this really isn't the time for this—"

"I think it's the perfect time for it considering Dunk is in jail and hopefully can soon be in rehab since he nearly killed me when he got behind the wheel of his truck—"

Jerry lifted his hands in front of him and nodded. "Yes, yes, Steven told me all about that. And I'm very sorry, but I had nothing to do with that. Nothing to do with Dunk's decision to drink that much. But you're understandably upset, and the band can definitely talk about what's going on. Just not now. This is not a good time, and I need you to leave."

Clay jumped to his feet, his chair falling backward, his eyes pinned on the screen, his heart threatening to beat out of his chest. "God dammit! No!" he roared, fear and helplessness coursing through every cell in his body.

The submersible driver slipped up behind Christina. With his hand clamped over her mouth, he expertly pressed against her carotid artery, and she slumped to the dock.

Jerry rushed forward. "Christ! What are you doing?"

"Getting rid of any evidence."

"No, no," Jerry cried, dragging his hand through his hair, looking around as though an answer to this predicament

would appear out of nowhere. "She's got nothing to do with anything. She knows nothing."

The man stepped directly into Jerry's face and sneered, "You need to remember who you work for." He glanced down at Christina's body. "Get her into the sub. I'll take her out to sea and dump her body where no one can find her."

"Ms. Monroe?"

Amelia stepped into the boathouse, her gaze landing on Christina's prone body on the floor.

"Jesus, no... God, no..." came Jerry's agonized voice as the man grabbed the teen, knocking her unconscious as well.

Watching the men kneel over the two women's bodies, the Keepers sprang into action. "Make the call!" Mace barked to Levi, who was already reaching for his phone. To Josh, he ordered, "Get the coordinates to follow."

Josh looked toward Clay. "Is she wearing her necklace?"

Sucking in a hasty breath, he nodded, not trusting his voice.

Mace, still growling, ordered, "Get to the boats." He turned to Babs. "She's got a teenage girl with her—"

"I'm on it," she replied, hustling down the hall with Drew.

As everyone jumped to obey, Clay's feet stood rooted to the floor, his eyes locked on the sight of Christina lying unconscious.

25

Awakening from a deep sleep, Christina blinked her eyes several times while remnants of a strange dream ran through her mind. The muffled hum of a motor sounded in the distance, and she wondered if she'd pulled the blanket over her head while sleeping. As she blinked more, light was discernible, debunking the idea that she was covered. She wanted to stretch but found her movements halted.

"I know you're awake."

Hearing the strange male voice next to her, she jerked her head around, wincing as the pain slashed through her forehead. She continued to blink, forcing her eyes to focus. A man she'd never seen was next to her, his hands on the instruments in front of him. Wearing a leather vest, she recognized one of the patches. *Was he from the same group that Steven talked to at the Ottawa festival?*

She sucked in a quick breath, her gaze moving away from him and toward the front. A glass dome surrounded them, and for an instant, she imagined they were in a helicopter. Movement outside had her swinging her head back toward the front, pain once again slamming into her.

A school of fish swam by.

Fish?

As understanding pushed its way past her incredulity, she realized she was underwater. A seat belt had her firmly strapped into her seat, and her hands were taped together in front of her.

Moving her head more slowly to still the pain, she asked, "What... what is this? Who are you? What are we doing?" The questions rushed unheeded from her mouth, her brain racing faster than she could speak clearly.

"Who I am is not important. What I'm doing is not your concern. Where we are is obvious."

She licked her lips, trying to force her mind back in time to the last thought she'd had. *The violin. Music. Amelia. I was with Amelia Bennett!* The pounding in her head continued as she struggled to remember everything that happened. *Jerry Kincaid. The boathouse.* The last scene she could pull to the forefront of her memory was standing in the boathouse, demanding answers from Jerry as to what he wanted to do with the band. *But what happened after that? How did I get here?*

"You were in the boathouse," she said, her words a statement that was really more of a question.

"You walked in on something you shouldn't have."

Something I shouldn't have? He and Jerry? What were they up to? Another thought slammed into her, and she battled to keep her gasp from slipping out. *Clay!* She had assumed it was Jerry's finances that he was investigating and how that affected the band. *He must've been looking into something else. Jerry must be involved in something he shouldn't, and I stumbled right into the middle of it!*

Trying to keep her body movements to a minimum, her gaze darted around the small space inside. There were plastic-wrapped packages stuffed all around her feet. Shifting her gaze slightly to the side, she could see the same plastic-wrapped packages were also behind the seat next to her. *Whatever he's carrying is probably stuffed behind my seat as well.* She had no idea what was in the packages but had seen enough news shows to imagine that it could be drugs. *This is how they're transporting drugs?*

A sound of murmuring came from the back, and she jerked around, grimacing at the pain. Seeing a leg behind her seat, she twisted further. Amelia, bound and blinking her eyes open, was in the back as well. *Oh, my God!* As Amelia's frightened gaze held hers, she fought the rising nausea, praying for strength. Giving a quick nod, she hoped she was offering comfort—comfort she wasn't sure she had.

She had no choice but to stay exactly where she was. If they were above water, she could fight, or at least attempt to. But here, she needed this man next to her to steer this tiny underwater craft. *Oh, God, no one knows where we are.* The image of Clay ran through her mind, causing her heart to pound even more. His beautiful face with his square jaw and intense eyes. His muscular arms that made her feel protected when they encircled her. His laughter and kisses. *I'll lose him before I ever have a chance to be completely his.*

Clay forgot every rule in the book on missions, his vision still filled with Christina being hauled over and lowered into the submersible. He had warred between the desire to stay and watch, afraid he would never see her again, wanting to memorize every nuance, and needing to rush to rescue her. Pushed along as he was surrounded by his fellow Keepers, they moved through the caverns, deep into the underground dock that Mace had built. They quickly divided as they boarded two specially-fitted high-tech boats filled with equipment that would rival the best the CIA Special Ops had to offer.

With Walker at the helm of one and Rank driving the other, they fired the engines and shot out into the open water. Until they were closer, there was little for Clay to do but pray. Sitting where the wind cut through and the splash of water slapped against him, he was soon joined by Tate and Blake as they sat on either side.

He leaned forward, his forearms pressed against his knees as his hands clenched together. "I should've told her."

"Told her what?" Tate asked.

"I should've told her everything about Kincaid. I know we're not supposed to discuss our missions, but this man had been around her. Had shown an interest in her. Was actually fuckin' involved with her band. We know there's a connection between Steven and him. I should've fuckin' told her."

"You had no idea, man. You gave her the information that concerned her at the time," Blake said.

"But we knew he could be dangerous, or at the very least, the people he's involved with are dangerous. I should've made sure she knew to avoid him. Then to call me if she saw him."

"This is not on you, Clay. We've all talked about this. She was never involved in this mission until recently, and then it was only on the periphery. You had no reason to alert her or alarm her."

"Then why is my woman trapped under the water right now?" he growled.

"You know the answer to that is it's them, not you. It's bad, shitty luck, but we're going to get her," Tate answered.

He leaned back, swiping the water from his face. "What about Amelia? Jesus, she's only a teenager—"

"She's not alone," Blake Insisted. "She's got Christina—"

Snorting, he said, "Somehow, that doesn't make me feel any better. Christina is not equipped for this."

Blake shifted around and got right into his face. "Do you think any of our women were equipped for this? We're all attracted to strong women, and that's what you've got in Christina. She's strong, smart, she can handle this."

Tate added, "What you gotta do is keep your head in the game and focus. We'll get to her."

Walker called out, "Got coordinates from Josh. Rank and I'll get to the area and begin circling."

Jumping to his feet, he spread his legs to brace against the movement of the boat speeding over the waves, barely feeling the rocking motion. Turning, he said into his radio so everyone could hear, "We have no idea how much of a charge he was able to get on the submersible. It sure as fuck wasn't a full one."

"His battery probably wasn't drained when he got to the boathouse. But if he has to rise to the surface to get a charge somewhere anyway, he'll keep the women with him," Drew said. "He won't risk rising to the surface to do something with them only to go back under."

Trying to ignore the idea of what *doing something with them* entailed, he opened his mouth to speak only to snap it shut when Mace called out.

"The FBI has picked up Jerry Kincaid. He'd grabbed his stuff and was just leaving the Bennett estate when they snagged him. He started to lawyer up, but it didn't take a lot of pressure when he found out he would be charged with accessory to kidnapping and attempted murder. He started to talk."

"We need to know where the submersible might get charged," he radioed.

"On it," Levi replied.

Clay's adrenaline spiked again, coursing through his bloodstream. As usual with a mission, knowing they were getting closer to her gave him courage.

Rick's voice came over the radio, "Josh says the submersible is not deep under the surface. If his charge is low, then he's not wasting power going deep. He's managed to ping them about three nautical miles south-west from where you are."

Josh interjected, "I've located Christina's tracer on her necklace... she's still with the submersible."

The air rushed from his lungs at that last statement. *He hasn't dumped her somewhere else.* The others began pulling on wetsuits, Clay thankful for the physical activity to help focus his mind.

Levi came back on the radio. "According to my FBI contact who's with Jerry Kincaid right now, Kincaid claims he has no idea where the shipments go once they leave him. He also has no idea where another charging point might be. According to him, he was paid to provide a place for the submersible to charge and that was all. The International Drug Task Force has picked up the Minotaurs that were just across the border waiting for the shipment of heroin to come in."

Mace added, "I'm searching areas between the Bennett estate and where you guys should intercept the submersible. There are several small docks that probably have electricity, but so far, Josh doesn't see him veering from his Northeast path—"

Josh jumped in, "He's just now changing course and heading slightly northwest. I can see a small, private dock in a cove. If it's got electricity and he has his own charger, then all he needs is to hook it up. Sending the coordinates to Walker and Rank."

Mace radioed, "You need to come in from behind them where his visibility is limited. If he gets to the surface and sees you, he might decide to harm the women."

The words were factual, but the idea of Christina dying at this man's hands sent Clay's heart rate spiking. Knowing her life could depend on his steady hand, he called upon all his training and slowed his breathing.

Walker veered out to sea so that he could come up behind the submersible, giving the Keepers a chance to get into the water unseen. Rank would keep his boat forward. Now that they were close, Walker could see the submersible on his sonar screen. As they quickly formed the mission, Clay, Blake, Tate, and Cobb checked their equipment, slid their feet into the fins, and moved over the side of the boat and into the water. With the submersible now slowing in front of them, they swam closer, carefully staying toward the rear, out of sight.

26

Christina cast her gaze around, assuming they were not far under the surface considering the light surrounding them. Fish swam by and it struck her that if she was not fearful for her and Amelia's lives, the trip could have been an adventure. Mumbled cursing coming from the man next to her sent that notion flying out of her mind.

"Your interference kept me from getting a full charge. We're going to have to surface soon."

Not understanding what he meant, she glanced toward the back seeing Amelia's wide-eyed, still-fearful expression. Turning back to the man, she asked, "If we surface for you to charge, can we go to the bathroom?"

Barking out a laugh, the man shook his head. "How stupid do you think I am?"

"If you have to travel in a submarine that stinks, perhaps you'll have a different idea," she said, her anger getting the best of her until he cast a glare toward her so evil she felt it sear over her skin. Deciding to stay quiet, she watched as they slowly began to turn toward the left while rising to the surface.

Suddenly, a clunking sound came from behind, and they jerked to the right, her side dipping down. She threw her hands forward to balance even though she was held tight by the seat belt, her scream blending with the screeching cry coming from Amelia.

"Dammit!" the man cursed, grabbing the controls and attempting to maneuver them.

"What's happening?" she asked, her chest heaving with fright.

"Something's in one of the propellers."

He continued to fiddle with the controls, and she looked down, hating the way the sub listed toward her side, her feelings as off-balance as the vessel. Suddenly, a dark form appeared at the corner of her vision and she screamed again.

"Shut the fuck up!" the man yelled, reaching over and grabbing her arm, squeezing tight. "I can't fucking think!"

Gasping, she blinked, looking back down, seeing nothing. A slight motion caught her attention and a hand appeared, pressing a silver lighthouse pendant against the glass where only she could see. *Clay! Lord, have mercy... it's Clay!* She had no idea how he found her or how he came to her rescue, but renewed energy radiated throughout her body.

She didn't know what to do or what might be expected of her but wanted to keep Clay's presence hidden. Glancing to the left, she saw the man turn his head toward her. She screamed again, this time lifting her hands toward the front of the dome.

He jerked around and stared out the front. "What?"

"I saw something!"

"What the fuck did you see?"

"A fish... some kind of big fish!"

"We're in the ocean, you fuckin' bitch! Of course, you're going to see a fish!" Focusing his attention back to the controls, he managed to get the sub to lift a little more. "I can't get the ballast right," he growled.

She could see light shining brighter in the water, and with a little more grinding of the motor, the very top of the sub lifted above the surface. Wishing Clay had a way to make his ideas known to her, she instinctively knew the rescue would go easier if she was not buckled into her seat and the man was disabled. Sliding her hands to her chest, she quietly unsnapped the seatbelt.

The submersible lurched to the side again, righting itself before listing to the side once more. Taking advantage of the man's attention focused on the controls, she whirled around with her wrists still taped together and hit him in the face, knocking his head to the side. Without giving him a chance to recover, she slammed her fists down onto his lap, hitting him in the groin.

Amelia cried out from the back seat, but Christina's focus stayed on the man. Suddenly, the sub bounced in the water, surrounded by dark figures. She looked up to see several fully suited scuba divers climbing onto the sides, their weight causing the submersible to bob up and down. Looking toward the top, she heard a noise and watched as the lid above opened, and a gun aimed downward, pointed directly at the man.

"Keep your hands where we can see them," she heard someone say but was unable to identify which Keeper was speaking.

"Christina," Clay called out, and she looked up, trying to see which one was him. "Are you and Amelia okay?"

"Yes, yes, but our hands are taped together."

The man was still groaning but looked up, growling, "Go ahead and shoot. I'll die either way. If I lose this shipment, I'm a dead man walking."

The weapon discharged, and both women screamed. Expecting to see blood gushing, Christina saw a small dart sticking from the man's upper chest. His eyes closed and his head slumped forward. Looking toward the hatch, the Keeper with the gun explained, "That'll keep him unconscious so we have a chance to get you two out first."

She turned around in her seat and scrambled toward the back, helping Amelia to get unbuckled. Half-dragging the teenager toward the front, she encouraged, "Stand in the middle here and you'll be able to raise your arms first. That way they can cut your hands free." Helping to steady Amelia as the submersible rocked back and forth, the teen followed her instructions. Once her hands were free, one of the Keepers quickly slit the tape and then pulled Amelia to safety. Christina watched as Amelia's legs and then feet disappeared, and she slid over the side into the water. Her gaze followed and saw that Amelia was wrapped in the arms of one of the Keepers, who was swimming away rapidly.

Christina quickly followed suit, scrambling to stand in between the two front seats of the submersible. The bobbing of the craft along with trying to balance on shaky legs with her hands still taped caused her to list to the side, crying out as she raised her hands over her head to grab onto anything to keep her from falling. Her hands were immediately held in a vise grip, steadying her as they were cut free. She was pulled upward, and she kicked her legs out, standing on the back of the front seat to give herself more push and stepping on the unconscious man in an attempt to escape. As her upper body passed from the submersible, she gasped as the first slap of cold water hit her face.

His arms banded tightly around her. "Clay! I can't believe you found us!" Her breath left her lungs in a rush as she slid from the top of the submersible and her body moved into the cold water. "Oh, fuck!" she cried, clinging to him.

"Hang on, babe, the boat is right here."

She looked in the direction he indicated, but the waves kept her from seeing anything as icy-cold water splashed into her face. Finally, a large, dark object moved closer and she could identify the boat maneuvering closer.

Teeth chattering, she said, "A... A... Amelia—"

"Don't worry. We've got her."

"H... he's got p... p... plastic-wrapped p... packages in there. I... I don't know—"

"Don't worry about it, babe, we've got it."

The cold was making it hard to think, but Clay was swimming rapidly toward the boat. "It was J... Jerry—"

"Stop," Clay ordered. "Babe, worry about you and nothing else."

She began to shiver but clung tighter to him. As long as she had him, she knew she had everything. As long as he had her, she knew she was safe.

Clay held tight, swimming quickly, glad to see that at the back of the boat, Blay and Babs had assisted Amelia out of Drew's arms and into the boat. Directly behind them, he twisted his body so their waiting arms could assist Christina up as well.

Clambering up into the boat after she was safely on board, he jerked off his gear, then pulled off his fins. Amelia and Christina had already been hustled down into the cabin, accompanied by Blay and Babs. His hands shook as he unzipped his wetsuit and was so desperate to get to Christina, he wasn't offended when Drew's hands landed on his shoulders to assist in pulling the suit off him.

"Babs will get the women stripped and in the warm shower," Drew reminded. "I know you want to get down there but give them a minute."

Drew's reminder that there was a teenage girl below was the only thing that kept him from rushing to Christina's side. Pacing the deck, it seemed like an eternity before Babs called out, "Clay, come on down."

Rushing into the cabin, he spied Amelia in thick

socks, heavy sweatpants, and a Go Navy sweatshirt, sitting next to Babs. Her wet hair was wrapped in a towel while Blay, their medic, checked her over. Her wide eyes stared up at him as he stalked through the room. Moving into the bathroom, he stepped over the girls' wet clothing that had been stripped and dropped onto the floor and moved directly into the shower with Christina.

Steam rose all around them as he pulled her into his arms.

"I'm fine, I'm fine, I'm fine," she repeated, her warm cheek pressed against his cold chest.

Letting the warm spray of water surround both of them, he held his lips against the top of her head and murmured, "You're not, but you will be."

After a moment, he flipped the water off, reached over to grab a towel, and scrubbed her body dry as though every movement would ensure her blood still circulated.

Finally, as he knelt and rubbed her calf for the third time while her fingers rested on his shoulders, she began to laugh. Looking up, the mirth on her face finally sent warmth through him.

"If you keep rubbing like that, I'll be lucky to have any skin left!" She bent so that her face was close to his, and her small hands cupped his jaws. "Clay, I'm okay."

Sucking in a deep breath, he felt as though he could breathe for the first time in hours. Smiling, he stood, then pulled her body flush against his and bent to take her lips in a soft kiss.

Babs had tossed his clothes into the small room as

well as some for her. Soon, Christina was dressed in similar clothes to Amelia with the exception of a sweatshirt with the word ARMY emblazoned across her chest.

He opened the bathroom door and she rushed out, heading directly to Amelia, and threw her arms around the young woman. They hugged and laughed, both appearing unharmed after their ordeal. He looked at Blay, who said, "Amelia is good. Temperature, blood pressure, heart rate, lungs. I checked for frostbite, but they weren't in the cold water that long. Her skin is a good color and her extremities are dexterous."

Christina looked up at Clay, and he explained, "Blay is our medic, babe. He's going to check you out."

He couldn't help but hover until Babs finally pulled him to the side. "Give them room, Clay. Let him do his job."

As soon as Blay was finished with Christina, giving her the same excellent bill of health as Amelia, Clay moved in and pulled her into his arms. Drew popped his head down to check on everyone as Babs was radioing their status.

"Amelia, we're going back to your parents' estate. They've been apprised of the situation and are anxious to see you. Plus, the FBI is there, and we'll be turning over the evidence."

Jolting, Christina blurted, "I didn't even ask! What happened to the man who kidnapped us? I don't even know his name! I don't even know what he was carrying in that submarine—"

"It's called a submersible, Ms. Monroe," Amelia said. "That's what Ms. Babs told me."

Babs laughed and said, "That's right. And as to what he was carrying..." Her voice faded as she looked toward Drew.

"The other boat is towing the submersible and carrying the prisoner. It was used to transport bricks of heroin."

Christina and Amelia gasped at the same time, both staring at Drew before turning their gazes toward each other. In unison, they exclaimed, "Mr. Kincaid!"

27

Clay kept his arms around Christina for the next half-hour as they traveled back to the Bennett estate. He continually pulled her in tighter until she finally twisted her head around and looked up at him, claiming, "Honey, I can't breathe!"

Mumbling, "Sorry," he loosened his arms slightly.

Her fingers held onto his arms and flexed. "How did you find us?"

"We had cameras on the inside of the boathouse. There was evidence that it might be used for a stopover in the transport of drugs."

"My parents' boathouse?" Amelia squeaked.

"They're not suspects—only Kincaid," he quickly said.

"But he's... he's my father's friend. They've known each other since they were kids." Amelia turned toward Christina, who reached out and placed her hand on the girl's arm.

"I know, sweetie. Sometimes people can change... or

maybe get into situations where they make really bad choices."

Amelia sucked in her lips and nodded slowly. Finally, she said, "My dad is going to be really pissed!"

Babs and Bray chuckled at her proclamation. "You're right, Amelia," Clay agreed. He knew he was pissed about Kincaid's involvement with Christina and could only imagine how Congressman Bennett was going to feel.

Twisting around again so she could face him, Christina asked, "You still didn't answer the question. How did you find us way out here?"

He hesitated, uncertain of her reaction to the truth. "We could track you with sonar," he said, lifting his hand and sweeping it over her cheek before dragging a finger down to the necklace resting on her chest. "This is special... there's a small tracer embedded in your Celtic cross. I know you might feel it was an invasion of your privacy, but—"

"But you wanted me safe, knowing Kincaid was a snake."

He nodded and she smiled, squeezing his hand before linking fingers with him. Grateful she understood, he leaned forward, placing a gentle kiss on her lips, glad they were no longer cold.

"Told you," Babs said, and he glanced to where she sat near Amelia. Cocking his head to the side in a silent question, she continued, "Perfect for a Keeper."

Grinning, he kissed the top of her head again. "Couldn't agree more."

Clay was used to missions ending where LSI turned

evidence over to the FBI and then slipped away, but the arrival at the Bennett estate was overwhelming. The congressman and his wife were waiting anxiously inside the main house, chosen to make sure any coverage by the press could be contained. Plus, the boathouse and guesthouse were now considered a crime scene and were being combed by the FBI. The boat Rank was steering with the prisoner and towing the submersible filled with over a million dollars street value of heroin was met by the FBI.

Mrs. Bennett flung herself toward Amelia as soon as the teen's feet made it through the front door. The congressman wrapped his arms around both of his women.

Clay escorted Christina inside, where she was literally pulled from his arms by the Bennetts, all exclaiming their concern for her. When they turned toward him, expressing gratitude, he gently moved her back into his embrace.

The FBI stepped in, but the congressman insisted the interviews take place in the family room where he could be assured of Amelia and Christina's comfort. As she was led forward, she smiled and tossed a wave toward him. "Wait for me?"

He winked, his smile wide. "Wouldn't be anywhere else, babe."

A week later

Christina opened the door to her apartment, welcoming Jamie and Mike inside. They greeted her with heartfelt hugs and then made their way inside to where Clay leaned his hip against the kitchen counter. She glanced over her shoulder, glad to see him shake hands with them. They had discussed this meeting and as much as she knew he wanted to insist on being present, he'd left the decision up to her. She wanted him there—not because she couldn't handle herself but because she knew how much it meant to him.

Hearing more footsteps, she turned to see Dunk approaching hesitantly. Opening her arms, his face filled with relief as she welcomed him with a hug as well. Closing the door behind him, she wasn't surprised to see Clay not so welcoming to the final arrival.

Ushering the band members to the living area, she said, "I know you haven't had the whole story... just what was in the news about Steven being arrested. I wanted to meet today so you can have the whole picture and to discuss what we want to do." Jamie and Mike sat on her sofa while Dunk perched on the edge, his hands clasped tightly together. She sat in a chair on the other side of the coffee table.

Clay moved to sit on the arm of the comfy chair she was in, his hand resting close to her shoulder. Plunging directly into the story, she said, "The investigation by the FBI is still ongoing, but what I can tell you is that Steven became involved with someone in the drug-trafficking trade."

The gasps from Mike, Jamie, and Dunk were audible, their eyes growing wide in unison.

"Jerry Kincaid, the man you knew as a benefactor for our band, had been embezzling from Congressman Bennett for several years. A drug cartel became aware of his thefts and convinced him that working for them would be in his best interests. All he had to do was provide a place where the drug-runners could recharge their craft and they would assist with laundering the money."

"Oh, fuck," Mike breathed, shaking his head slowly, then jerking his gaze back to Clay. "Steven?"

Nodding, Clay replied, "Yes. I'm not sure how Kincaid and Steven struck up a partnership. It seems to have occurred right after he heard your band and saw it as a way to move money through your books. I have no idea if Steven was aware of the full extent of Kincaid's illegal dealings, but he was very aware that the band's books were being cooked to hide money."

"That fuckin' moron!" Jamie bit out.

"Do we actually have any money left?" Mike asked.

"While the money that Steven allowed Kincaid to siphon through the band's accounting is now being held, he did have another account that appears to have most of our actual earnings in it," Christina said.

The gathering was quiet for a moment, the three visitors seeming to take in the information, lost in their thoughts.

"He pushed it."

Dunk's voice cut through the silence, drawing everyone's attention to him. He lifted anguished eyes toward

Christina and said, "I take full responsibility, but he pushed it."

"Dunk, what do you mean?" she asked, her brow furrowed as she watched him carefully.

He scrubbed his hand over his face and cast his gaze around the others before settling it on her. "Steven kept telling me that tossing back the whiskey during our performances made the crowd go wilder. Kinda like when they go nuts when you're dancing around, Tiny. I knew I was losing control. My dad was an alcoholic, so you'd think I'd know better. But he was right. We'd finish a song, I'd slam back a beer or whiskey, the crowd would scream and shout. We'd finish a set, and I'd let the fans buy me drinks. Where we were playing, we'd often get a cut of the house, so it was more money." Shaking his head, he added, "The fucker was using the band to launder drug money and pushing me to drink just so we could get more."

"Oh, Dunk, I'm so sorry," Christina said. She stood and walked closer, sitting on the coffee table, reaching over to place her hand on Dunk's arm. "How can we help?"

He shook his head, wincing. "Damn, Tiny, you don't need to worry about me. How the hell you can even sit here with me is a miracle after what I did."

"I want you to get help. What happened was awful, but it's over and we can move past it."

"Even him?" Dunk asked, inclining his head toward Clay.

Clay sucked in a deep breath and replied, "I'll have my eye on you. She's more forgiving than I am, but I'm willing to be led by her example... but you've got an alcohol problem and need to take care of it."

Dunk nodded emphatically. "I've entered AA. My driver's license is suspended, and I have community service to perform. But I entered AA on my own."

"Then that's a good start," Clay said.

"What about the band?" Jamie asked. He ducked his head and said, "With everything going on, I guess it seems ridiculous to ask about the band, but... well, I just wondered."

Standing, Christina walked back over to Clay's side and smiled at him. He wrapped his arm around her waist and squeezed. She knew what she had to say might not be met with gladness, but with Clay's support, it made it easier to face her bandmates. Facing them again, she said, "I love playing my violin. Whether I'm in the symphonic orchestra or with Amhrán M'anama, I love touching other people with the music I create. But I have a life here in Maine. A life that's important to me, and while an occasional trip is fine, I have no desire to be part of a group that requires a circuit of national or international travel and touring. So, this is where the four of us have to come to a decision. Steven is out, so there's no lead singer at this time."

Cocking his head to the side, Mike asked, "So, exactly what decision do we need to make?"

"At this point, any one of the four of us can walk away. Or any combination of us can stay in and create a new version of Amhrán M'anama. We can audition for a new lead singer, one who has our same goals and values. Or we can just stay instrumental. And if the three of you want to continue without me, that's fine too."

Dunk immediately said, "I'm just honored that you're offering this invitation to me as well. I've got some family in this area, and I need the support from them and friends to make sure I stay on the AA path. So, I'm willing to continue to be the drummer with the same goals that you have, Tiny."

Nodding, Mike said, "I love the bagpipes, but my vocation is my shop. Like Dunk, I've got family in the area and have no problem continuing this being our part-time gig."

Jamie rubbed his chin and grinned. "I couldn't have said it better. I'm in."

"Well, all right, boys. It looks like Amhrán M'anama is still in business."

Clay squeezed her hip slightly and reminded, "Contract, babe."

"Yes," she nodded. "I'd like for us to have a contract that spells out what we want as a band, including how we handle the money through a reliable accountant, payments given to each of us, and agreements on travel and recordings."

"God, yes!" Jamie enthused, nodding emphatically.

"Absolutely," Mike and Dunk agreed with equal enthusiasm.

After warmer goodbye hugs, she closed the door as the three left. Turning back to Clay, she walked over and slid her arms around his waist. Leaning her head back, she held his gaze. "Thank you for not pounding Dunk into the ground."

He snorted. "It was hard. But I'll have my eye on him. One step out of line, and he's out."

"I love you, you know," she said. Smiling, she lifted on her toes. Bending, he closed the distance, taking her lips in a deep, heartfelt kiss.

Two Months Later

All the Keepers and their women were filling one side of the bar. Laughter and chatting amongst friends had him wish Christina was sitting with him. They had searched for a house together, still near the coast but convenient to both. Not too large, but big enough for a family one day. Finding one they both loved, they'd closed on the property the week before. Their friends helped them move and then Christina delighted in hosting their first Lighthouse party.

She would still drive into Portland for the practices and symphonies during the orchestra season, but with the other members of Amhrán M'anama living just to the north of Portland, they'd found a practice site that was nearby to cut down on her commute.

Now, the noise in the bar came to a halt as soon as the owner approached the microphone and introduced the band. A light shone down on Dunk. Clear eyed and smiling, he twirled his drumsticks in between the beats of the rhythm he pounded. Two men with long hair, kilts, and boots hopped onto the stage, the sound of their bagpipes joining the drums. Mike and Jamie grinned, continuing to play as the new vocalist, Clark, jumped to stage, headed to the microphone, and began belting out a song.

Everyone was clapping, but Clay held his breath as he always did, waiting for Christina's appearance. He was never disappointed, and tonight was no different. In a short, plaid miniskirt with her black tank, sky-high heeled boots, long, dark, wavy hair flowing around her face, and ruby-red lips, she danced and twirled as the music flew from her violin. At the end of the song, she lowered her violin, her gaze immediately finding his, and a wide smile curved her lips.

As always, the crowd went wild with shouts of 'Tiny' filling the air. He grinned. To him, she was simply his Christina.

For the next exciting Lighthouse Security Investigation book, click here!
Cobb

Join my reader group on Facebook!
Maryann Jordan Alpha Fans

For all the other Lighthouse Security Investigation books:
Mace
Rank
Walker

Drew
Blake
Tate
Levi
Clay
Cobb

Jaxon

Jayden

Asher

Zeke

Cas

Lighthouse Security Investigations

Mace

Rank

Walker

Drew

Blake

Tate

Levi

Clay

Cobb

Hope City (romantic suspense series co-developed

with Kris Michaels

Brock book 1

Sean book 2

Carter book 3

Brody book 4

Kyle book 5

Ryker book 6

Rory book 7

Killian book 8

Saints Protection & Investigations

(an elite group, assigned to the cases no one else wants…or can solve)

Serial Love

Healing Love

Revealing Love

Seeing Love

Honor Love

Sacrifice Love

Protecting Love

Remember Love

Discover Love

Surviving Love

Celebrating Love

Follow the exciting spin-off series:

Alvarez Security (military romantic suspense)

Gabe

Tony

Vinny

Jobe

SEALs

Thin Ice (Sleeper SEAL)

SEAL Together (Silver SEAL)

Letters From Home (military romance)

Class of Love

Freedom of Love

Bond of Love

The Love's Series (detectives)

Love's Taming

Love's Tempting

Love's Trusting

The Fairfield Series (small town detectives)

Emma's Home

Laurie's Time

Carol's Image

Fireworks Over Fairfield

Please take the time to leave a review of this book. Feel free to contact me, especially if you enjoyed my book. I love to hear from readers!

Facebook

Email

Website

ABOUT THE AUTHOR

I am an avid reader of romance novels, often joking that I cut my teeth on the historical romances. I have been reading and reviewing for years. In 2013, I finally gave into the characters in my head, screaming for their story to be told. From these musings, my first novel, Emma's Home, The Fairfield Series was born.

I was a high school counselor having worked in education for thirty years. I live in Virginia, having also lived in four states and two foreign countries. I have been married to a wonderfully patient man for thirty-five years. When writing, my dog or one of my four cats can generally be found in the same room if not on my lap.

Please take the time to leave a review of this book. Feel free to contact me, especially if you enjoyed my book. I love to hear from readers!

Facebook
Email
Website

16583993R00184